THE DANGER
GAME

IAN BULL

STORY MERCHANT BOOKS
LOS ANGELES • 2020

PRAISE FOR *THE PICTURE KILLS*
BOOK 1 IN THE QUINTANA ADVENTURES

"The settings are stellar and richly detailed. We're gripped from start to finish...pacing is spectacular, and story excels. Characters are multi-dimensional, and settings gleam."

—Writer's Digest National Book Competition

"A thrilling page-turner with real literary value...combines the international intrigue of Lee Child, the procedural know-how of Michael Connelly and, yes, the Hollywood insider's expertise of Jackie Collins, with a plot that takes the reader on a Bond-like adventure across the globe."

—Amazon reviewer

"The book comes together in a shocking, hair-raising climax that only later will the reader realize had been set up by the author chapters in advance."

—Amazon reviewer

"Steve Quintana is...a new thriller hero who's human, prone to mistakes, frailty, and self-doubt, yet with Scot Harvath power, Angus MacGyver ingenuity, and Ethan Hunt resilience that makes him ripe for a continuing literary series."

—Amazon reviewer

The Danger Game

www.IanBullAuthor.com
www.CaliforniaBull.com

Twitter: @IanBull3
Instagram: California Bull

ISBN-13: 978-1-970157-18-5

Story Merchant Books
400 S. Burnside Avenue #11B
Los Angeles, CA 90036
www.storymerchantbooks.com

THE DANGER
GAME

IAN BULL

To my wife, Robin, and my daughter, Lily.
Thank you for your love and patience.

A NOTE FROM STEVEN QUINTANA

You don't need to read *The Picture Kills* and *Six Passengers, Five Parachutes* to enjoy *The Danger Game*—just let me give you the highlights:

In *The Picture Kills*, I was a top Army Ranger reconnaissance photographer turned Hollywood paparazzo. Taking photos of celebrities was an easy way to get rich, while trying to forget my past.

That's how I met the beautiful and talented Julia Travers. While doing my job, I snapped shots of Julia boarding a yacht with her ex-boyfriend, Xander Constantinou. Except she wasn't running off with him for a secret rendezvous, he was kidnapping her and taking her to his private Bahamian cay. Julia's best friend and manager, Trishelle Hobbes, was days away from being kidnapped, too.

Swearing that no one would ever be harmed by my photos again, I set out on a rescue mission with Carl Webb, my best friend and a fellow former Ranger.

Keep in mind, the last person Julia wanted to see was me—the paparazzo who was ruining her life in the tabloids.

In mounting a rescue attempt, Carl and I wound up shot, stabbed, and nearly dead. But we saved them, and Julia and I developed a deep, permanent bond.

Six Passengers, Five Parachutes picks up eighteen months later. My bond with Julia deepened into love but not so much a relationship. I blew that one. (Having a celebrity girlfriend is as hard as it sounds.)

Instead of working on being the "perfect boyfriend," I did what I do naturally, and left to track down Julia's kidnappers incognito. They figured out my identity and sent men to kill me. Long story short, I ended up on a plane programmed to crash with five convicted criminals and five parachutes—you do the math. One of us wasn't leaving alive. Oh, and they televised the whole thing. At the helm of this deadly moneymaking scheme were TV producers Robert Snow and Tina Swig, taking orders from this supervillain known only as Boss Man.

I somehow escaped. Unfortunately, Tina Swig and Boss Man did, too.

After that, Julia gave me another shot—leaping from a crashing plane changes a guy.

And our lives were perfect for the next two years....

THE DANGER
GAME

CHAPTER 1

STEVEN QUINTANA

Saturday, March 9, 10:00 a.m. (PST)
California

I t's time to pull the trigger on *Operation Bacon*. I'll sneak two pounds of fried Canadian pig inside Julia's trailer, and we'll enjoy the fatty flesh before her big press conference. Julia tries to be vegan, but she can't turn down the luscious pork from the land of her people. I love being a bad influence.

I walk through a maze of tables arranged on the grassy bluff. Chatty journalists sit in chairs, enjoying their catered breakfast while ignoring the majestic Pacific Ocean below. I sidle up to the chef's station where Chef Rafa is whipping up omelets. He hands me two paper plates taped together. "There's a lot of pig in there, Esse, so it should stay warm."

"I owe you, brother." I slide out of line and weave back through the tables.

It's going to be a busy day. After breakfast, Julia and Trishelle will announce that their new company, A-OK Productions, will be producing its first movie, *Under Withering Fire,* about the Vietnam War, to be shot here in Malibu. Trishelle is Julia's best friend, manager, and producing partner, and she convinced Julia they should host the press conference onsite, which is, coincidentally, not far from our home. The weather, eleven days before spring, is perfect.

I'll be the stunt coordinator. It will require focus, planning, and zero schmoozing, which is perfect, for now. This is *not* my career—flipping cars for my movie star fiancée is not the long-term plan, but at least we're together.

Carl Webb appears from nowhere and steps in front of me. "I've seen that look before. You're on a mission."

"I'm sneaking bacon into Julia's trailer. We're going to chow down."

"How about you and I joyride that Ferrari parked over there later? That'd be nice." He points at the red stunt car that Julia's character will be driving in the movie.

"Don't get too excited. It's got a Ford Fiesta motor. It's just a prop I drove here for the press conference."

"Too bad," Carl says and leads the way through the last tables toward Julia's trailer.

Carl was the team leader of our Army Ranger reconnaissance team. He now runs Global Webb Securities. We've saved each other's lives enough times that we don't need to wear friendship bracelets to remember.

He also looks like a football Hall of Famer in his thousand-dollar suit, while I'm in jeans and a T-shirt. At least I have a thick head of black hair. He's as bald as Mr. Clean.

A small blonde with a big voice blocks our path. "Wait. You're those Rangers."

"Used to be," Carl says. He tries to pass, but she puts her hand on his chest.

"Gwen Thompson, CBC correspondent. You're Carl Webb, and you're Steven Quintana. You rescued Julia once."

"Yup. In the Bahamas. Almost four years ago," Carl says.

"And Julia rescued *you* from that crashing plane," Gwen says, pointing at me.

A man eating at a nearby table, yells. "*Celebrity Exposed* says that was all fake!"

"Nope. It all happened," Carl says.

"Then prove you're as amazing as they say you are," Gwen says.

"Hand me a piece of paper with something on it," I say, accepting her challenge.

Trishelle appears behind us, holding a clipboard. "Gwen, can I answer any questions?"

"Give Steven Quintana whatever's on your clipboard."

Trishelle hands me a piece of paper. "It's just the call sheet for today's event."

I look at the four quadrants of the page, moving my thumb to each corner, then hand the paper to Gwen. "Quiz me."

She rolls her eyes and looks at the page. "Nearest emergency room."

"Providence Saint John's, 2121 Santa Monica Boulevard."

"Who is the production assistant, and what's his call time?"

"She's a woman. Toni Fleischaker. Her call time was 5:45 a.m. at the crew parking lot at Gladstone's at the Beach, in the crew shuttle van at 6:00 a.m."

Gwen seems impressed. "You have a photographic memory."

Carl nods. "And that's only one of his superpowers."

There is no such thing, but I don't admit that. I had an eidetic memory as a kid, but it's fading with age. The Army taught me how to memorize something fast and keep it in my brain for a day or two.

"Thank you for the show, gentlemen!" Trishelle shoos us away, but not before trading a wink with Carl. We leave her behind to smooth things over.

Carl and I dart past the last table and up the stairs into Julia's trailer. I put the warm plates on the Formica table, grab a red Sharpie, and draw a heart. Julia busted me hard for not giving her a Valentine last month, so maybe this will make up for it.

The bedroom door opens, and Julia emerges. We lock eyes and grin. She's dressed as her character: low jeans, a tie-dyed shirt, and a headband around her wavy, blonde hair, like a war protestor from the 1970s. My knees knock like a swooning high school girl. We slam into each other and kiss.

"You send me. Honest you do," I whisper.

Carl motions like he's gagging.

Julia sniffs the air. "Did you bring me bacon?" She rips the plates apart and pops a greasy piece in her mouth as her eyes roll back in her head.

She notices Carl. "Hello, Mr. Webb! You look wonderful, as usual. Steven, what are you going to wear?" She looks at me like I'm naked.

"What for? I'm not making any speeches."

"To meet the minister and the wedding planner after the press conference. They're making a special trip out here."

Even with my memory training, I still forget the scary stuff, like marriage. She wants us to get hitched right after production, and then adopt a child by the end of the year. Parachuting into war zones with Carl was less daunting.

"What about you? You look like a hippie."

Julia puts her hands on her hips. "I have a proper outfit steamed and ready."

Carl grins, enjoying my discomfort. "Let me cut the tension." He pulls an envelope out of his jacket pocket and thrusts it between us. "Major Glenn Ward found the names of the man and woman who caused all your problems. Just tear it open."

Julia and I stare at the envelope like it's radioactive. Major Glenn Ward works for Army Cyber Operations and consults for Carl on the side, with the Army's permission. Eighteen months ago, when I was trapped on a crashing plane, Glenn's expertise helped save my life. Now, after months of work, Carl and Glenn have tracked down the sick masterminds who created *Six Passengers, Five Parachutes.*

Neither Julia nor I reach for the envelope. It reeks of bad luck.

Carl flicks it up and down. "Boss Man's real name is Douglas Bushnell."

I saw Boss Man only once, standing next to his jet on an airfield in Mexico. That was right before he and Tina strapped me into a flying bomb alongside five killers and broadcast it on Pay-per-view. That was a bad day.

Carl stops flicking. "I understand if you don't want to open it. You two are on a winning streak. But, now that we know his name, we can catch him, no matter how rich he is. But only if you want."

I don't touch it. We're still wounded. Escaping to a lake house in Canada and living off-grid for a year until our nightmares pass is the best solution. Not for Julia. She pushes through the pain instead. She produces a movie, plans a wedding, and preps for a family, all while paying a fortune to catch the bad guys who gave her the pain in the first place.

We stare at each other.

Julia exhales and grabs the envelope. I half-expect it to burn her, but it doesn't. She rips it open. I hope whatever is inside won't spoil our lucky streak.

CHAPTER 2

JULIA TRAVERS

I rip open the envelope, wishing it was Tina Swig's head. I want to catch her even more than Boss Man. She put Steven on that plane. I won't be happy until I can say, "I beat you," right to her face.

Blood pounds in my head as I pull out the information—photos of yachts, maps, and a dossier of billionaire Douglas Bushnell. I shake it at Carl. "What about Swig?"

"I saved the best for last. Yancy Mendoza located Swig in Wisconsin. She snuck back into the country and is hiding in a motel next to a river. Yancy and Victor are watching her now, gathering evidence, and will call the FBI to arrest her within a day."

Six months ago, I hired Carl and his firm to find Boss Man and Tina Swig. He hired Major Glenn Ward and offered LAPD Detective Yancy Mendoza a bucket of money to take a sabbatical and join our team. Carl then assigned Victor Marsh, a young hotshot at Global Webb Securities, to help Yancy.

Steven knocks for luck on the Formica. "You wanted everything settled by the time we get married, and we're almost there. Nothing to weigh us down anymore."

There's a knock, and the trailer door opens. Trishelle sticks her head in. She spots Carl, and they smile. "Hello, again. Planning on staying a while this time?"

"As long as you'll let me."

Carl and Trishelle had a brief affair and continue to hook up when the timing is right. I don't know how they do it. I'd get too jealous.

A middle-aged woman in a blue suit stands behind Trishelle on the bottom step of my trailer. Next to her is a tall, blond man in a seersucker jacket. They peer inside. I

Trishelle raises her voice a tad too high. "Julia, good news! Pastor Eileen Campbell and Toby Jenkins both came early!"

"I didn't want to miss the Hollywood press conference!" Toby yells. "The pastor only agreed because I insisted!"

Pastor Eileen and Toby back up to avoid getting flattened by all of us, tumbling out of the trailer. Pastor Eileen stares at my hippie clothes as if I'm dressed like an alien.

"I'm in costume. I was going to change for you later."

Steven offers his hand and saves me. "Hello, Pastor, I'm Steven. Thank you so much for coming all this way on a Saturday." He can't dress, but his parents raised him right.

"Steven, the war hero? Call me Eileen," she says, pumping Steven's hand.

Trishelle claps her hands. "Everyone! Let's head to the podium on the bluff, and we'll start the conference!" She steers Toby by the elbow, and we all follow behind.

"You're a very striking couple," Pastor Eileen whispers to Steven and me.

We smile at each other. I feel like I'm floating. A word pops in my head: *success.* I'm producing my movie with my best friend, I'm marrying the love of my life, and we're starting a family. It's a lightness I haven't felt before. Then I remember Tina Swig and the heaviness returns. It'll feel better when the FBI arrests her. Then we'll really be in the clear.

As we pass the journalists on the way to the podium, a Sousa March starts on the hillside behind us. Everyone looks up the slope, searching for the source of the blasting music. Trishelle and I look at each other with wide eyes. An intruder is sabotaging our day.

Gwen Thompson groans. "They didn't secure the hillside! Amateur producers!"

"What's going on?" Pastor Eileen asks.

"Someone is trying to disrupt my event. It happens all the time when crews shoot in Los Angeles. Usually, it's someone looking for a hand-out," I explain.

"Find that guy and give him this, please!" Trishelle yells, holding up a hundred-dollar bill.

Journalists aim their TV cameras at the hill. This guy is not just ruining my event, he's creating an even bigger story. This doesn't feel right, though. Intruders harass crews in urban Los Angeles, but this jerk came all the way to Malibu to ruin my press conference?

I glance at Steven. He's wearing his thousand-yard stare. What does he see? He grabs my hand and points at a crew guy with a tattoo on his neck, walking past us with an extension cord. The hair on my neck goes up. I never hired him. He disappears behind my trailer.

Steven tries to follow him, but I tug his hand to stay. He scans the crowd again. All I see are overworked journalists. Steven points to my right—there's a man with a tattoo down the right side of his face and bolts coming out of his lower lip. He kneels like he dropped something. Another new face. A cold shiver runs through me.

Almost two years ago, Peter Heyman drugged Steven, drove him into the Sonoran Desert, and handed him to his tribe of tattooed followers who looked just like these two fake grips.

Steven points halfway up the hill covered with waist-high green grass. I see the glint of metal from his face first; the rest of him blends into the hillside because of the camouflage get-up he's wearing. It's Peter Heyman, the asshole with a god complex, leader of a tribe of survivalist wannabe trans-humans living off the grid.

Peter sees us, grins, and makes a shooting motion with his finger.

Steven lets go of my hand. Trishelle, Toby, and Carl are behind us, but Pastor Eileen is next to me by the Ferrari. Steven creeps toward the stunt car. The chassis is low to the ground. There's a clicking noise.

"Take cover!" Steven dives and tackles Pastor Eileen and me, and rolls us under Chef Rafa's cooking table, covering us with his body.

The journalists laugh.

The Ferrari explodes.

The shock wave hits my back and knocks the wind out of me. Debris rains down. People scream. There's another explosion farther away, and then another.

It was bad luck to open that envelope.

CHAPTER 3

TINA SWIG

Saturday, March 9, 12:30 p.m. (CST)
Wisconsin

I t's zero degrees outside my motel room, and it's time to go running. The path by the frozen river is rock hard and easy to run on. I'll shake for five minutes and then be fine.

I find my leggings and yank them up over my underwear, then find my sports bra and pull on a T-shirt. I love the cold. Some people can't wait to leave Wisconsin, but the freezing Midwest doesn't bother me.

I did move to Los Angeles for my career in TV, but I never loved Southern California. It's too hot, and there's too much cement.

Is there fresh snow on the ground? I pull open the drapes and check. Nope. That white van is still on the far side of the parking lot. Dumb and Dumber are inside, spying on me while smelling their own fast-food farts. I change motels every two nights, and they keep tracking me. It's all part of my plan. Stupid investigators, working for Julia Travers: watch me all you want, Yancy Mendoza and Victor Marsh. You sound like a yuppie mail-order catalog. I pretend to look at the clouds then drop the curtain.

CNN says another snowstorm is coming, which is perfect. I pull a fleece over my T-shirt, put on my socks with the little cotton-ball tassels, and slip into my running shoes. I run eight-minute miles and look good while doing it.

When is Douglas going to text me? He should have started the fun on the movie set by now. On cue, my phone buzzes. My man can read my mind. I got myself a lean and mean billionaire, the only man I ever met who can match me.

My thumb opens his text: *Fireworks have begun. Enjoy your run, darling.*

I put my laptop on the desk by the window. I open the drapes and let daylight flood the room, then sit down and type. I want Dumb and Dumber to see me from their van.

I go into the bathroom and look in the mirror. I look damn good for thirty-eight years old, better than I did five years ago when I was working my ass off for Robert Snow. He was a brilliant producer but a failure as a man. He almost ruined my life too. But, now, eighteen months later, I feel younger and stronger.

I look good with long, straight, black hair, but I miss my curls. I had to change my look when Douglas and I went into hiding, so I cut it, darkened it, and added extensions. I find hair ties in my toiletry kit and put my hair in two pigtails.

I pull my knit cap on, leaving pigtails dangling out on either side. It's another simple trick that the pavement people don't get—if you want to keep your fingers and toes warm, wear a hat. Your brain is what burns up all your calories.

I lay two large Ziploc bags on the side of the sink. I turn on the water, wet my hands, and run my fingers through my pigtails until they're dripping wet. They'll work their magic later. Last of all, I reach past the curtain covering the bathtub and open the tiny window to the outside. The bathroom gets cold right away. I turn off the light and leave the bathroom door open a crack. I grab my motel key, walk outside, and lock the door.

I don't even glance at the van as I cross the road and find the path next to the Pine River. Within a hundred steps, I find my rhythm. I'll go five miles. That'll give Dumb and Dumber time to make their move like they always do, but today there's a surprise for them.

This wouldn't be necessary if Julia Travers's obedient little gang of former soldiers and cops like Dumb and Dumber weren't turning over every rock to find Douglas and me. Thus, we must create a week of confusion—and our lives will be ours again.

Always have a plan—that's my motto.

I pick up the pace. My lungs love the cold air. The Pine River is frozen solid, with pine and birch trees surrounded by snow that's hip deep. My friends and I used to float on innertubes down this river in summer, towing a floating cooler of beer behind us. It was fun. We'd end near the town of Leon, carpool back, and then party at one of the fancy, summer houses. My friends all peaked at eighteen. Today, they're fat, drunk housewives. Not me; I'm peaking now.

Did I make it in California? Almost. I helped create TV shows that made over a billion dollars. Never got the credit but made some money. I fell in love and married Drake Shelby, a lame soap opera actor with an even lamer name. I thought I was marrying up, but he was shallower than a puddle of spit. We had a son, Devon, who was born with cerebral palsy. That didn't fit my narcissistic husband's vision for his perfect actor life, so he left. Fine, leave. I take care of my own.

Then, Robert Snow appeared. He launched my career, but I was smart enough not to marry him. He just bossed me around for ten years while I clawed my way up the ladder. I slept with him when it was necessary. It wasn't often, thank God. Then he screwed up and almost ruined everything for Devon and me. That was the second time I believed I was working with a man who was smarter than me, but I was wrong again. *Find someone smarter than you.* That's easier said than done, especially when you grow up with shitty male role models.

I got it right this time, though. There are less than a hundred men on the planet smarter or richer than Douglas Bushnell.

What's happening right now in California is sweet revenge. I'd love to be sitting on that hillside with Peter Heyman watching all the madness at that press conference. Steven Quintana and Julia Travers must be freaking out.

I run to the A&W stand, which is 2.5 miles, and turn around. I used to come here with my sister and stepdad. He was the original loser, but I was too young and stupid to know. Then I figured out he was abusing my sister and got smart. Once mom died, I didn't need them in my life and left home at seventeen. They're probably stuck living in a trailer right next to this river. Good riddance.

Either Marsh or Mendoza is in my motel room right by now, digging through my stuff. They've gone into my rooms at the last three motels. That's illegal, but they can't help themselves, they want so badly to find out who Douglas is. I don't feel bad about what's going to happen.

When I told Douglas my plan, he laughed so hard he couldn't breathe. Then he kissed me and took me to bed and treated me to his delicious love-making.

I get back to the motel forty minutes earlier than usual and approach it from the back. My step ladder is waiting in the snow, under the open window to my bathroom. I climb up and slide in through the high window and land in the tub without a sound. I practiced this at the last three motels, whenever the panel van wasn't around.

I pull open the curtain and step out of the tub into the dark bathroom. I peek through the crack I left open in the door and see Marsh, the skinny one, sitting at my computer. Mendoza is in the van watching the running trail, waiting for me to come back into view so he can radio Marsh to leave.

I pull my scissors out of my little bag and glance in the mirror. My wet pigtails are now frozen hair icicles. I cut them where the ice starts, giving me two short frozen spears, one in each hand. I drop each one into its own baggie and zip it shut, then wait thirty seconds for the bag to get ice cold.

I ease through the door, walk six steps across the cheap shag carpet, and plunge one plastic-covered spear into his left side, under his rib. He gasps and pushes back. Before he can look up, I jam the other frozen spear into his right ear. His head turns. He looks surprised and then goes blank. That does the trick.

I pull the chair back and use all my strength to haul him onto the bed. He bounces on the cheap mattress. The icicles stick out of him like shish-kabob skewers. There's no blood flow—the ice prevents that.

The walkie talkie on his belt chirps. I pop the earpiece out of his right ear. Mendoza's voice comes through: *"Marsh? Do you copy?"*

I reach inside Marsh's jacket and take out his weapon. An M9 Beretta, which means this clown is ex-military, not a cop. I find the walkie on his hip and push the call button six times. I grab a pillow off the bed and step back next to the motel door.

Mendoza runs up. He grunts as he almost slips on the icy sidewalk. Los Angeles moron. Probably never seen snow in his life. The door eases open. Mendoza sees Marsh on the bed and rushes in.

"Hey, Sexy," I whisper. When he turns, I push the pillow against his chest and pull the trigger. He grabs my wrists, but he's dead before his knees hit the floor.

He's bleeding fast, so it's hard to drag him closer to the bed. A drop of his blood lands on my shoes. Damn it, they're new. Asshole. Now I have to toss them.

I dump him at Marsh's feet. The open window in the bathroom will turn the room ice cold, so their bodies will freeze before they can stink up the place.

Time to set the scene. I take their phones and wallets. I find the keys to the van in Mendoza's pocket. I also find a Glock 22, probably his service weapon from when he was with the LAPD. I pull out a small tub of bleach from under the bed, wet a towel and wipe down every surface twice. I cleaned motel rooms while I was in college, so I know how to disinfect.

I pre-paid for the room with cash and told the manager that I don't want to be disturbed, so no one will open the door for ten days. That's all the time we need.

What else can I do to maximize confusion? I clean Marsh's gun twice with the bleach soaked towel, then slide the weapon into his right hand.

Mendoza lies in a pile at his feet, his blood already thickening on the carpet. I step around Mendoza and unbuckle Marsh's belt buckle and pull down his pants, so he's naked from the waist down. His dick is hard. I heard that happens. This will create at least another half day of confusion, hopefully. The tortured vet shoots his ex-cop lover.

I heard Mendoza's got kids, but cop widows get good pensions. I don't know about Marsh, except that he worked for Carl Webb, which was his first mistake.

Julia Travers and Steven Quintana made this necessary. They know too much about Douglas and me. They know my name, which I hate. Do they know about Devon? Few people do. He must remain safe, first and foremost. Do they know Douglas is Boss Man? I have no clue. But one week of chaos will make all this worry go away.

The room is a refrigerator. I look at my watch; it's been twenty minutes since I stabbed and shot them. I test the black hair icicles sticking out of Marsh's right ear and left side. They are softening, while his body is hardening. I pull them out fast, and no blood flows onto the bleached and frayed motel bedsheets. The plastic bags aren't punctured. I got the heavy-duty kind, so no DNA transferred. Douglas made me practice on pigs in a restaurant freezer in Palermo. It was gross at first, but it helped me get used to how to stab, and how long to wait before I yanked out the icicle. The holes will contract, making them hard to find and even harder for them to figure out exactly what happened. It will be all over the news, probably a week from tomorrow. They'll need a day to identify the bodies, and we'll have disappeared by then.

I toss the hair, wallets, phones, and weapon into a garbage bag along with the pillow. I pocket the keys, grab my carry-on, and do a final check. I'm ready to go.

I toss my carry-on and the garbage bag out the bathroom window and climb back out. I practiced this too. I lean the step ladder back against the woodshed, then sweep away my footprints in the snow. The storm comes tonight will leave another two inches of snow and leave no trace of me. The *Do Not Disturb* tag is still on the doorknob.

I walk across the parking lot to the van. No one sees me at 2:15 p.m. on a frozen Saturday. Everyone is watching their kids' hockey games, except for the motel manager who's watching an evangelical preacher on TV. And the local clown cop never patrols here. I get behind the wheel of the van and drive away.

I'll drive to Chicago. Along the way, I'll download everything from their phones and the computers in the van. Then I'll smash it all and toss the pieces into trash bins at different gas stations. I'll find a high-end truck stop with showers where I can trim the rest of my hair short again and put on the fancy clothes in my carry-on. I'll leave their empty van in a garage by the airport, enjoy a hot meal in the first-class lounge, then board my flight and get back to my man. Living well is the best revenge.

I drive along the road hugging the river. The sun peeks out from behind a cloud and reflects off the ice crystals on all the trees, making it look like they're covered in diamonds. It's pretty. I wish Devon could see it with me.

My phone buzzes with a text: *How was your run?*

I text back a thumbs-up emoji.

As I said, I always have a plan.

CHAPTER 4

CARL WEBB

Saturday, March 9, 4:00 p.m. (PST)
California

Malibu City Hall has a long lobby. My black shoes echo off the tile floor. Surfboards hang from the ceiling, but it's still a government building.

What the hell happened on that bluff? Trishelle seized all my situational awareness, and I dropped my guard. I slipped my arm around her waist, heard the corny march music, and then the explosions came.

I reach the end of the lobby and stare at the photographs of the elected officials on the wall. The City Manager is cute. My brain yells at me. *Get your head in the game.*

It was a blur after the explosions. I hovered over Julia and Steven, but the pastor and the wedding planner were the most shaken up. Then, the paramedics arrived and pushed me to the side, and the sheriff deputies showed up and drove Julia and Steven away. I get it; that's standard protocol for VIPs, but I made sure to follow them here.

I loosen my tie. At least the air-conditioning is good in here. My suit is too new to get sweat stains over crap like this.

Two LAPD detectives arrived next, which means the cops are grilling them. Massive explosions can be a crime, but they've been here for hours. I should get them some food. They're going to be hungry when they get out.

A car beeps, and I step outside. Trishelle exits her gray Audi and strides across the parking lot toward me. She's tall, curvy, and the best damn girlfriend a man like me could hope to get, precisely because she wants to be my girlfriend and nothing more.

She takes off her sunglasses and grants me one kiss in the shaded entranceway. She doesn't flash me her coy smile, which is how she usually gets me to stay for two weeks.

"This is not what I had in mind when I arrived. I thought I'd get a list of my duties as a best man, and then you and I could check into a hotel."

"Me too. But this is bad."

"How many people got hurt? I heard three explosions."

"Nobody. The car exploded, an empty oil drum went up like a rocket, and one of Chef Rafa's refrigerators blew up and sent a metal door flying, but that's all. People ran around screaming, but when paramedics and firefighters from Point Dume Station got there, no one needed first aid."

"That's good then, right?"

Trishelle spits in French. "Except I lost control of my own production. The journalists loved it. They interviewed the cooks, the PAs, even the pastor. That pisses me off."

"Why?"

"Those explosions are now the news, not our press conference." Her forehead knits, revealing her worry. "And the fire chief treated it like a crime scene. They had their tape measures out, they took pictures, and they put pieces of burnt crap into plastic baggies. I heard him tell a firefighter that we're lucky it's winter because if we'd pulled this stunt in summer, it would've started a fire."

"A stunt?" A snicker sneaks into my voice.

She pokes me in the chest with a pointy fingernail. "A dumb stunt to promote the movie and get easy media coverage. That's what they're saying. That reporter from the CBC said that Julia tried to *terrify* her. The sheriff deputies heard that and hauled Steven and Julia in. Now those gorillas are interrogating them, thinking they planned it all."

Two sheriff deputies, a man, and a woman exit the main doors and give us the once-over. Trishelle and I walk down the stairs and back to her car. I open the passenger door and get in. "Come on, let's get them some coffee and donuts."

"Julia doesn't like donuts. But you can poison Steven if you want," She puts on her sunglasses and slides behind the wheel. I'm barely buckled when she revs the car and pops it into gear. We tear past the two deputies, who gape at us.

"Trishelle, chill out. We don't want to get arrested too." I glance over my shoulder, half-expecting them to hop into a squad car and chase us down.

"We are under attack, Carl."

"Let's not go there yet."

"Boss Man and Tina Swig could be behind this."

"Except we have them on the run. Mendoza and Marsh are tracking Tina Swig in Wisconsin. She'll be arrested tomorrow."

"Peter Heyman, then. That survivalist nutball who strapped Steven into that plane."

"He's hiding in the Mexican desert with his tribe of wackos. How would he profit from messing with Julia and Steven right now? It's too risky."

Trishelle heads to the center of town and parks in front of the Malibu Country Mart. "I don't know. But this shit makes me so hungry I'm going to eat an entire meatloaf sandwich."

She gets out of the car and walks fast. I fall in step next to her. "We feed them first. Then what, handsome?"

"The LAPD and the County will figure out if they have enough to press charges. Meanwhile, they'll be watching Julia and Steven to see what they do next."

"Don't the police have anything better to do?"

"Maybe not. This may be the most exciting crime to hit Malibu this year."

"So, what do we do?"

"We keep them separated, so they'll be nothing for the police to see. I'll take Steven to his bachelor apartment. You take Julia back to the beach house. No visitors. Only answer calls from me. They shouldn't talk to each other, either."

She shrugs. "Is that really necessary?"

"Just for a few days. If the DA brings charges. they'll subpoena their phone records, so why give them anything to subpoena in the first place? Let things settle. By mid-week, we'll have a bigger picture of what happened and what to do."

"You're the security expert."

What I don't mention is that keeping them on lockdown is the best strategy if someone is really trying to hurt them. But there's no reason to get her worried about something I can prevent.

We walk up the steps to the Malibu Country Mart, but she puts her hands on the screen door before I can open it. My brunette looks cool with her Jackie Onassis shades. "I want to talk about us. What are we doing, anyway?"

"We're having a sophisticated and passionate international love affair."

"That'll work, but only for a little while longer," she says, then opens the door for me. "Come on. I'll buy you a meatloaf sandwich."

Damn. I thought I'd dodged that bullet on this trip.

CHAPTER 5

STEVEN QUINTANA

Saturday, March 9, 5:00 p.m. (PST)
California

Detective Adrienne Gum flashes a thin smile as she comes back in the room. She opens her black jacket, flashing the gold badge on her belt, then drops the legal pad on the table and sits down across from me.

"Where's Julia?" My olfactory bulb is picking up her perfume in the air.

"With another detective. He's checking her story while I'm checking yours."

"We're not the ones you should be questioning. You want Peter Heyman."

Detective Gum twirls her pencil and narrows her green eyes. "Steven, you say that you knew that the car was going to explode. Yet, you don't know anything about the explosives planted in the trunk, refrigerator, or oil drum. That doesn't make sense."

"The car chassis was close to the ground. There was clicking. It was a feeling."

"Have you always had a feeling when bombs were about to go off?"

She's taunting me, hoping I'll get angry and rise to her bait. "When you're in Afghanistan, if you don't want to die from an IED exploding next to your Humvee, you develop a sixth sense about spotting them."

This silences her, but she still smiles. "Did Julia Travers ask you to do it?"

"She didn't ask me anything."

"She's the producer and star, and you're just the stunt coordinator. Maybe you're jealous of her success. Maybe you planted the dummy bombs to raise a ruckus."

"Like I said, you should be looking for Peter Heyman. Yancy Mendoza can confirm everything. He's been working for Julia to find Douglas Bushnell and Tina Swig."

"This conspiracy sounds very elaborate. But the answers are usually closer to home."

"Are we done then? I've answered all your questions."

"Yes. You can go." She stays seated, letting me find my own way out.

It feels good to walk out the front doors into the California sunshine. Carl appears and hands me a cup of coffee and a paper bag. "Caffeine and half of a meatloaf sandwich. It's good."

"Thanks." I eat the sandwich in four bites, then chase it with a sip of joe. "Julia is still in there. We need to wait."

Carl points at two black BMWs parked side by side in the parking lot. "Her agent and lawyer just got here, so they'll be in there a while. Trishelle will wait for her." He nods at the Audi parked in the shade of a tree. Trishelle smiles and waves from the driver's seat. I wave back.

"I saw Heyman on the hill."

He looks surprised. "Metal-face? Are you sure?"

"Absolutely. His cheek was glinting in the sun. He pointed at Julia and me just before the explosion."

Carl glances around as if Heyman might be watching from behind a bush right now. "Then you're not safe, especially out in the open. Let's go."

CHAPTER 6

JULIA TRAVERS

Saturday, March 9, 5:00 p.m. (PST)
California

My agent, Rick Telles, and Saul Berlin, chief counsel for The Griffith Agency, shift in their seats on either side of me. Detective Niall McCusker tugs at his rumpled suit and stares at the paper in his hand, then he looks at me with his tired face and asks the same three questions yet again.

"Did you have a permit for the explosive devices?"

"No, because we were attacked! There were men on the set I didn't recognize, men who work for Peter Heyman. He pointed at us from the hill!"

"So, you had no fire marshal on set? No federal permit from the ATF either?"

"It was a press conference. We didn't expect bombs to be going off. Steven and I were right next to the Ferrari that exploded. If he hadn't tackled Eileen and me and pulled us under the table, we could have been killed."

McCusker shakes his head. "The trunk was reinforced with plates. All the energy of the explosion went up instead of out. All that diving was dramatic, but you weren't in danger. He also grabbed you before the bomb went off like he knew it would happen."

Saul exhales like a deflating balloon. He puts his hand up. "Can we speak to our client privately, please?"

McCusker stands up. "I'll be back in two," he says and walks out the door.

Saul and Rick bring their chairs so close I can smell the ham sandwiches they had for lunch. "*Celebrity Exposed* is reporting that the explosions could be a publicity stunt arranged by you and Steven," Rick whispers.

My pulse pounds in my temples. "*Celebrity Exposed* was *not* invited to the event. They're liars, especially the editor-in-chief Larry Naythons."

"*Celebrity Exposed* knew about the explosions as soon as they happened," Rick says. "They sent a crew from Los Angeles and streamed interviews live to the internet. Six people from your crew insisted that the explosions were a stunt that Steven arranged."

"The crew had four people, and Trishelle and I hired them ourselves. Heyman and his people infiltrated the set. It's all fake."

"Slow down, Julia. Let us help you," Saul says. He's a cross between Gandhi and Tony Soprano, lethal and calm in any situation. Yet, there's a glimmer of concern.

McCusker comes back in, plops down, and sighs like an exhausted grandpa. "Okay, let's get back to it. Steven Quintana served in Afghanistan, correct?"

"Yes. I don't remember when or for how long."

"The stunt car, refrigerator, and oil drum all had deflection plates. Our bomb expert says that soldiers built and installed similar deflection blast plates on the bottom of vehicles in Iraq and Afghanistan."

"So?"

"Do you think it's possible that Steven did all of this without consulting you?"

I stare at McCusker. His smug mug tells me that he already believes it. Saul and Rick purse their lips and narrow their eyes.

I look back at McCusker. "That's impossible. Steven would never do that."

"Are you sure? Take your time answering."

I turn back to Rick and Saul. "You back me on this, right?"

"We represent you, Julia, not Steven." Saul and Rick each flash me an eyebrow raise, giving me permission to sell out Steven to protect myself.

I close my eyes. *Steven, hang on. We'll be together soon.*

CHAPTER 7

TINA SWIG

Monday, March 11, 7:10 a.m. Central European Time
Near Palermo, Sicily

Sicily is gorgeous, especially with spring on the way.

"You have friends in San Vito Lo Capo?" my Uber driver asks.

Nosy bastard. I lie to him. "My grandfather. He goes to church every Sunday."

"Beautiful Norman church there. Wonderful children's choir. Sublime."

He drops me off at the church, and I walk two blocks to the beach. The sun is rising over the long stretch of white sand. The sound of music and children singing comes from behind me. They start choir practice early, poor kids.

Carlos, the young Italian bosun, appears in his formal, white uniform with the black and gold epaulets. "Miss? May I take your bag for you?" He's discreet; he never asks my name and never asks questions except to serve me. No one on the yacht is allowed to know my name. They can call me *Miss T.* or *ma'am*, never *Tina*. A long dock runs out into the bay, where a motorboat is docked. "The tender is ready."

He helps me into the small boat, and onto a cushion. It's just past seven in the morning on Monday, March 11, and the sea is calm. A huge rock, *Monte Monaco,* rises like a massive pimple from the bay, marking one end of a beach that stretches all the way to Mount Erice on the opposite side. The rock is lit up yellow in the rising sun, and out in the bay is our yacht, *Reckoning,* ninety feet of pure bliss. It's a moving mansion. We go to sleep in the same bed every night and then wake up off the coast of Malta or the Aeolian Islands or Ustica or Tunisia.

Douglas is right; it's perfect for our work right now. We blend in with all the other yachts. No one cares where we go; we're welcome to come ashore and spend our money in every port, no questions asked. Life is good when you are rich and anonymous. And it's about to get better, now that the explosive fun has begun.

Carlos helps me off the tender and onto the swim platform. I climb the five steps to the main aft deck, walk past the covered dining tables, and through the glass doors into the main salon.

Computer screens and TV monitors are recessed into mahogany cabinets along one wall, displaying everything from our satellite communication to the ship's internet traffic. We're a moving international internet broadcast company, but right now, it's the quiet before the storm. Our high-tech frat boys—Min, Ismael, and Elliot—are ashore whoring it up somewhere, like sailors on leave. They'll be back on board and at their keyboards tomorrow, ready to ramp up the madness.

Douglas emerges from the master suite with his cropped, brown hair and perfect, two-day stubble on his handsome face. He wears loose pants and a raw silk shirt. He looks like a yachting billionaire, which is what he is.

"Hello, my sweet genius. How was your flight?"

"Uneventful."

He kisses me. "That's the best kind of flight to have."

Rebecca, his redheaded steward, enters carrying a glass of champagne on a silver tray. She doesn't make eye contact as I take the glass, then slips away before I can thank her. She's always discreet, but never this modest.

"Were you just fucking her?"

"No. Do I seem guilty?"

"She does. And there's nothing to be guilty about, even if you were. You had billionaire tastes before I met you. I just want the chance to keep pace."

"Rebecca's been with me a long time and is very loyal. But no, I wasn't fucking her. I have a marathon with you coming up, both in bed and out, so I need my rest."

Douglas is fifty-eight (I think), so he'd better get his rest. Otherwise, I might kill him with all my kindness. I never want him to doubt choosing me. "What have you been doing since we traded texts?" I ask.

"Monitoring the chaos in California. The police have questioned Quintana and Travers, so our fake news is working."

"You look a little tired, my love."

"I was up most of the night while you were flying, but I did my Krav Maga and followed it up with a thermal heat bath. I feel good after only three hours of sleep."

"No cold thermogenesis?" Workers from Rome installed a special freezing chamber in the master bathroom before I left.

"That's every second day, along with the juicing. It seems to be working."

There's no debate. He only seems five years older than me, not twenty.

Carlos returns to the salon after putting away my things in the master suite. He bows and then heads down to the crew quarters. It's just Douglas and me now. We won't hear from the captain or first mate. They stay on the bridge or engine room and never come into the living areas. Every need, from the air temperature to the depth of the anchorage to shore communication, Douglas controls with his touchpad. He issues a command, and they comply. Rebecca and Carlos serve our personal needs, while a chef stays in the galley below deck. Rebecca supervises a housekeeper, a woman who changes the linen and cleans our rooms when we're elsewhere on the yacht.

Douglas takes me in his arms. "Hello there," he whispers, sending an erotic pulse up my spine that explodes in my brain.

"We'll start stage two soon. Do you have their phone numbers?"

"I do. All four of them."

He smiles. I do love to please him. I don't tell him how I get my information, and he doesn't ask. We each have our secrets. It's safer that way.

He releases me. "Go visit Devon. Rebecca is serving breakfast on the sundeck in thirty minutes, and I want both of you there."

Up a short flight of stairs is the middle floor, with a sundeck and two smaller bedrooms. I knock at the first door, hear a grunt, and let myself in. It's a teenager's bedroom, with World Cup football and *Marvel* superhero posters on the wall, and two computer screens running. The drapes are open for a change, and the water outside is like a sheet of blue glass. Devon is strapped into his cherry-red wheelchair with the built-in computer monitor, but he's gazing at the view.

"Hello, my gorgeous son. I missed you."

He hits the power toggle with the palm of his right hand, spins around, rises to my height, and then zooms right at me, stopping one inch short. He grins.

"Show-off. Happy to see me?"

He slides his teeth over a mouthpiece, which works like a computer mouse. His tongue types out words that the computer turns into speech. It's a neat little device Douglas invented for him.

"I don't like it when you leave. Where did you go?" The voice of Paul Newman comes out of the computer speaker.

"I was securing your future. Us against the world, right?"

"Us against the world," he says. It's our little phrase.

"I like Paul Newman. Did Uncle Douglas give you your new voice?"

Devon nods. Douglas has done a lot for Devon—the hip wheelchair, the computer, and the voice alteration software. We can load a two-minute recording of any person's voice into the computer, and, within minutes, the computer will sound like that person.

Devon is handsome, with sandy brown hair. He's a fantastic seventeen-year-old genius and the light of my life. But, he's also a quadriplegic with dyskinetic cerebral palsy since he was born breech with the umbilical cord wrapped around his neck. My condescending jerk obstetrician should have known and handled the crisis. But he didn't, and I blame myself for not standing up to him earlier in my pregnancy.

Since then, I've dedicated my life to making Devon's productive and happy, and to punishing any fool who gets in my way. I took that doctor to court, ruined him, and made sure his wife knew he was cheating on her.

"I spoke to Professor Carlton today," Devon says, throwing in a Southern drawl. "He wants me to try one of the Millennium Prize Problems from the Clay Institute."

"Really? Which one?" We memorized all seven challenges, a mother/son hobby. Whoever solves even one earns one million dollars.

"The Hodge conjecture. Belgian mathematician Pierre Deligne first predicted that for projective algebraic varieties, Hodge cycles are rational linear combinations of algebraic cycles. I have an idea for a computer model that may lead to a proof."

"That's so exciting! When are you starting?'

"Tomorrow. I was staring at the view, thinking about the code I must write."

"I'm so glad we found Professor Carlton. You're going to have a degree from Cambridge University before you're twenty."

"And I'm going to win the Fields Medal before I'm thirty." Devon's grin covers his whole face. He's in bliss, which means I'm in bliss because, when his brain is working in hyperdrive, he transcends his wheelchair.

"Uncle Douglas wants us on the sundeck for breakfast in ten minutes, my love," I say and give him a long kiss on the forehead. I pull back. He smells like perfume. Rebecca's perfume. His skin flushes red.

Now her guilty look and Douglas's odd answer make sense. Did Douglas initiate their encounter? Did Devon do it on his own? Douglas must have at least given it a nod of approval since nothing on this yacht ever gets by him. He may have even suggested it and instructed Rebecca to proceed. How far did this encounter go? And how upset should I be? I shoot Devon a sideways glance. He flushes a deeper red and grins.

"I won't ask. As long as you get that Fields Medal, darling."

CHAPTER 8

CARL WEBB

Sunday, March 10, 10:30 p.m. (PST)
California

I offer Steven a paper plate filled with spicy beef and broccoli. He sighs and takes it. We're on the back deck of his old bachelor pad, sitting in Adirondack chairs overlooking the beach in Tivoli Cove. We've been here all day, lying low, doing nothing. It's the safest choice after yesterday's madness, but his legs are bouncing like pistons, he's so restless.

I need to distract him. "Quintana, why do you keep paying for this place?"

"The surf. Imagine catching that wave right now."

The wave moves across the cove. It starts to break, but the face stays glassy as it passes us, and keeps going. The shoulder finally closes out as the wave hits the sand.

"That's the best left-breaking wave in Malibu. Ten seconds of serenity." He sighs. He sure as hell ain't serene right now. I offer him a pork bun, but he turns it down. "I need to talk to Julia."

"She's with Trishelle."

"Is that why you're babysitting me? To keep us apart?"

"Yep. You're on lockdown."

"Radio silence too?"

"For now. If you want to talk to Julia, tell me, and I'll tell Trishelle."

He sips his Corona. "I get it. Heyman can't hurt us both this way."

I finish my beer and toss the dead solider in his blue recycling bin. "He won't hurt either of you as long as I'm involved."

Steven gets up and stands by the wooden railing. There's no one in the cove, but he hugs the shadows. "I bet Heyman is out past Palm Springs, running his Humvee through Patton's old tank training ground. He's a desert rat, that's where he'd go."

"Or he's on the coast highway, looking for you. Let other people find him."

Steven sits back in his chair and opens a water bottle. "I don't get it. Heyman goes to all this trouble to try and pin three fake explosions on me? How bad can it get?"

I mirror him and sip water too. "If someone was really scared, it could be assault. There are county laws about setting fires and federal laws that cover explosive devices."

Steven laughs. "Bring it on. I've been shot three times. I fought six killers on a plane. I could do six months for that bullshit standing on my head."

"And they'd have to convict you first." Heyman could be up to far worse, but I stay quiet. No need to rile him up.

"As long as Julia's safe. I will do what's required."

We clink water bottles. "Anything, Anytime, Anywhere. Want to know how we figured out Boss Man's name?"

"Tell me."

"Major Glenn Ward gets the credit. Boss Man was in La Paz, Mexico, during the broadcast of *Six Passengers, Five Parachutes*. We traced every airline and hotel during that time and got nothing. Then,

Glenn remembered that Boss Man used a yacht when he was in Hong Kong. Glenn got NSA satellite photos and traced every yacht in the La Paz Harbor that week. There was one that never registered with the harbormaster, a white yacht with a unique hull, with a sharp bow and stern. We spotted her in other photos in other harbors, where she did register. And we got her name: *Clairvoyance*. We then examined satellite photos of when Boss Man was in Hong Kong and found its exact twin in Asia: *Second Sight*."

Steven's eyes open as big as plates. "Robert Snow whispered *Clairvoyance* and *Second Sight* before he died. I thought he was talking to God. Those were yachts?"

"Yup. *Clairvoyance*. Owned by a shell company that's owned by Douglas Bushnell. Another shell company owns its twin, *Second Sight*."

"If we find his yachts, we find Bushnell."

"We've been looking. The yachts are either in a warehouse or he scuttled them."

"Is Bushnell rich enough that he can sink two mega yachts?"

"Yes. But, if he likes living on yachts, my guess is he's hiding on one now."

"And when they arrest Tina Swig, she'll tell them where to search." Steven stares at the waves. He's still for the first time in hours. I may be getting through to him.

"Exactly. Mendoza should've already alerted the FBI about Tina Swig. They may be bursting into that motel room right now. Then we'll find Bushnell, and Peter Heyman, in that order. There's no reason to go racing through the desert. Stay low. Trust us."

"Thank you, Carl."

He shouldn't thank me yet. Mendoza hasn't checked in with me.

CHAPTER 9

JULIA TRAVERS

Sunday, March 10, 10:30 p.m. (PST)
California

It's odd being home without Steven, on the longest, loneliest Sunday of my life. It'd be nice to open the curtains and see the ocean, but Trishelle refuses. We move into the study instead. "I need something. Coffee. Ice cream," I complain.

"I'll grab two pints of chocolate from the garage freezer."

"Brilliant. Make mine vanilla."

"Boring, but okay." Trishelle leaves me alone in the wood-paneled office with the computer that no one uses. The clock on the wall ticks.

My phone rings. It's Steven's number. I answer so fast I almost hang up on him. "Are you okay? They don't want us talking!"

"They're bringing federal charges against me. I'm going to prison, Julia."

I've never heard him this upset. "We'll fight it. We'll hire the best lawyers."

"They found my fingerprints on all the bomb material."

"How?" My mind goes to a bad place for an instant, and then I pull it back.

"Heyman…." His voice drops out and comes back.

I rush into the hallway, desperate to find better reception. "Steven! Say that again."

"Heyman called me. Says he has my prints and is going to set off more explosions."

I pace in the long, white entranceway, wishing Trishelle would come back. "Steven, listen. You're with Carl. I'm with Trishelle. They can't blame us."

"He'll kill people unless we pay him off. He wants one hundred thousand dollars at the Wilshire and Western Metro station. I have fifty. Bring another fifty."

"No! Where's Carl? I have to talk to him."

"I've never asked you for anything, Julia. I need help. Be on the last Purple Line train entering the station at midnight. I'm getting on my motorcycle now." He hangs up.

Trishelle comes in the door from the garage. She has no ice cream but holds her phone. "Carl just called. He said Steven is gone, and then hung up."

"Call him back. Steven's heading to the Wilshire Wiltern Metro Station."

"I did. I hit redial, and it just rings." Trishelle looks terrified.

I see my reflection in the entranceway mirror, and it's way worse. I only have ten thousand dollars stashed in this house. "How much money is in the safe in the production office?"

"Thirty thousand. But I need that to grease palms for the entire six-week shoot."

I'm wearing diamond earrings. That adds up to over fifty. I grab the car keys off the entrance side table. "Let's go."

Chapter 10

STEVEN QUINTANA

Sunday, March 10, 11:15 p.m. (PST)
California

Tiny waves lap on the beach. Big waves crash in my brain.

I hid in a tree in Bosnia in a snowstorm for three days, until my camera froze solid. Carl and I hid in the mountain jungles of Colombia for a week and only spoke six words. In the Bahamas, Julia and I hid all night in a cave in a freshwater sinkhole. I'm trained to wait, but I hate waiting.

"Get some sleep, Quintana. I'll sleep out here in the hammock."

Carl won't sleep. He'll stay on watch all night. We're both in that zone of hyper-awareness, ready to move, but stuck in neutral.

His phone rings. He gives the screen a puzzled look and shows me. Trishelle Hobbes. He pushes aside the Chinese takeout cartons and sets the phone on the wooden table between us. "Trishelle, what's up?"

"Where are you? I can't see you."

"At Steven's place in Malibu, where I'm supposed to be."

"You just called again and hung up. I'm standing by the escalator, waiting."

"That wasn't me, Trishelle. Where are you?"

"The metro station by the Wiltern Theater. Julia just took the money down."

Carl jumps up and motions for me to stay put. With the phone to his ear, he walks down the three wooden steps to the beach.

Carl was my commanding officer for seven years and was always right, but this time, his plan isn't working. Julia's in trouble, and I'm done waiting.

I walk inside and open the oven. On the racks are my cameras and my motorcycle keys. I grab the keys to the Bonneville and a helmet on my way out the door.

I dart up the wooden stairs to Tivoli Road and run under the covered parking and put the keys in the motorcycle. There won't be traffic this late on a Sunday. If I drive a hundred, I'll make it in forty minutes. Carl runs up the stairs as my bike takes off.

"Quintana, get your ass back here!"

Sorry, Master Sergeant, she needs me, and I'm the only one who's dealt with Heyman before. I hit Pacific Coast Highway, accelerate past a Bentley, and the windblast hits my chest. I lean over the handlebars and crank it open all the way.

CHAPTER 11

JULIA TRAVERS

Sunday, March 10, 11:55 p.m. (PST)
California

The emptiness echoes inside the metro station. Tile murals cover the walls, faces of the people of Los Angeles, six feet high. Where's Steven? They stare back at me, not answering. It's quiet; the Wiltern Theater is three floors above and dark tonight.

I zip up my blue tracksuit, pull the brim down on my Dodgers cap, and hope that no one recognizes me. Steven will toss Heyman his money, and this nightmare will be over. But how did he get Steven's prints?

At the far end, two homeless women hide under their hoodies next to their roller bags, trying to sleep on a stone bench. I ache for them. They're my mother's age. One whispers and the other laughs, which warms me inside; they have each other, at least. At the other end of the platform, two teenagers kiss.

So here I am, Steven. Where are you?

The long escalators hum. A glass bottle falls down a cement staircase somewhere in this cavern but doesn't break. A siren passes by on Wilshire Boulevard, far above. I so want to be back in Trishelle's car with Steven next to me.

A dusty wind kicks up and a light appears in the tunnel. It's midnight. Steven can do amazing things, but can he control the flow of metro trains now? A three-car train pulls into the station. The doors slide open, and I step on.

The car is empty. He had better show up, or these doors will close, and I'll be riding the Purple Line alone, back downtown.

Footsteps echo off the marble. Someone is leaping down the steps, five at a time. Feet appear, then legs. It's Steven. The train beeps and he leaps on just as the doors close.

I hold up the backpack like a proud kid. "I got the money!"

He leaps back at the closed doors and tries to pry them open. "That wasn't me on the phone. They got your number and faked my voice."

My stomach turns. I almost throw up. *Fuck.*

He gives up on the doors and crouches into a fighting stance in front of me. Every muscle in his back tenses up, ready.

My face flushes hot with shame. "I'm sorry."

"There are cameras in here, mounted above the windows."

I see the small, square cameras. How did he spot them?

The train pulls out of the station. The overhead lights flicker as it lurches to the right. Steven plasters his face against the glass, peering outside. "We're leaving the main track and going into a service tunnel. Who knows you're here?"

"Trishelle is waiting in a car on the street."

He checks his phone. "Shit, no bars."

My muscles tremble with a new rush of adrenalin, but there's nowhere to run.

The lights flicker. The door at the other end of the train car opens. A tall, bald man with a scar of metal across his face—making him look like a circus freak—steps through. Peter Heyman. He tried to kill Steven before and he's back to try again.

Steven runs down the aisle at him. Heyman grins, showing even more metal in his freaky face. He raises a gun and shoots Steven in the chest. He falls on his face in the aisle three feet before reaching Heyman.

I dive between the orange metro seats and force myself onto the hard rubber floor. Heyman appears above me and shoots me next, right in the thigh. I look down—he darted me, like a rhino in Africa. My mind slows. The train tilts.

No, I'm tilting. The train goes black.

CHAPTER 12

TINA SWIG

Monday, March 11, 9:00 a.m. (CET)
Sicily

I ignore Rebecca as she clears the breakfast dishes. Chef baked brioche with orange zest and stuffed them with amaretto gelato. Instead of coffee, we had coffee granita. It's an indulgent Sicilian breakfast that's often served on a hot day, not our usual healthy meal of green smoothies and coconut milk, but today is a special occasion.

I walk down the side staircase and stand alone on the aft deck, enjoying the last few black ice shards of my granita. They look like tiny versions of the hair icicles I used on Marsh yesterday, and my brain flashes back to his surprised face. Yuck. Why does my mind do that?

Douglas exits the main salon and hugs me from behind. Douglas. He's the one man who can give me memories worth remembering.

"Come in, darling. All our planning is paying off. The rabbits ran right into our trap."

"I want to savor the last moment before the game really begins. Want a taste?"

I feed him the last spoonful, which he enjoys.

He touches my hair. "I miss your long hair."

"I used it to kill someone."

"You had to. They were putting our lives at risk, and Devon's too. Tell yourself that, and those irritating images won't plague you much longer."

He's right, as usual. "I'll be right in," I whisper.

He hugs me, then walks past the tinted glass doors back into the main cabin.

I glance up the stairs to the sun deck. Devon is locked in his room, solving his impossible math problems. He's also bored. This yacht is not enough. The key is to keep challenging him and keep expanding his world.

I look at my watch. It's 9:00 a.m. in Sicily, so it's midnight in Los Angeles and they've boarded the train. My phone buzzes with an encrypted text from Walter.

They were not followed.

Perfect. No cops saw them.

Now show me your tits.

Snide little Walter. He's my secret weapon in Los Angeles, from my time producing TV. He found their phone numbers for me, the clever little prick. Our two-week affair was miserable while it lasted, but it has paid off over the years.

I yank down my top and click a selfie of my exposed boobs, making sure to give him a side-shot with plenty of stretch marks from breastfeeding. Why make them look good for him? I send the photo and text him. *Beat off to that, loser.* He likes being abused.

Time to play the game. I walk back through the glass doors into the main salon. Our three tech geniuses—Min, Elliot, and Ismael—sit in front of their big 5K monitors.

"Talk to me, boys."

"The darting went great. We have awesome footage from the train," Min says, glancing over his shoulder. He's a handsome Korean-American kid who dropped out of Stanford to program for us. His first-generation immigrant parents are furious, but they'll change their minds once he buys them a new house.

"Elliot, how many nodes did you use before you placed the calls?"

Elliot, my white jock, sits in the middle. He's got thin orange hair and wears a football jersey, which makes him look like an NFL hooligan.

"I circled the globe. We have bots on servers on three continents."

"Is Peter Heyman happy?" Douglas asks as he joins the group.

Ismael, the last one in line, answers, "He's frothing at the mouth, he's so excited." Ismael is my preppy African-American nerd who always wears button-down shirts; yellow, blue, or pink. He's the only one of the three who knows how an iron works, and found one downstairs in the crew quarters.

"Let's get them to the studio. And keep that footage coming."

I love when a new project launches, before your life changes forever.

CHAPTER 13

CARL WEBB

Trishelle tugs open the curtains. White light attacks my retinas. I pull myself up to a sitting position on the couch.

"Sleep well?" She goes into the kitchen and snaps on the coffee maker.

"I would have slept better if I could have slept with you."

"It wouldn't have helped."

She's right. We ran around the metro station with our heads cut off, and got back here exhausted at 3:00 a.m. I lay on the couch in the dark, listening to her tossing in the guest bedroom. I thought I heard music, then fell asleep just before dawn.

My eyes adjust to the light. It's weird to be in a beach house while a crisis is happening. Julia and Steven's place isn't huge, and the neighbors' houses are close. But, it's overpriced California, so its price tag is still in the millions. The house starts on a hillside and juts out on stilts embedded into the rocky part of the beach. You walk in the front door, down a white hallway, past a master bedroom, dining room, and guest bedroom, and reach a living room with two, deep-gray couches with way too many pillows. What makes it feel big is a wall of sliding glass doors that lead to a narrow balcony and the vast Pacific Ocean on the other side. There's a small galley kitchen next to the dining room with its own smaller windows that overlook the water.

And the Pacific Ocean is still out there, flat and blue, stretching forever. It doesn't care that Steven and Julia are gone.

How did Heyman pull this off? There's been radio silence from Mendoza since midnight Saturday. Mendoza must catch Swig, so she can lead us to Bushnell. That's our sliver of hope. Finding Bushnell requires searching satellite photos of vacation spots around the world, looking for a yacht with a pointed bow and stern, if that's even what he's on. That requires people at the NOAA, at the National Reconnaissance Office, the National Geo-Spatial Intelligence Agency, and NASA.

My staff in Miami may know people at some of these agencies, but that's a Hail Mary pass. I grab my phone off the vast coffee table and speed-write a text.

Trishelle pushes the toaster button down and pours something in the kitchen. This is the first time I've been with Trishelle when we haven't ripped each other's clothes off. Our best friends are missing, which kicks our relationship into new territory. She comes back in the living room and hands me a cup of coffee.

"That was fast."

"It's instant espresso. Real coffee is brewing."

We sip and trade stares. I want to yell at her but don't. Anger is too blunt a tool for the precision work that this situation requires.

She reads my mind. "I'm sorry. Julia is my best friend, but I still work for her. I can't stop her, only steer her."

"Why didn't you call me sooner last night?"

"Because you were calling me. At least I thought it was you. They were phishing me with your number. The voice even sounded like you. He'd say two words and hang up, and then I'd hit redial. I didn't get a clue until we got to the station. I got played."

"He played all of us. It's not your job to keep them safe. It's mine. I should have warned them, but I downplayed the danger."

Trishelle puts down her coffee, walks into the guest bedroom, and comes back with a guitar. She pulls open the sliding door a few inches, letting in a clean ocean smell and the sound of waves and seagulls. She sits on the edge of the opposite couch and strums. The breeze blows a few strands of hair across her face.

"I've heard that song before. It's good."

"You haven't heard it before, because I'm writing it now."

"Were you playing it last night?"

"When I couldn't sleep."

I fall into a mini-trance, watching her play, then shake myself out of it. "Trishelle, I love ya, babe, but we don't have time for 'Kumbaya.'"

Trishelle keeps playing. "You're the one who just woke up. I've been busy thinking, and this is how I think. Last night you called McCusker. Did you call the woman detective? What's her name?"

"Gum. I called them both. I only got through to McCusker. He said that unless we witnessed an abduction, we can't yet say they were kidnapped. But he's on it."

She keeps working the same musical notes. "Call Gum then."

I fight not to react. Trishelle's phone, which is on the coffee table between us, dings with a text. She grabs it. "It's from Rick, Julia's agent. He says to look at the *Celebrity Exposed* website—and, that if it's true, we're 'fucked.'"

We race to the study and pull up chairs to an oak desk with a huge desktop computer. Trishelle calls up the *Celebrity Exposed* site. The lead article fills the screen:

Travers and Quintana Pull Plug on Big Budget Movie for Phone App

by Larry Naythons

Actor and producer Julia Travers, who was on a winning streak with three hit movies in a row, is dumping the silver screen for the smartphone, in a risky move that may prove profitable if her new venture is a success, or a career killer if it fails. Together with fiancé Steven Quintana, she is launching Tales by Travers, *a new storytelling smartphone application that allows users to influence and even help write episodes of their new streaming series.*

"Do you want to see me in a romantic comedy? A thriller? An adventure? We give it to you," Travers told Celebrity Exposed.

Quintana, who has zero Hollywood credits, insists that letting random submissions drive the creative process won't lower the story quality. "We will pick the best ideas submitted and turn them into very short episodes for mobile devices," he says.

The first series will be a self-referential exploration of Travers and Quintana's own adventure-filled past called The Danger Game. *Travers and Quintana will play "Julia" and "Steven," fictional versions of themselves who've been kidnapped and sealed inside a bunker/film studio. The obstacles they face and whether they "survive" or "perish" will be decided by fans who contribute ideas and dialogue through the app.*

"Blowing up a successful movie career seems foolhardy, but she could be at the forefront of a new kind of storytelling," says Joe Weiss of the Hollywood Reporter. "It represents total ownership from story through distribution."

And that ownership could pay off. Julia Travers is known around the world. If twenty million people buy her app for five dollars, she can make $100 million before the first episode airs.

The Tales by Travers *app dropped at midnight, and sales are brisk, according to AppTracker. The first episode of* The Danger Game *will drop today, with a new episode every two days or less.*

Story submissions may be where they make the most money. Users will pay a dollar to submit an idea, ten dollars to submit a page of dialogue. If either is selected by the producers, that fan will earn five thousand dollars. With up to twenty million people watching and submitting, Travers and Quintana's take could be half a billion dollars within the first week.

Journalists went to Malibu yesterday for a press conference to promote Under Withering Fire, *Travers's new movie, but instead endured a terrifying fake "attack," which they insist was a promotional gimmick to kick off the first episode of* The Danger Game. *The movie was supposed to be distributed by Warner Bros. The studio will not comment.*

Chris Grivakes, an independent counsel who works for the studio, did say, "Travers and Quintana have been accused of fabricating drama in the past and turning a profit on it."

Grivakes may be referring to Travers's kidnapping three years ago, and Quintana's involvement in a "fight to the death" competition show, set on a crashing plane. Rumors arose that both events were fabrications designed by Quintana and Travers to raise her Q-rating.

The Danger Game *may be the next logical step. Considering how fast entertainment is changing,* The Danger Game *may be the safest place for Travers and Quintana to be.*

"Who is Larry Naythons, and why is he writing this fake crap?" I ask.

"Before he met Julia, Steven worked as a paparazzo. He'd sell his photos to Larry Naythons. He's only gotten bigger since then."

"Along with his bullshit. You and I are going to visit Larry."

Trishelle inhales like she's been stabbed. "What if the article is real?"

"There is no way that Steven and Julia are creating a game for the internet."

"No, I mean, maybe they've been kidnapped, for real, to be in this game."

I stare at her. Bushnell did bankroll *Six Passengers, Five Parachutes.* Heyman helped him run it. They could be doing this together.

Trishelle reads my mind. She grabs her phone and types it into the search engine. "The game app is for sale. I'm buying it." She downloads the app. "The first episode airs tonight at 8:00 p.m. That's in ten hours."

She shows me her phone. Julia and Steven are on a movie poster, green and red, trapped in a dark room with glaring lights above them. In red scrawl, it says *The Danger Game.* Underneath is the tag line: *The world is watching.*

"Tabernac," she whispers. "It's happening again."

CHAPTER 14

STEVEN QUINTANA

Kidnapped 14 hours ago

Julia sleeps beside me. Her breathing is slow. It's pitch black, and we're on a cold cement floor. We've been this way for eight hours. The floor is too cold to sleep on, so I taught her how to rest on her knees and elbows. If your knees are far enough apart and you tilt forward, you can rest your face in your cupped hands. You can fall asleep like that if you're tired enough.

She tilted over a few times, but then her brain and body adjusted, and she's in a deep sleep that will last about thirty minutes until her hands and arms fall asleep, and her brain wakes her up again. I squat next to her like a caveman, so if she tilts and falls, she'll land against me.

My Ranger training came back. How to survive capture. How to go without food and water and sleep. How to make lists and prepare, so you don't give up hope.

She snorts and inhales, and I catch her before she pitches face-first onto the cement. She whimpers and crawls into my arms, and I plop down on my butt, holding her. "You slept. That's good."

"I'm scared."

"I'll get us out of here."

"GOOD LUCK WITH THAT!" A loud voice, an inch away from our faces, screams.

We scramble across the cold floor in the dark. My forehead smacks into a cement wall, and white light flashes through my brain.

Now the voice whispers, and, again, it sounds an inch away. *"If you want to eat, drink, sleep, piss, or shit, then obey me. If you want clean clothes or to bathe, then obey me. Most of all, if you wish to escape punishment, obey me."*

It's Peter Heyman. I shout into the darkness. "Still can't get a job, Peter? Maybe people would hire you if you took that piece of metal out of your face!"

Someone stabs me in the calf, and a jolt of electricity convulses my body, sending my knees into my chest. They can see me in the dark. I put my hands on the floor and sweep my heel fast in a low roundhouse kick—and knock my attacker off his feet. I roll fast, get on top of him, and slam his head against the cement, which jars his night-vision goggles off his forehead.

Julia screams. They're shocking her now. I almost get the goggles on when they prod me six times in the back, sending me convulsing across the floor. I bang my head again and hear the goggles shatter. Someone yanks them off my forehead.

"This is a wonderful start!"

The overhead lights snap on. After hours of darkness, they are like white-hot suns. My eyes blink, fighting to work.

"Now, you are docile. You want your eyesight back more than you want to fight," Peter's voice whispers. *"You are so predictable."*

My vision returns. Julia and I are in a large, square room, twenty-five yards across. The walls and floor are painted bright green. Three men, dressed in black with hoods and goggles, surround me and point electric cattle prods at my face. Julia, ten yards away, is surrounded by another three men.

"*UP!*" Peter shouts, and all six men fly up and away, like Peter Pans. They wear harnesses on their chests and back, and the retracting wires yank them up to a metal catwalk above us.

Glass shards are on the floor next to me—the remains of the shattered goggles, gone now with the men. I roll onto the shards, hiding them under my still shaking thighs.

Julia and I lock eyes. Her blonde hair is stringy, her face is dirty, and the crotch of her blue track pants is dark. She crosses her legs. She wet herself.

"Don't worry. I did it too. It's hard not to piss yourself when asshole cowards are jabbing you with twenty thousand volts." I shift and feel the shards of glass poke into the back of my thighs. There are three of them; one is long, two are short. I must hide them somehow, in my pocket, my underwear, or in my mouth. Sweat drips into my eyes, and I wipe it away—it's not sweat, it's blood.

Julia touches her own forehead. "You're cut."

I glance at the wall. There's a red mark where I collided with the cement. I shout up at the metal catwalk. "I left a red mark on your pretty green wall!"

"*We can paint it,*" Peter whispers. I can't see him, only the silhouettes of eight men on the catwalk above me moving in front of the white-hot lights.

"We're in a green screen room," Julia says. "They're filming us."

I look at the walls. Every few feet there is a six-inch circle of wire mesh.

"Those are microphones and speakers," Julia says, pointing at the circles, and then at the catwalk. "And those are cameras above us."

In between the bright lights, there are ten cameras mounted on a big ring, which hangs halfway down from the ceiling.

"*Very good. Our cameras can capture every angle and close-up, no matter where you are in the room.*" Heyman's voice is coming from all the mesh circles. *"Your kidnapping is episode one, which ends with that little fight you gave us. It will be airing around the world."*

Julia laughs. "You're trying this again?"

"Killing us on camera hasn't worked yet!" I yell. I run my hands along the back of my piss-soaked jeans and find the shards of glass. I slide them into my socks.

Heyman cranks up the volume on his voice. *"THIRD TIME'S A CHARM."*

Buckets on ropes lower from the ceiling—one in front of me, one in front of Julia.

"Mine has water and sandwiches," Julia says, emptying plastic water bottles and plastic-wrapped food onto the floor. Her bucket rises back up the catwalk.

My bucket stays. "Mine has toilet paper, alcohol, and bandages."

"Eat, drink, and relieve yourselves. We'll send down the script for episode two. Do that well and you'll get clean clothes and a mattress to sleep on."

"Script? You kidnapped the wrong guy. I'm no actor."

"'We're all poor players, strutting and fretting our hour upon the stage, and then we are heard from no more.' You are no different, Quintana. Yours is a story told by an idiot, full of sound and fury, signifying nothing."

Julia forces herself to stand. "You're an idiot, Peter Heyman. Don't you know that it's bad luck to quote anything from *Macbeth* before your actors perform? Now your project is doomed to failure!"

"It is you who are doomed if you do not do as you are told."

"'It is not in the stars to hold our destiny, but in ourselves!'" Julia shouts up at the men on the catwalks. *"'And this room means nothing to me! You can bound me in a nutshell and I would count myself king of infinite space!'"*

Heyman laughs. *"'Were it not for your bad dreams.' I also know Hamlet."*

A lever flips. They plunge us into darkness again.

64

CHAPTER 15

JULIA TRAVERS

Kidnapped 15 hours ago

I'm glad we're in the dark. I don't want Steven to see me, like this, squatting over a bucket. Then come the snickers. The pigs on the catwalk above can still see us with their green goggles. They see everything. They hear everything.

I finish and clean myself. How are we going to get out of this?

Steven taps my arm. He's ripped open the sandwiches and water, which we devour. I choke on the stale bread, and Steven jams an open water bottle into my hand. My throat guzzles half of it before the sandwich even goes down.

My hands find the bandages and alcohol. "Let me clean that cut."

"Can you find it?"

"Yes." My fingers run across his skin until they find the gash. I rip open three bandages, put them against his forehead, and stretch them across the wound, pulling it taut. It feels like it will work.

"There." I kiss his forehead.

"How sweet." Heyman's voice shocks me, and I fall back on my ass.

"I need stitches. You want me to act with a cut on my forehead?" Steven yells.

"We'll fix it in post. It's all special effects."

"Turn on the lights! To see if I put the bandages in the right place!"

"We see them. What you did will suffice."

"We need sleep!" Steven yells.

"There are two sleeping mats behind you. Rest. You have a lot of work in front of you."

Steven and I crawl until we find the folding mats they dropped from the ceiling. They're only an inch thick, but they feel like plush mattresses from a four-star hotel. My body wants to shut down, but it's too afraid to sleep.

What can I do? I can fight back and defend myself. I can hide my feelings. I can act. I can distract. Will that be enough?

Heyman whispers, *"Thanks for the help with the bombs on set, Quintana."*

"Nice try, Heyman. Julia knows the truth."

"What Julia thinks doesn't matter. The world thinks you set off the bombs and that you two are producing this entire show. That means no one is coming for you. Your only hope is to obey."

My mind twists, trying to unravel all the lies. Steven wraps his arms around me and whispers, "He's trying to break us. We can't let him."

I nod and close my eyes, willing myself to believe, and to sleep.

CHAPTER 16

TINA SWIG

Tuesday, March 12, 4:00 a.m. (CET)
Sicily

Min, Ismael, and Elliot work at their stations while I pace behind them. Most TV producers hide their idiocy by being screaming assholes when quiet precision is best. "How many downloads so far?"

Min sits at the first desk, tracking the app purchases. He blinks, trying to focus. "Come on, Min. I went for a five-mile run on the beach yesterday while you three were sleeping off your hangovers. I told you, be sharp for the Monday night drop in California. If you yawn, I'll cut your balls off."

Min sits up straight like he's got a yardstick up his ass. "We're at ten million and climbing. A lot of downloads from India."

"How many in the US?"

"We'll hit a half-million downloads by midday. We've been open eighteen hours. Not bad for a Monday game release. That *Celebrity Exposed* article helped."

"How are the platforms reacting?"

"We're on all of them. No one is rejecting us, at least for now."

"As long as they get their cut, no one will question us for a week."

I go to Ismael next, at the last monitor. He tracks story submissions. His monitor refreshes with a dozen new buys every few seconds. He turns in his swivel chair. "We're getting over a hundred submissions a minute, both story ideas and dialogue. "

"I am not surprised."

"I can't track all the storylines they submit. There are too many," Ismael says. He runs his hands through his thinning black hair, yanking out a few tight curls with each pass. If he keeps worrying this much, he'll be bald before he earns his millions.

A sweaty Douglas walks into the room, dressed in black workout clothes. He sips a green drink—which he insists on making himself at the wet bar in our master suite—straight from his VitaMixer. "Don't worry, we have thought of everything."

Min, Ismael, and Elliot turn to Douglas, mesmerized. They don't worship me in the same way. I'm just the woman who invented this entire game.

Douglas finishes his drink and wipes away a green mustache. "Stories people submit automatically go into a database. Search for the word 'shark.' Let's see how many people think we should feed Julia and Steven to sharks."

Ismael types into his keyboard and hits return. His screen fills with dozens of submissions. Ismael scrolls through several pages. "It looks like about three hundred and fifty submissions—"

"—That's three hundred and fifty paid submissions from people who want to see Steven and Julia battle sharks, with no clue of what's in the first episode. We may start with them naked on a frozen mountain. We can paint them purple and have a Druid priest slice their hearts out inside Stonehenge. Whatever we make them do, someone out there will be thinking it too."

Ismael's eyes widen. "We reverse-engineer. We find the submission that best matches what you're already planning."

Douglas points at him. "Exactly. And we declare that person the winner and send them money in bitcoin."

"Can we try some more ideas?" Ismael asks.

"Go ahead," Douglas says.

"Try 'raped by aliens,'" Min suggests.

Ismael types and gets an answer. "Ten have those words in the submission."

"Try 'baptism by fire,'" Elliot says.

Ismael types and gets another answer. "Four have 'baptism by fire.'"

"There is nothing new under the sun," Douglas says.

Their eyes widen as they lean back and look at each other, huge grins on their faces. "It's sick, bro…it's ridiculous…dude, this is fucking epic."

"She's the wizard who designed all this, gentlemen, not me. Pay attention to *her*."

The boys swivel and stare at me now. Sweet Douglas knows that we are a team. That's why I love him so.

I start with my K-pop star. "Min, you, maintain the app and the sales. I want to know how many people are online at any time, so we can tweak the stories and the price if there's a drop in interest."

"I understand."

I move to my red-haired football fan in the middle. "Elliot, you maintain security. We must stay online but remain impenetrable. No losing money."

"Firewalls up and running."

"Hackers will try to get on the servers and recode the game. They'll submit the same story a million times and try to crash the system."

"They won't succeed."

Douglas wags his finger at him. "They better not."

Elliot bows his head like a dog who just peed the carpet. Douglas keeps going.

"And if law enforcement ever believes that Steven and Julia really have been kidnapped, governments will get involved. If they do, I will pull the plug and we will disappear, but I'm the only one who will decide if and when that happens. You will keep us secure and keep them guessing until then. Understand?"

Elliot nods at him, then at me.

I move to preppy Ismael in the last chair. His pink shirt is well-ironed today, with a perfect crease down both arms. "Ismael, you maintain the story database. There will be three story submission and dialogue winners a week."

"How do I pick the best dialogue?" Ismael asks.

"We use keywords that go with the episode we're already doing. How long will it take to write a program that selects for all that?"

Ismael turns to his keyboard and types so fast I think he must be messing with me. "Give me a keyword for something they will encounter," Ismael says.

"You're done already?" I ask.

"The code for most of it was already written. I just cut and pasted it in."

"In one scene, they will encounter lava," Douglas says.

"Cool," Elliot and Min both say.

Ismael types it in and hits return. "There are sixty dialogue submissions with lava."

"Good. You guys can read one hundred and twenty pages a day between you. If any are similar to what we're already doing, we'll declare that person the winner."

"This feels like real Hollywood," Ismael says.

Douglas laughs. "It's the future of entertainment, gentlemen."

I snap my fingers, and they turn to me like trained puppies reacting to a clicker. I pick up a dry erase marker and write on the whiteboard mounted above Elliot's monitor. "Our goal is to earn one billion dollars in bitcoin in ten days or less," I say as I write all the digits out: *1,000,000,000*. "That's one hundred million dollars a day. Min, you said we'd sold about eleven million units so far?"

Min looks at his monitor. "Yes. We make four dollars a download, so we've made almost forty-five million dollars so far."

"Ismael, how much have we made in story submissions?"

Ismael looks at his monitor. "It's hard to say. Maybe fifteen million?"

I write *Day One, Status: 60 million*. Then I recap the marker. "We're sixteen hours into our first day and over halfway to our daily goal. When the first episode drops in two hours, we will skyrocket. I don't want it to ever lag. No matter how it's received, we must keep this pace or faster. We pull the plug at a billion dollars. And, if we make it, you boys get one percent each. That's ten million dollars."

They spin circle in their chairs, dab fists, snap their fingers, and sing to each other in frat speak. "Hella cool...we got skills...our game's legit...super-sick way to represent!" The wave of adolescent excitement crests and passes through the room.

"Can we see the first episode?" Min asks.

Douglas clicks a remote. "Of course, you can. It's ready to air."

A panel opens above the three computers, revealing a large monitor that powers on. Pulsing tension music begins. Images from the metro train pop on screen. A camera moves through a train car. Peter Heyman is wearing it. Steven Quintana and Julia Travers appear at the other end of the car. Steven runs at the camera as Heyman darts him in the chest. Heyman walks down the aisle, peers under the seat, and darts Julia. The music gets louder. A montage shows Heyman and his cronies blindfolding and gagging Steven and Julia and tossing them in the back of a van. Then, they are carried onto a private jet. The monitor cuts to black, and then infrared night vision cameras show the heat off two bodies, a man and a woman, flailing their arms. It's Julia and Steven trying to find their way in the darkness.

They find each other and hug. "Where are we?" she whispers.

Steven teaches her how to sleep on her knees and elbows. "I'm scared," she says. Steven answers, "I'll get us out of here."

Heyman's voice blares, *"Good luck with that."* Men descend from the ceiling and jolt them with electricity. Steven smashes his head against the wall as Julia screams. Steven trips one attacker, but the others surround both Steven and Julia and shock them until they submit. Peter Heyman's voice echoes: *"If you wish to escape punishment, then obey."*

Julia screams: *'It is not in the stars to hold our destiny, but in ourselves!'"*

The music climaxes as a bright red title fills the screen: *The Danger Game.*

Douglas clicks his remote. The monitor turns off, and the panel closes. "That's just the tease. We'll finish the full episode soon."

Min and Elliot elbow each other like half-wit brothers, but Ismael raises a finger. "Where does the game take place?"

"Yeah," Min adds. "Where are Steven and Julia right now, anyway?"

Douglas clicks his tongue in gentle disapproval. I love it when he does that. "They're in a distant part of the world. That's all that's safe for you to know."

They grin at each other. These boys like their dangerous adventure.

CHAPTER 17

CARL WEBB

Tuesday, March 12, 9:00 a.m. (PST)
California

M y phone sits on the coffee table set to speakerphone. Trishelle stands in the kitchen doorway, her arms crossed. Over the phone, McCusker's voice sighs. "So far, we still have no real evidence of a crime." I imagine him slumping in his mud-gray suit.

"Have you even looked?"

"It's been less than forty-eight hours, Webb."

"Have you reached Mendoza in Wisconsin? He'll confirm everything I told you."

"He works for you, Webb, not me. You track him down. This is one of six cases I'm working on. And I don't have time to watch crap on the internet."

"What's that supposed to mean?" I ask, just as he hangs up.

"It means no one believes us."

We've been spinning our wheels for a day, working the phones, calling his family, calling her family, convincing McCusker and Gum to visit the train station, finding Steven's motorcycle, and we've made zero progress. I need help.

I follow Trishelle into the kitchen and find fresh coffee and hot waffles with maple syrup. When did she do that? I devour them standing up, making sure I don't drip on my white shirt. I didn't realize I was this hungry.

Trishelle plays her guitar while standing in the open sliding glass door.

"Time to leave, babe," I say, wiping my mouth.

"I've been waiting an hour, handsome. That's when I cooked for you."

We're not talking about what's really on our minds. Last night we watched the first episode of *The Danger Game*. There was tense music, rushed editing, and slick graphics, which made the whole piece of shit look like fiction.

McCusker believes that it's fiction, too. That's why he called it *"crap on the internet."* If he believes that it's crappy fiction, so may everyone else.

I want a text from Mendoza so bad that my phone seems to vibrate in my pocket, but it's still sitting on the coffee table. I'm getting ghost-texts.

On Friday night, he called and said he had tracked her to yet another motel, alongside a river northeast of Minneapolis. How many rivers are there east of Minneapolis? How many motels? My Miami staff is working on it, but not fast enough.

A boat passes by in the cove outside, and a paparazzo on the bow snaps Trishelle's picture. She flips him off. She then plays that musical phrase again—and finishes it. She smiles with triumph like she solved a puzzle.

"Does playing music help us find Steven and Julia?"

"No, but neither do your phone calls—or you driving around. You were in the car three hours yesterday."

"I was doing necessary research."

We stay in our lane and stay quiet the rest of the way to Marina del Rey and the sprawling new high-tech offices of *Celebrity Exposed*. We slip into the loading zone next to the parking structure.

I unbuckle. "Wait here."

She grabs my forearm. "I'm coming with you."

"Damn, you've got a grip, Trishelle." I pry her fingers off my jacket and put them back onto her steering wheel. "He'll recognize you. He printed six issues of you and Julia sunburnt in your bikinis after Steven and I rescued you in the Bahamas. You sold a lot of fish-wrapping for that prick."

"What about you? You and Steven were there too."

"He won't remember me. Today, I'm just an anonymous law enforcement agent, asking questions." I pull open my suit jacket and show her the gold badge in its leather case hanging on my belt.

"Is that real?"

"Yup. I'm a Los Angeles Sheriff's Deputy. Sheriff McKenzie deputized me himself, to be called into service whenever there is a crisis. And this, babe, is a crisis. Listen to your podcasts, and I'll be back in thirty minutes."

She leans forward for a kiss. "Break his nose for me."

I smack her on the lips and leave the car.

I wipe my lips with the back of my hand while running up the cement stairs. She marked me. Let's hope her lipstick traces bring good luck.

I wait in the stairwell by the second floor, which is reserved parking for *Celebrity Exposed* employees. I came yesterday and plotted this. It was part of my "running around" that Trishelle complained about, so it had better work.

It does. Within six minutes, Larry Naythons parks his Jaguar in spot 632. He chirps his car lock and walks to the elevators. He is lean and fit in a blue suit with curly, dark hair, a JFK Jr. look-alike. He's nothing I can't handle. I leave the stairwell and block him ten yards before the elevator. He looks up from his phone.

"Larry Naythons? I need to talk to you about the article you wrote about Steven Quintana and Julia Travers." My fists land on my hips, so my jacket falls open, showing the badge on my belt.

Larry slides his phone into his jacket pocket. "I answered all your questions yesterday. If you want me to reveal my sources, I won't."

"Except you're not a journalist."

"The state of California says I am." Larry turns and points at his Jaguar. "See my California license plate? See the PP written inside the triangle, and then the four numbers? That's a press photographer's plate. I can legally drive into a disaster zone, and the police can't stop me. And neither can you right now."

When he tries to pass, my hand goes up to block him. "Why not just answer my questions here? Instead of me making a scene in your office?"

"What's your name and your badge number?"

"Carl Webb. My badge number is 656."

Larry smiles. "Mr. Webb, I have time for you. Is that a real badge?"

"It certainly is. And I've arrested people using it."

"Then you're a real cop, just like I'm a real journalist. Let's go to the roof. The view is better up there."

We head up another four flights, and he's right; you can see down the row of buildings lining Balloña Creek to Playa del Rey and the ocean, which is a straight line of dark blue against light blue, marking where the two paint rollers met.

"I have this view from my office."

"It almost makes your job worthwhile."

"What was your plan anyway? Beat me up in the stairwell until I talked?"

"Or scare you into thinking I might."

"Is that how you run your Global Webb Security firm?"

"When I have to."

"I heard you moved your business from the Bahamas to Miami."

"We do a lot of security work in Latin America. You keeping tabs on me?"

Larry leans against the ledge. "I don't dislike you, Carl. Or Julia or Quintana, even though he punched me in the chest once. We all benefit. It's a symbiotic relationship."

"More like parasitic."

"I've published just as many positive articles about Julia as negative ones. And about her producing partner, Trishelle Hobbs, too. She's from Vermillion Bay. Her family moved to Thunder Bay when Trishelle was in high school, which is where she and Julia met. Did you know that?"

"No." This showoff knows more about my girlfriend than I do.

He crosses his arms and stares. My reflection is perfect in his sunglasses. "I know because we ran a whole series on all of you after Quintana, and you rescued Julia and Trishelle from that Bahamian cay."

"You printed that we staged it."

He wags his finger. "Wrong. I printed that there were *rumors* that you had staged it, and, in the same series, we printed the truth. I can't help what people believe."

"They've really been kidnapped. It's not some game that they've invented."

"Or maybe they sent you here to tell me that. Julia is very creative."

"Did you see the first episode? It was horrible."

"I saw bits of it while I was cooking dinner last night. The production value is cheap, but it's supposed to be gritty. They accomplished what they set out to do, I think."

"I'm not talking about the quality of the show. What's actually *happening to them* is horrible."

He shrugs. "I've seen worse, but I didn't see the whole episode. I was on deadline."

"You don't care about the truth. You only care about getting clicks." I poke him on the arm for a reaction.

Larry pushes my hand away and pokes me back. "I publish facts. History determines the truth. But let me give you my own facts, Deputy."

We each cross arms in a face-off, two angry guys in suits and sunglasses, mirroring each other on a gravel rooftop. "Lay it on me, journalist."

"I employ a hundred people in this building and five hundred across the country. We give them health insurance, a pension, and assistance with home loans. And we've won every libel lawsuit brought against us. That's the truth I like."

The sun beats down on my sweating bald head. I should have worn a hat. I look over the edge and see Trishelle's car down below. It's good she didn't come. She'd be clawing his eyes out. Larry looks at his watch; he's losing interest in my dilemma.

"You quote both of them in your article. How is that possible?"

"They called and offered me an interview. That was the same day as the explosions on the set of their movie, a few hours after the police spoke to each of them."

"How do you know it was really them?"

"Because they said so."

"That wasn't Julia and Steven. That was Peter Heyman or Douglas Bushnell or people working for them. They altered their voices."

"I had no reason to doubt them. Did Julia Travers call me pond scum like she usually does? No. Did their answers sound rehearsed? Yes, but so does every interview with any celebrity pushing a project. It's all canned and rehearsed hype."

"You have doubts, admit it. You think she'd walk away from a huge movie? Stage explosions? That's crazy."

"Everything that happens with Julia Travers and Steven Quintana is crazy. They asked me to run the story, so I did."

My voice is earnest. "What if you're wrong? What if I'm the one telling the truth?"

He sighs and uncrosses his arms and pushes his sunglasses up on his forehead. I'm getting somewhere. "I've made mistakes in the past, and this is a crazy story. If you come up with something newsworthy, with sources to back it up, I'll print it."

"Was the phone call to your office or your personal phone?"

"Office. I'll pull the phone record. Don't be surprised if it's a blocked number."

"I have my ways. And I promise that the truth will be a better story."

"I look forward to it, Deputy Webb. You should get out of the sun. Your head is turning red." He walks away, his feet crunching on the gravel. I'm going to need help.

CHAPTER 18

JULIA TRAVERS

Kidnapped 42 hours ago

"I can't make it! The lava! It's too hot! It's too hot. I'm going to die…."

I fall to my knees. My brain dredges up a memory of my grandmother on her death bed until my eyes flow like faucets and bubbles come out of my nose.

Steven stands on a green box ten feet away. We're both dressed in silver heat suits, but our faces are exposed, which makes no sense if we were really this close to lava. Steven looks like a terrified zoo animal.

"If I jump, will you catch me?"

He nods. He has no clue how to do this.

"Say the line, Quintana," Peter shouts from somewhere above.

"Jump, and I will catch you!" Steven yells, sounding like Dwayne Peabody, the worst ham actor in my high school drama class in Thunder Bay, Ontario.

My lungs hyperventilate, preparing me. My eyes shift from the green box under my feet to Steven on his box, six feet away. I teeter on the edge, imagining it to be a rock in the middle of a flowing lava river.

"The box will move in three, two, one…"

The wire that runs through my box moves on its pulley, jerking the box beneath me, dislodging my fake rock in the lava river. I leap to Steven on his box, and he catches me. We hug. "You saved my life again for the hundredth time."

Steven grins, trying to emote "happy," but his eyes are wide with stage fright. He looks up at the ring of cameras surrounding us.

"Don't look at the cameras," I whisper. "Say your lines."

Steven grimaces, defiant.

"Say your line, Quintana."

Steven sets his jaw. "I am sick of rescuing you. You are always the woman in peril," he says, his acting so bad he makes Dwayne Peabody's work look worthy of an Oscar.

"Push me."

"What?"

"Push her, Quintana. Don't make me work to edit this."

Steven pushes me, and I throw myself into a back splat on the green cement floor, howling as if I'm being consumed by lava.

"Cut. We have another episode."

I strip off the silver suit and toss it in a corner, leaving me in just my sweat-drenched underwear and a T-shirt. "Now do I get a shower?" I yell up at Heyman's silhouette.

"Quintana's acting is piss poor. If you want to bathe, he has to act better."

Steven scowls as he pulls off his silver outfit. His red T-shirt is soaking wet. We've both lost ten pounds in perspiration today. They hung us from wires as we pretended to be floating in outer space; we wore mountaineering clothes and pretended we were climbing a granite wall, and even battled puppet alien invaders, all while leaping around in a green, cement room for fifteen hours, I'm guessing. They gave us little food, less water, and a lot of electric shocks from the cowards in the black ninja outfits.

"What about a bed? Hot food? We can't work unless we're fed, clean, and rested."

"Drop five."

Five men in black, with hoods and goggles, drop from the catwalk on their wired harnesses. Two corner me while three surround Steven, circling us like we're zoo animals. They poke me in the legs and the back with their cattle prods, jolting me with burning electricity. My hand flies up and hits my face. Steven grunts as he battles them.

"Stop."

The men fly back up to the catwalk. Steven runs to me, covering me with his arms. We pant like racehorses trying to catch our breath.

"Act or die. That's the best incentive for any actor."

"Your show will never work!" I yell. "No one can do this!"

The warehouse falls silent. The metal in the catwalk creaks. The men up high look like spiders, backlit against the bright overhead lights.

"What do you want most?"

"A shower. I need to be clean—"

Steven interrupts me. "A mattress, with blankets. We need to rest. And we need to rest together, so we each know that the other is safe. We can't go days without sleep."

"Slap him, and you'll get a shower."

"You want more violence. Of course," I say.

"Stand and face each other. Slap him as hard as you can, or you get nothing."

Steven stands up and lifts his chin, like a defiant boxer. He gets it now. Take the pain and you get something in return. He nods at me to proceed.

I get up and slap him, hard. He staggers back. A red handprint rises on his cheek.

"Again."

My other hand flies out and slaps the other cheek, so hard my palm stings.

"Again."

My hands slap again until my palms are on fire. What must his face feel like?

"We can edit that. You will get a hot shower soon."

"Thank you, Great Oz."

"Quintana, you want a bed? Punch Julia in the stomach."

Steven raises his chin, defiant. "No."

"You bombed her movie set when I offered you money. Punching her is easier."

Steven blinks, flitting from confusion to anger. "He's trying to set us against each other. Divide and conquer." He yells at the ceiling. "No!"

"Drop five." The five ninjas with cattle prods drop back down from the ceiling. They stay on one side of the room.

"Do it, Steven. We either work together or we die!"

He shakes his head.

"I'd rather get punched by you than prodded by them. Do it!"

He closes his eyes and prays. His fist flies out faster than I can see, hitting me in the gut and lifting me off the ground. My head bangs against the cement floor. My mouth gasps like a fish, but there's no air in my lungs. I roll onto my hands and knees and try to inflate them. I can't.

I try again. Air fills my lungs. I breathe deep.

Tonight, we sleep in a bed.

CHAPTER 19

TINA SWIG

Wednesday, March 13, 7:00 a.m. (CET)

Devon zooms his wheelchair across his carpeted stateroom and stops an inch before the smoked-glass window, then spins and zooms at me. I stand my ground. I'm used to this. He stops an inch before hitting my shins.

"Stop it, Devon. Find a more intelligent way to be a rebellious teenager."

"Do not mock me," he says, with an evil alien voice.

"I'm not mocking you. I'm challenging you to be a rebel with your mind, instead of threatening violence against this beautiful yacht or my shins."

He rises up and down on his wheelchair as if riding a slow-moving pogo stick. "Be a rebel with your *mind*," he says, imitating me with a silly cartoon voice.

"Very clever."

"I'm sick of this boat," He sounds like Paul Newman again, so I know he's serious.

Outside the window is the jagged, black-and-green, volcanic island of Ustica, with its small ancient postcard town, lit up gold with the rising sun. I love these views, but it's boring for a teenager.

"Something else is bugging you. The code you wrote isn't working."

His brown eyes well up.

"It's been two days since you've asked Rebecca to send Professor Carlton an encrypted email. Are you stuck?"

He puts his lips over the mouthpiece. "The Hodge conjecture remains a conjecture."

"Take a break from it. Do something else."

"I can't. I'm stuck on this boat."

"There's a full media library. Watch a movie, play a video game, read a book."

"At least let me cruise the internet."

I'd rather let him play doctor with Rebecca again but don't say it. That would be crossing a teenage privacy line that would be unforgivable.

"Not yet. Douglas and I have important business right now."

"You act like Russians are trying to infect us with a Stuxnet virus."

"You must wait, Devon. It took me two decades to achieve success, and then we almost lost it all when my first project for Douglas crashed and burned. Now we've climbed out of the ashes and built this new project. And, once this succeeds, we will have everything. Us against the world. All I want from you is eight more days. Maybe less."

He turns his chair, ignoring me.

"I have to get back to work. I'll check on you again in a few hours."

"Fine," he sighs. His cerebral palsy won't let him sigh, but Douglas built that choice into his computer. It makes me love them both even more.

I move to kiss his forehead, but he backs away. Time to leave. He's a big boy. He can live without YouTube and his *Nightstream* game for a few more days.

I go downstairs and into the galley and pour myself a magnificent mug of coffee with a whisper of cream, then walk out on the sundeck. The morning light hits the turquoise water surrounding Ustica, which is just five hundred yards away. I spot a lovely beach. Maybe Douglas and I can have a picnic there.

I should check in with Walter, my slimeball in Los Angeles. He's got photographers watching Trishelle Hobbes and Carl Webb in case they make a move. But I'm too busy to send him another boob shot. No news from Piggy is good news.

I enter the main salon, where Min, Ismael, and Elliot are crowded around a monitor. Douglas stands behind them with the remote.

"My love, the second episode of *The Danger Game* is ready."

"Is the first episode still making us money?" I ask Min.

"Downloads have dropped off twenty-five percent, but we've made about forty million, total," he says.

I point and raise an eyebrow at Ismael. He grins. "Story submissions skyrocketed after the first episode. Fans submit dozens of times a day. We're at sixty million."

"We made our hundred million on Day One! And episode two is ready twenty-six hours after the first episode aired, which makes us late by just two hours."

Douglas smiles. "I'm sorry for its tardiness, my love. This episode has a lot of computer rendering. We farmed out the work to different companies around the world. They all said the green screen was impeccable. Bravo to you on the production."

"Thank you, my love. Hit *play* and let's see this thing."

Douglas clicks the remote, and the large monitor lights up as it emerges from its walnut cabinet. A male narrator speaks over images

don't want to die," Steven whispers. The wind blows his thick hair as his body sways above the green fields far below.

The camera zooms in on Julia's face as she arches an eyebrow. *"Except you're a loser. You're just a hanger-on, using me to get ahead. You know what you are to me, Ranger boy? Deadweight."* Julia yanks her hand away, and Steven screams and falls to his death.

The scenes look as real as any big-effects Hollywood movie. Julia Travers is as believable as Faye Wray was, facing a fake King Kong. Quintana is terrible, however, which makes the scenes that much more cheesy, tongue-in-cheek, and stupid.

Good. I don't care, as long as we make a billion.

The third scene starts. Julia and Steven stand at opposite ends of a sprawling field of grass that stretches down to the blue Mediterranean twenty miles away—each is dressed like ancient Greeks, with white tunics fringed with gold. Julia carries what looks like a swaddled baby in her arms. The baby cries, and Steven moves toward her. Every blade of grass bends with the breeze as Steven walks through the yellowing field. Julia holds out the child. *"Come see what the gods have bestowed on us."*

Steven kisses her on the cheek. Julia pulls back the swaddling cover and reveals a red baby with barbed, yellow teeth, orange eyes, and sharp horns. *"Isn't he beautiful?"*

The baby snaps at Steven's hand, biting it clean off. Steven holds up the bleeding stump and screams. *"He's a monster!"*

"Don't you call him a monster!"

Julia slaps Steven hard across the face. He holds steady while she slaps him. Steven punches her in the stomach and sends her flying. The baby hits the ground, then leaps up and attacks Steven's face, ripping it apart.

"Yo, that was a sick jump scare!" Min laughs.

"Took me totally by surprise." Elliot laughs.

"It was decent," the more reserved Ismael insists.

Min and Elliot groan at his critique. "You jumped, dude, I saw you."

Ismael shakes his head. "I did not. And that scene was lame until they punched each other. Those hits weren't rendered. They really went off, so that was cool."

The next scene starts. Julia and Steven wear spacesuits and float inside a damaged space station. Rows of machines on the walls are blackened with bomb blasts. There's a gaping hole leading to the vacuum of space outside. Hand-sized pieces of green steel float past them. Julia grabs one of the pieces and examines it closely. *These are fragments from a Soviet rocket. Whoever attacked us did it with old technology.*

"Be careful. There's a lot of jagged metal in here," Steven says.

"Don't tell me to be careful. I know what I'm doing."

"Are you sure? Exercise caution, please."

Inside her glass space helmet, Julia rolls her eyes. She gives him a mock salute. *"Yes, sir, Mr. Man!"* she yells, and as she brings down her hand, her spacesuit hits a jagged piece of metal on the wall of the spacecraft, ripping it open at the wrist. Her glove pops off, and she screams as she holds up her bare hand in the vacuum of space. Steven grabs her wrist as her hand turns red and swells to ten times its normal size. She screams. Her hand explodes, sending out a billion blood droplets that cover their spacesuits. She flails around in space, then bumps against more jagged metal. The glass front of her helmet cracks, and the air inside escapes. She howls until there is no air left to carry the noise. Her head swells to the size of a basketball, and then it explodes like a cartoon.

"She always had a big head," Steven says, deadpan.

Elliot, Min, and Ismael punch each other like ten-year-old boys.

"That was so wrong it was right," Min says.

"Probably slept her way through NASA,"

"She should have listened, but, no, she had to talk," Elliot says. The misogynistic scene where the uppity woman dies is the one they love the most. It perpetuates the worst of tech-bro culture, but boys like them will watch it.

Douglas sees my face and knows what I'm thinking because he rubs his forefinger and thumb together. He's right. We're making money, so why do I care?

"That wasn't scientifically accurate," Ismael says.

Elliot throws his hands up. "Who cares? It's way cray that Julia Travers's head explodes like a balloon! That'll be on YouTube forever. Her career is *o-ver.*"

Douglas whistles and raises his arm high like a football referee, stopping their frat-boy banter. "Can the comments! Last scene!"

Douglas hits *play* again, and lava comes on screen. It's the last full scene we shot yesterday with Julia and Steven wearing silver heat suits. They step on rocks to cross a lava stream, which in real life would incinerate them instantly, but, hey, this is Hollywood. Julia leaps from her rock into his arms. Julia whispers, *"You saved my life again, for the hundredth time."*

Steven stares at her. *"I'm sick of rescuing you. You're always the woman in peril."*

The boys groan. "Man, he is *so* bad. Not good-bad. Bad-bad," Ismael says.

Min nods. "Bible, dude."

Elliot nods twice. "Bible squared."

Steven pushes Julia into the lava stream. She bursts into flames and dies.

"Her dying makes it entertaining," Min says.

"Not by much. That boy needs some acting classes," Elliot says.

The monitor turns off and recesses back into the cabinet. The boys look at Douglas.

"Thank you for the witty commentary. Will it make money?"

Shit, yeah, dude!" Elliot yells. "And I'm not blowing smoke just because you're the Boss Man. The shit is lit."

"Her career is dead, but WTF?" Min says, laughing. "It's so fucked up, it's Gucci. People will make memes from it. It'll be on Twitter in a hot minute."

I cough to remind my bros that Mama is here. "Ismael, who's our winner?"

Ismael sits up straight, remembering his job. "Only one person in sixty million submitted multiple entries that matched all five story beats: fighting a puppet, mountain climbing, a killer baby, dying in a spacesuit, and crossing a lava stream. Mr. A.J. Catalone from Salt Lake City is today's winner."

"Wire him his money, then post his story on the website. Elliot?"

Elliot smooths his jersey. "Yes, ma'am?" These boys are scared of me, which I like.

"Upload episode two. Let's make another 100 million."

Douglas puts his arm around me. "Think we can keep this pace up?"

"I think we can squeeze out enough episodes to reach a billion before they drop dead or kill each other."

CHAPTER 20

STEVEN QUINTANA

Kidnapped 50 hours ago

My body jolts awake. The room is dark. I exhale, calming myself out of fight-or-flight mode. They're watching us with heat sensor cameras, so I close my eyes and rest my cheek against Julia's back. She sighs and pulls my right arm tight around her. It feels good to spoon her under the thin wool blanket. It's the only real comfort we have.

How long have I been sleeping? My body says eight hours. They worked us for fifteen hours straight, and, as each hour passed, I thought we'd found the basement of our exhaustion. Then, we dug deeper and found yet another level below that.

The idiotic horror we endured made me admire Julia even more. She did what they asked with complete commitment, with no shame. She wasn't pretending to be in ancient Greece; she carried herself like a queen from another time. She really was floating in outer space and battling a sock puppet. I envy how she can become someone else and project herself somewhere else. It allows her to escape, which I cannot.

Her talent is what got us this mattress and blanket, and the shower, and the food. They threw us packaged sandwiches, and we wolfed down five each. The hot shower felt fantastic. I let the jets pound my back until my muscles were par-boiled.

Julia kisses the back of my hand, then squeezes it three times—three syllables, which means *I love you.* I squeeze her hand three times back. She sighs and falls back asleep.

We should have gone to that cabin and gone off-grid. She should have waited to do the movie, and I shouldn't have agreed to be stunt coordinator. I shouldn't have chased her into the metro, trying to be the hero.

My mind interrupts my chattering monkey brain. *Stop. Focus.*

We're alive. We have food, water, and time to rest, and time to think. And strategize.

Start with what we know. We're in a cinderblock room in a warehouse that must be 20,000 square feet. Above us, is an interlocking grid of metal walkways from where the men in black watch. Above those walkways, is a sloped tin roof that has skylights every few yards. Weak, yellow light seeps in through the dirty windows when the sun is up. My body has a good internal clock; the sun rises and sets close to the same time as LA. I don't think we've changed time zones.

When they let me out of the green screen room for my shower, I followed a maze of wooden walls. There was no loose wood, no glass or metal—nothing I can use as a weapon. What I do have are three pieces of sharp glass: two the length of my pinky finger, one the length of my forefinger and thin as a needle. They were in my socks, and I managed to get them into my mouth while undressing for my shower. My tongue pressed them in place until I could transfer them back into the clean socks that they left out for me. Dangling one sock in my teeth while I pulled the other one on helped make the switch back.

Eyes are always on me. If I had cut myself and drawn blood, they would have made me bleed even more. Still, what can I do with three pieces of glass in my socks?

Back in the green bunker, a mattress and blanket were waiting. I collapsed. Julia came in next and fell into my arms and we were asleep in seconds.

Julia trembles as she wakes up, then freezes. Her heartbeat quickens, throbbing through her whole body. I exhale a warm breath on her back, and her heartbeat slows. She's awake like me now, thinking. We may not have a way out, but between the two of us, we have one good brain.

I nuzzle close under the blanket and draw a heart on her thigh with my right forefinger. She squeezes my hand three times. She gets it. We can communicate.

I trace out the capital letter *A* with my finger, then tap on her back—first, a dot, then a long press for a dash. One dot, one dash— the letter *A* in Morse code. She does it back to me. She gets it.

I then draw a *B* with my right forefinger and tap out dash, dot, dot, dot – for the letter *B*. We lie still, both pretending to sleep while I teach her the alphabet, and she repeats it back to me. She makes a light snoring noise as she taps back, acting while she's learning. We do it again and again. It's something, and we must try.

CHAPTER 21

JULIA TRAVERS

Kidnapped 54 hours ago

We need sleep but this is more important. Learn this, and we can communicate. If we can communicate, we may live.

He teaches me letters and then words. I keep at it, squeezing them back to him as fast as I can: *Julia, Steven, love, marriage, baby, family*—words from our wish list. Sometimes, he drops the vowels, and I can still understand the words.

I tug his hand close when he tries to pull away. He's tired, but I'm not done. One of my first acting jobs in Los Angeles was playing the "girl next door" on *Forever Love,* a daytime soap opera. I'd memorize thirty pages of dialogue and regurgitate it on-screen day after day. Learning Morse code isn't that different.

Three hours after the lesson started, I initiate our first conversation:

You relax.

You bossy. Stop.

Just say words. No act.

Us team. No fight. No listen to Heyman. Focus. Do job.

He's right. We have to be a team. I squeeze out my words:

My job. Keep us alive.

How?

Acting. Distracting.

Yes. You distract.

Your job?

Get us out.

Promise?

Promise.

He's escaped insane situations before, but this seems impossible.

CHAPTER 22

CARL WEBB

Wednesday, March 13, 6:00 a.m. (PST)

I tried running on the beach before sunrise, but it didn't calm me down. Pacing through the house works better. I start at the front door, walk past the office, the bedrooms, the dining room, and through the living room until I reach the sliding glass doors to the tiny balcony overlooking the cove and the ocean beyond.

Yup, the Pacific Ocean is still out there.

At least it's raining. Calm, blue water and rolling, green hills irritate me. It's too perfect, day after day. I like these sheets of gray rain that match the shit we're in.

Concentrate. Find Steven and Julia.

I turn on a heel, walk back to the front door, spin on my other heel, and start pacing all over again. Heyman kidnapped them Sunday night, three and a half days ago .... Bushnell is pulling the levers, but no one believes us .... McCusker acts like they're fugitives.... Still no trace of Tina Swig or Mendoza or Marsh.... The Miami office is calling every motel, trying to locate a white, panel van or records of a single woman staying alone. I want to drive the entire length of every river myself but can't be in two places at once.

I reach the balcony again. The ocean is still out there.

"He'll get here when he gets here," Trishelle says, irritated. She lies on one of the deep couches, an arm draped across her face to block out the morning light. Her notebook is open. While I went running, she wrote lyrics.

"You can write at a time like this?"

"You went running in the rain. We handle stress differently."

We'd watched the second episode of *The Danger Game*, and it kept us awake most of the night. While Steven looked and sounded like a robot, Julia humiliated herself in scene after dreadful scene. Fighting puppets, birthing monster babies, dying in lava, and exploding in spacesuits.

"It was horrible, but I couldn't turn away," I say.

"That's the point. They're forcing Julia to commit career suicide and probably making hundreds of millions while doing it."

The security system dings. Someone is outside the main entrance. I check the monitor and see Glenn waving from the front seat of his black, government-issued Chevy Caprice. I buzz open the gate and watch him drive through before closing it again.

Trishelle, exhausted just a second ago, beats me to the front door. She's wearing one of my tailored shirts and smells clean. When did she have time to shower and steal my clothes? I still smell like a locker room from my run.

She swings the door open, and Glenn strides in with a computer bag on his shoulder and walks straight back into the living room without a hello. He looks like a tall Tiger Woods right down to the red shirt, black pants, and cap—except he's a phenom with tech instead of golf. He sits at the dining room table and opens his laptop. "Houston, we have a problem."

Trishelle cocks her head. "My name is Trishelle Hobbes, not Houston."

"I wasn't calling *you* Houston. That's from *Apollo 13*, the space mission where the fuel tank exploded, and they got home using the LLM for main propulsion. I'm using understatement to emphasize the size of the problem we face. Plus, my CO is only giving me one week of emergency leave to help you."

Trishelle raises her eyebrows at me but holds her tongue.

Glenn is a major in the United States Army in cyber-operations, but he lacks social skills. His subordinates call him Major Ass Burger (a play on Asperger's) right to his face. But his expertise helped save Steven's life once before, so I called in a favor with his CO at Fort Belvoir in Virginia, who flew him out here. My time as a Ranger and my company's security work still gets me pull with the Army brass.

"Are you upset with me? If I'm missing a social cue, please inform me."

"Let's just start with hello," Trishelle says.

Glenn stares at us like we're a weird bird species he's studying. "Oh, yes. Standard greetings. Hello, and hello. I brought three large, new computers plus an extra monitor for each of us. Please get them out of the car. This place will have to be headquarters."

"Will you be sleeping here too?" Trishelle asks, half-joking.

"Yes. Commuting to a hotel wastes time. I can sleep in the guest bedroom or on the couch. That way, you two can continue to have sex together without interruption."

Trishelle walks to the front door to escape him, with me close behind. She opens a big umbrella, and we step outside into the driving rain. It's big enough to shield both of us from the water bomb that's drenching the coast.

Computer boxes fill the trunk and backseat, along with empty Mountain Dew cans and Flaming Red Hot Cheetos bags. She holds the umbrella while I lift. "Is he really the best we can do? He almost screwed things up for Julia the last time he worked for you."

Rainwater runs down my nose. "He helped save Steven. He's the one who figured out that Boss Man's real name is Douglas Bushnell. And he's the smartest cyber specialist I know. And he works for DARPA."

The rain stops like someone flipped a switch, and the sun bursts through. Trishelle closes the umbrella and lifts out a monitor box, showing off her cut arms. "DARPA? Sounds like a carpet cleaning company."

"Work with him. He's the best, Trishelle."

Back inside, Glenn sits on the couch and types on his laptop, oblivious to us. We put the first boxes on the dining room table.

"I'm ready to share my deep thoughts, Handsome."

"The ones that come while fiddling on your guitar? I'm ready."

"Tina Swig isn't in Wisconsin. I think she's with Douglas Bushnell, and they're doing *The Danger Game* together."

Her idea hits me like a punch in the face. Have I been too focused on finding Swig and expecting her to lead me to Bushnell? We head back outside. "Keep talking."

"Robert Snow was the producer who created *Six Passengers, Five Parachutes*. When we stopped it, everyone split up and went underground."

"Save your own skin. It's what people do." We lift out monitors from the trunk next. They're big, but the boxes have handles at least.

"But, Tina Swig was Robert Snow's creative partner. The best way to save her skin might not be to stay hiding, but to find another partner with deeper pockets."

"And you think she hooked up with Bushnell and created *The Danger Game*?"

"He was Snow's boss. She does the work, and he takes the credit and makes the money. Women have been doing it that way in Hollywood for years."

104

"Why would she take the risk again?"

"Maybe she needs the money. Maybe she wants revenge."

We stand in the gravel driveway, each holding a heavy box. "Mendoza's phone mailbox is full. Other people can't reach him either."

Her thin smile can't hide that she's scared too. "She's probably with Bushnell on his pointy yacht. You've got people looking?"

"The National Reconnaissance Office is helping me. Let's get Glenn started." I don't say it's just three analysts helping me in their spare time—guys my Miami staff found. We head back inside.

Mendoza quit the LAPD for me, and I hired Marsh for his first civilian job. My pulse pounds. Where are my guys? I take ten calming breaths. Fear is not what this parade needs right now.

Glenn jumps up as we put the last boxes on the table. "I got inside the game app distribution platforms. *The Danger Game* is the fastest downloaded application, with ten million people around the world downloading it since it dropped Monday at midnight. It costs $6.99 a pop, so after distribution gets its cut, they've already made fifty million dollars just on the downloads."

"Can you follow that money?"

"They ping it around the globe through so many nodes that, unless I have a hundred NSA computers chasing them, it's pointless."

"Is there another way to find them?"

Glenn sits back down and types, his eyes locked on the screen. "Return engagement is high—over half of the people who buy the app watch again, sometimes multiple times, then make story submissions. There are about one hundred and fifty million submissions so far worldwide, I estimate. That means they've made two hundred million dollars on story submissions, with only two episodes so far. At this pace, they'll make a billion in less than a week—"

He'll keep going unless I stop this. "Glenn, you're not researching an article for *Forbes*. You're here to help us find Julia and Steven."

Glenn closes his laptop. His face flushes red. "I don't know how."

"We need to pull out all the stops, Glenn. Think."

"I've been thinking since you called me in Virginia!"

"Think some more. That's why I hired you!"

Glenn walks into the living room, falls backward onto the couch and closes his eyes. He's shutting down. Yelling is a mistake with him. "Work with me, Glenn. Please."

He dips his chin and pushes his head back deeper into the pillows. I blew it.

Trishelle picks up her guitar, sits on the arm of the couch, and strums a new tune.

"I've another thought. Want to hear it?"

"Babe, we should stay in our lanes, don't you think?"

She shoots me a look that says; *it's my turn now, so keep your mouth shut.*

Glenn lifts his head and squints at her in the sunlight. "That sounds nice."

"Is the sun bothering you? We could close the curtains."

"Yes. Please make it as much like a cave as possible."

I yank the curtains shut. I'll tin foil the windows if it keeps them talking. Glenn opens his eyes as the room darkens, listening to her play.

Trishelle strums her new tune. "I like caves too. The creatures inside live and die in darkness, so they use other senses besides sight to navigate. But, because we rely on sight, they remain invisible to us. Yet, they're right there."

Glenn sits back up. "Yes! And that's Douglas Bushnell is doing, like all cybercriminals. They render themselves invisible. Yet, they're still here." He casts his eyes down. "But I haven't figured out how to find him."

Trishelle sets the guitar aside. "It's not just Bushnell and Heyman. We think Tina Swig is with them too."

Glenn's eyes widen. "That makes sense. And makes it even harder for me to find all three."

You can't."

"Yes, he can, Trishelle. That's why Glenn is here."

"He just told us he needs NSA computers to do it." She turns back to Glenn. "You can't chase the money. Can you chase them through the app?"

"It's just like the money. I make a story submission, then chase it through different internet exchange points, but they disappear into the darkness fast."

"Like trying to see an animal in a cave." Trishelle moves next to him on the couch. They're almost knee to knee, which makes him shudder. She scoots back.

Glenn nods. "Exactly. And they run away and keep making episodes."

"So, we *stop* trying to find them. We try to beat their *game* instead. Do you play games online, Glenn?"

"I'm the best *Nightstream* player on the East Coast."

"I bet you can play *The Danger Game* better than they can. There must be a way to dominate their game. Take it over. Turn their game into a game of your own."

"Brilliant! That's it!" Glenn jumps up, infected with her idea. "But I can't do it alone. We need to crowdsource this thing."

I feel clueless. "What would this crowd do?"

"Imagine millions of players buying their app and playing online, but dedicated to spoiling their game—thus saving Steven and Julia."

"Do people do that?" I ask.

"Some people play online games just to make mischief. They disagree with the game itself, so they spoil it for the other players. It happens in shooter games all the time. You're about to shoot someone and score points, and they interfere. It's called 'griefing' because the spoilers give you grief."

I look at both of them. "Okay, I get it. Nice idea. But we can't just make a billion submissions and crash their website. We want to save Steven and Julia."

Glenn flicks his fingers, releasing his pent-up energy. "He's right. We have to steer the outcome. Our millions of recruits must play *their* game but *our* way."

"And what way is that?"

Trishelle jumps in. "Maybe our spoilers can flood their game with storylines in which Steven and Julia aren't tortured. That way, Steven and Julia may live long enough for us to rescue them."

Glenn shakes his head. "It's called *The Danger Game*. They won't back down, no matter what our spoilers send in."

"And for me to rescue them, I need to know where they are, Trishelle."

Glenn paces the length of the dining room, turning at each end like a lion in a cage. "But her idea is good. Real good. I just have to figure it out."

"Then what do you need, so I can get it for you?" I ask.

Glenn stops, his face so close to mine I can smell Cheetos on his breath. "I need Corporals Darna and Rafael Hilaro here. Today. They're stationed at the Defense Language Institute in Monterey, California."

"Why them?"

"I met them at the Black Hat conference in Las Vegas. They're the only ones who can beat me at *Nightstream*."

"And what will they do exactly?"

"We will build a rival game dedicated to griefing *The Danger Game*. We must code the game, and put it online as fast as possible, and they're the only ones who can do it with me."

There's one colonel stationed at the Presidio of Monterey Army Base who owes me. His number is still in my contacts. This better work. I'm running out of favors.

CHAPTER 23

TINA SWIG

Wednesday, March 13, 4:00 p.m. (CET)

At noon today, Douglas jumped into the tender, and Carlos drove him to the island of Ustica. Without me. No announcement, he just went. He was gone for three hours, and, upon his return, he went straight into the master suite to take a shower.

He has a lover there. Maybe she follows him, appearing in ports when he calls for her. He may have two or three lovers following him, all as loyal as red-haired Rebecca.

I don't confront him. She's not in my face or in my bed or using my toothpaste. He's being discreet, which I appreciate.

I also went to Ustica this morning for a run. I had to ask Douglas for permission, then go to Carlos and request a ride ashore, who then talked with the captain and first mate—men with whom I've never spoken. They just salute and disappear. The ship's bridge is also off-limits, which means Douglas is probably up there spying on me with hidden cameras placed around the ship. I think they're inside the light fixtures.

I ran the ancient stone steps on Ustica for fifty minutes, and Carlos watched me from the tender the entire time. I didn't let up until my lungs ached in my chest.

This tension is not freedom. Now I understand Devon's frustration. But it goes with the territory, and we're too close to the destination to turn back. Just a few more days and we'll be off this yacht. Then, we'll both have the life that I promised him.

I make sure to be in the master suite when Douglas emerges from the marble bathroom after his shower. There are no cameras here. I examined every bend and divot in the wood and plaster.

The door swings open, and Douglas comes out wearing a white robe. He walks to the bar and mixes his green drink. "How are the tech bros? Keeping you busy?"

"We're flooded. People want dragons, mermaids, zombies, and ghosts."

"And we'll make money with every one of their silly requests. We don't want to kill the goose laying the golden eggs too soon, right?"

Most of the story submissions are for torture and murder. But we're saving that for the final episodes. "What's the body-hack today?"

"I did six minutes in the cryo-chamber that Carlos installed."

The marble bathroom has a tall hexagon-shaped metal chamber that's just big enough to fit a human. It stays cold when he gets out, and it cools the master suite a few degrees. "Isn't six minutes a long time?"

"You have to work up to it." He sips his drink and smiles, showing off that adorable, green mustache.

"I'm excited for the next episodes. It will be hard to top the last one."

"That last episode was hard to produce on a tight schedule, although it did give us the huge audience we wanted. Now, we can crank out episodes with more words and fewer special effects."

"I'd rather just make them suffer."

Douglas finishes his green drink and pops his NAD+ pill to keep his cells working at top capacity. "They'll suffer. This is *The Danger Game*, after all."

"I don't like them acting."

"People pay and send crappy dialogue, so let's give them crappy dialogue. It's easy, and it keeps the gamers playing. The scenes still have pain and suffering."

The show is at risk when Julia Travers speaks. She gains power. When Douglas created the opening for the show, he shouldn't have put in those overwrought lines from Shakespeare that she howled up at the cameras. She's too compelling. That's why she's a star; she's genuine, and the audience wants to see more. Even the tech bros at their monitors lock eyes on her when she comes on screen. They feel for her.

We should stick with the cartoon idiocy that worked so well in the second episode. That absurdity makes them look silly, so their pain feels fabricated like the fight scenes in a superhero movie, and no one believes their situation is real. If we give her lines, she can make it real again, and take over the show.

Douglas reads my face. "Say it, my love."

"I want episode four to be over the top. Like episode two."

He beckons me to him. I get off the bed, walk into his arms, and kiss him. His breath smells like fresh kale. "The game will still end with them dying, but I want to make as much money as we can along the way. We may even hit two billion."

"I'm not a gambler like you."

"My biggest gamble so far has been on you, and it's paid off."

I lay my head against his chest. "You're the perfect fit."

"And so are you." He wraps his arms around me. He's getting aroused, which arouses me. Whatever happened this afternoon wasn't enough, which I like.

"Devon is struggling with the Hodge conjecture. He's getting cabin fever too."

"Invite him out of his lair. Carlos can take him ashore."

"He wants to use the internet."

"Not until the game is over. If he wants to send or receive email, Rebecca or I can do it for him, encrypted."

"He knows that. But he's a teenager."

"I've made sure that he has wonderful distractions here to stimulate him."

He means Rebecca. I almost say something. Instead, we fall back onto the bed.

CHAPTER 24

STEVEN QUINTANA

Kidnapped 56 hours ago

I float in dark, warm water, not knowing where my skin ends, and liquid begins. My body expands until the water and I become one.

"Wake up!" Peter Heyman's voice is the fish hook in my brain that yanks me awake. I roll away from Julia, off the mattress, and onto my knees on the cold cement. Julia's panting nearby. We're full of adrenalin with nowhere to go.

The overhead lights snap on, blinding us. I cover my eyes and flip my middle finger skyward. "Fuck you, Heyman. Who turned you into such a monster?"

"My brother. He'd beat me senseless. He wanted to turn me into him, and it worked."

"He must be very proud of you."

"I killed him. The trouble is, I keep wanting to kill him."

"You should have thought of that before you did it, you murdering moron."

Julia pokes me in the ribs. "Don't aggravate him. It doesn't help our situation."

"She's right. Act if you want to live."

"I don't act to live. I live to act," Julia says. "Bring it on."

"Learn from her, Quintana."

"I'll try."

"Try harder. Your show is a hit, and we want to keep it that way."

"What do you mean?" Julia asks.

"The Danger Game. It's what you're shooting. Act or die. That's the premise. People love it. Your head exploding in your spacesuit got thirty million views."

Julia's face turns red hot. I ache for her. After all her hard work, they can destroy her career in less than a day.

I point at the dark form on the catwalk, who seems to be Heyman. "You can't stand that she beat you people twice already! And she'll beat you again!"

Julia touches my arm and her eyes bore into mine. "I don't care about beating them. Performing is how we stay alive right now. *That's the job."*

Heyman shouts at full volume. *"Smart woman."*

Two scripts drop from the catwalk and hit the green cement floor with a thump.

"Memorize the first twenty pages and you get breakfast. Then, we start shooting."

The scripts are thick. I skim through mine, glancing at a few pages. It's all dialogue. My body temperature jumps ten degrees, and the sweat spigots turn on. I'd rather be poked with more cattle prods than do this.

Julia picks up her script and laughs as she turns the pages. "Yesterday, you humiliated us with stupid action scenes. Now you want us to do legit theater?"

"Your public is requesting it, mistress thespian. Start memorizing if you want to eat."

Julia takes her script and goes to a corner.

I can memorize fine; it's the acting that scares me. Julia feeds off it but not me. My skill is staying hidden, observing, recording, and remembering.

Then, it hits me. But people watching me may be good. Friends are watching, looking for a way to help us. Maybe I can use these words to reach them.

I sit down against a green wall opposite Julia. We trade glances, but I look away. They're watching, but I can hide in plain sight.

CHAPTER 25

JULIA TRAVERS

Kidnapped 57 hours ago

I sit in my corner and leaf through the hundred pages they dropped from the scaffolding. There are dozens of scripts inside that we must memorize.

One's a thriller, another a slasher, another a drama. We blaze through the first script in an hour. I confront Steven for cheating on me. We fight like cats for ten pages, then I shoot him and laugh while he dies. That earns us more stale sandwiches and water.

Act or die.

Will they really broadcast all this? Doubtful. Maybe they're gathering enough material to create digital versions of us. Then they can kill us and still make our holograms perform forever. At least I'd be out of my misery.

Sipping warm water keeps me from trembling as we memorize the next script. Steven crouches against the wall on the other side of the room. He looks like a teenage boy from here, with his script between his knees, mouthing the words. It makes me wonder what our son would look like. He may look like Steven does now, except curled up with a book worth reading. That vision gives me hope.

"You have ten minutes. Then you do script two."

Up in the scaffolding is the silhouette of a bald man in a long trench coat. It's Peter Heyman, lording over us.

I'd like a sweatshirt to sleep in. If I could sleep better, I could think and find a way out of here. But that's Steven's job. He better be thinking of something.

Steven stares at his script. He keeps mouthing the words and then touching the page like he's counting. The tip of his right index finger is red. He's bleeding. Somehow, he managed to cut himself and he's touching his bloody fingertip to the paper. I can see it from this angle but, because he's crouching against the wall with the script between his knees, no one in the scaffolding can see.

They better not or they'll kill us in an instant. Whatever he's doing, he better tell me in Morse code tonight.

"It's time." Heyman's voice sounds like we're in a horror movie, which we are.

We leave our scripts and face off in the middle of the room. A half-apple box, painted green, drops down from the scaffolding. It's for me to stand on, so our eyes are level, and I'm not staring up into Steven's face.

"Stand on your marks."

We get in place and exhale. Steven looks different; he's not a scared rabbit anymore. His eyes are set with that thousand-yard stare he gets in warrior mode. I think about losing him, and my eyes well up with tears.

"Action."

"Start?" Steven asks, then blinks.

Heyman yells, "*'Action' means start, moron! It's your third day!*"

"I can't remember! I have to start over!"

"Then do it, idiot."

Steven keeps blinking. "I am leaving you," he says like a bad robot.

120

I grab Steven by both arms. "What can I say to make you stay?"

Steven plows ahead. "The things we had, have never, ever been worth anything. Let's not kid ourselves that we can change. I have napped through my life like a sleepwalker. But I'm awake now. Nothing can rescue us."

Those aren't his exact lines. He can memorize anything, why is he messing this up? "You won't even try?"

Steven grabs me back, pinching my muscles. "Don't you get it? I hate you. I will kill you for what you put us through."

The lines are stupid, but his harsh voice triggers me. I fall to my knees, sobbing. "Please. I beg you. Don't kill me. I love you...."

He wraps his hands around my neck. The veins on his neck and the muscles in his face bulge as his hands tremble—but his fingers don't tighten. I hold my breath and bug my eyes out, pretending. I claw at his hands and hit his forearms, then go limp. He lets go, and I fall to the floor, staying still for thirty seconds. I finally gasp, filling my lungs.

"Unsatisfactory."

Steven looks up. "We performed exactly what's on the page."

"You changed some of the words, Quintana."

"I'm trying. You're lucky I memorized as much as I did."

"And you did not strangle her to unconsciousness."

"I was acting. Acting is pretending."

"Don't pretend. Strangle her."

"Why not make us kill each other?"

"We'll get there."

The point of today's episode hits me. Yesterday they humiliated us. Today's scripts are about making us suffer, and Heyman is going to make sure it's as real as possible.

"You will strangle her into unconsciousness. Now."

"No."

121

"Drop."

Five ninjas drop from the catwalk with their cattle prods and surround Steven. One jams him under the arm, and Steven's arms contract, so he slaps himself in the face.

Steven says something in Spanish and it enrages the man, and he keeps poking him until Steven falls to the floor, convulsing.

Heyman blows a whistle, the ninjas step back, and then fly to the ceiling, hauled up by the wires and harnesses. I fall to my knees and cradle Steven's head. He blinks in rapid succession, forcing himself awake. He smiles, a moment of tenderness that gives me hope. He blinks again, fighting to stay conscious. "We…we are trapped…we're somewhere in hell. South of hell. No…it's of…no…below hell. Worse than hell. No border. No door. No way to escape. No way out."

He's not making sense. I stroke his face. "Steven? I'm here. Right here."

"No one will rescue us. No one can find us."

"Don't give up. I love you."

"I love you, too…." He blinks again, trying to stay conscious, but he drifts away.

"Very touching. We'll add sappy music and make it a scene."

Heyman blasts an air horn, which startles Steven awake. He rolls away from me and pushes up to feet. "Why am I the one who's always torturing her? Strangling her? Punching her?" he shouts up to Heyman.

"Because that's what people want to see."

"Let her punch me. Strangle me. That's drama. They want to see her fight back!"

"If you need her to punch you, so be it. But fewer people want to see her hurt you."

Heyman is right. Men hurting women in literature, movies, and TV outnumber women hurting men by a thousand to one. I point up at Heyman's silhouette on the metal catwalk. "*"Hate is a bottomless cup; I will pour and pour. Of all creatures that can feel and think, we women* are the worst treated things alive.""

"*Typical. You give yourself the best lines, actress.*"

"They're not my lines. They belong to Euripides. And the truth about how men treat women hasn't changed in twenty-five hundred years."

"*Quintana, shut her up. Strangle her now.*"

"What's wrong, Heyman? You don't like it when a woman knows more than you? *'I know indeed what evil I intend to do, but stronger than all my afterthoughts is my fury, fury that brings upon mortals the greatest evils.'* And I swear I will have my revenge on you."

"*Strangle her, Quintana. Otherwise, you both get nothing.*"

Steven looks scared. My eyes tell him to be strong. He must trust me, and not fight them. I stay on my knees, and he puts his hands on my throat.

"I won't hurt you. I'll just cut off your air," he whispers.

"Do it."

"I'll get us out," he mouths and tightens his hands on my neck. The blood stays in my head. There's a rushing sound in my ears. His face goes out of focus. Black.

CHAPTER 26

CARL WEBB

Wednesday, March 13, 9:00 a.m. (PST)

How many hours does it take to tweak three damn computers? Glenn's been at it for hours. The smell of bacon, home fries, melting cheese, and butter come wafting in from the kitchen. I hear knives cutting fruits and vegetables, eggs cracking, and the sizzle of ingredients hitting hot pans. Trishelle is *making* as she says. First music, and now food. And when she's *making*, she comes up with great ideas, so go for it, girlfriend.

My job is to *make things happen,* but I'm stuck on the starting line. I call Mendoza's number one more time—no answer. The FBI and the LAPD stopped taking my calls. I need them to believe us, so I can tap their power to find Steven and Julia, but I can't do that until I find Mendoza and Marsh, and I haven't heard from them in over four days.

The Miami office is calling motels in Wisconsin. Three people in Washington are downloading satellite photos of vacation harbors around the world for us, so we can search for Bushnell's yacht. What else can I do?

"We need to air out the cave, Glenn! Fresh oxygen is required!" Trishelle yanks open the curtains, slides open the glass doors, and flips off the two guys on the Boston Whaler sixty yards offshore. They blow an airhorn back at her and motor away. She gave them the photo they wanted. Maybe they'll sell it to Larry Naythons at *Celebrity Exposed.* The air coming in is cold but invigorating. Glenn shivers but nods his thanks.

To keep Glenn working at top speed, I retrieved a half-finished bottle of Mountain Dew from his car, which he finished in one gulp. The caffeine and sugar combo launched him into hyperdrive.

My phone buzzes with a text from Colonel Johnson in Monterey: *The Hilarios are ten minutes out. I flew them to Port Hueneme Army Base and requisitioned them a car.*

I show Glenn the text.

"Just in time. These computers are almost ready for massive data."

"So, you work with these corporals?"

"The Hilarios do a lot of big data analysis and language translation for me."

"What will they be doing exactly?"

"First, they'll upgrade Julia's internet line. A portion of every fiber optic cable is set aside for national security traffic, which we can borrow. We need it to carry two gigabytes per second, encrypted."

The outdoor gate dings. On the security monitor are two uniformed soldiers inside another black Caprice. As I buzz them in, Glenn darts out the front door so fast that I have to run to keep up.

A man and a woman exit the car. They look similar; they're brother and sister. Both are slim and trim, about 5' 7", with trim black hair. They look Filipino and swagger like gunfighters. They wear green fatigues as if they're still on base, with Corporal stripes on their sleeves. They salute Glenn (even though he's wearing civvies), and he salutes them back.

"Major Ass Burger, we killed you in *Nightstream* last week," the man says.

"He's right, sir, we wiped your ass right off the planet," the woman says.

Glenn is around thirty, and they seem to be in their early twenties, but casual enough with him to give him a bad time, which Glenn doesn't like.

"It took both of you to do it, teaming up against me."

Time for me to interrupt. "Yo, we have work to do. Glenn, talk to me."

"These are Corporals Rafael and Darna Hilario. They are twin brother and sister cyber experts who each speak six languages— English, Spanish, Tagalog, Thai, Cantonese, and Mandarin. They also think they're better than me at the online video game *Nightstream,* but, in fact, they are not."

They each wear two patches on their arm sleeves: a pentagon-shaped one with three spears for Cyber Operations Specialist and a Defense Language Institute patch. Those mean that the Hilarios are brainiacs who never hold weapons but can program your phone to blow up in your face if you speed dial a terrorist.

"Should we start on the outside of this sick mansion?" Rafael asks.

"Yeah. This crib is lit," Darna adds. "You got a bitchin' side gig, sir."

"Just begin," Glenn says, and walks back in the house, slamming the door.

Rafael and Darna snicker as they take out their green duffel bags from the trunk. I guess they're staying too. I'll move to the master bedroom, so they can all sleep on the sofa like a pile of kittens. I go inside and leave the door open for them.

Trishelle lays out cheese, omelets, home fries, bacon, toast, marmalade, sautéed mushrooms, hot sauce, and a fruit salad, along with black coffee, milk, and brown sugar. "Come and get it! I timed it perfectly, Glenn, for you and your friends!"

"You sound like a mom, Trishelle."

"You should sound more like a dad. Time to lead, Handsome. You're on point."

Glenn plops down, grabs a fork, pulls an omelet close, spoons on some home fries, and chows down. Trishelle and I trade looks. It's like we have a teenager in the house.

Darna walks in. "We're done. You now have the fastest internet in the county."

Rafael is behind her. "Any food left? Us *Nightstream* champs get hungry." They sit on either side of Glenn and the three millennials race to scarf down the remaining food.

Glenn pushes his plate away. "The Hilarios and I traded texts as they traveled south. We will now explain our strategy to save Steven and Julia."

Trishelle pushes a glass of water across the table. "Finish chewing first."

He downs the water and starts. "Here in this room, we'll create *The Rescue Game,* complete with website and app."

Trishelle rubs her hands together. "Give me the details."

"Millions of people want to watch Steven and Julia being hurt and killed. Those people are already playing *The Danger Game.* However, many more people are opposed to games like this, like all of us. The goal is to recruit an army of like-minded people to our platform with two goals – keep Steven and Julia alive, and help them escape."

"How do you know people will join our army?" I ask.

"Because we'll design a game that's *good*. That's all gamers care about. Are Steven and Julia really in danger? Is it fiction? *No one cares* as long as the game is fun to play. And the more players, the greater the chance they'll get out of this alive."

"Can you build this game fast enough?" Trishelle asks.

Glenn scoffs. "I program games for DARPA that build neuroplasticity to heighten mental acuity. My games train people to spot hidden missiles in satellite photos that computers miss. We can build this game. Trust me."

I hold up my hand. "How is *The Rescue Game* going to find them?"

"We have a three-prong strategy," Glenn says. "Darna, will you please start?"

Darna finishes her food and types while she talks, never making eye contact. "Strategy one: we tell our players to study *The Danger Game*. Examine the type of cattle prods the bad guys use. The color of the paint on the walls. A quirk in their rendering technique on the green screen. The light bulbs in the ceiling. Anything can be a clue."

"Keep going. You're convincing me."

Rafael types and talks next. "Strategy two: we tell our players to study Steven and Julia's behavior inside *The Danger Game* episodes. Micro facial expressions. The flush of their skin. Their pupil dilation. We could find proof that they are really in danger, which we can show authorities. Or a message. Probably from Steven."

Glenn takes over as Rafael and Darna's typing picks up speed. "During the Vietnam war, American prisoners of war who were forced to confess on camera, communicated the letters T-O-R-T-U-R-E in Morse code by blinking during their filmed confessions, telling the world what was really going on."

"I like this. What's the last prong?"

Glenn walks away from the computers, leaving Darna and Rafael at the keyboards, muttering words like *JavaScript, Ruby, Python Code, Objective C.* "The final prong is the most important. Bushnell and Swig make most of their money from story ideas that people submit. So we flood their game with story submissions that will still make them a lot of money, but also give Steven and Julia the best chance to escape and be rescued."

Glenn grins with pride. The only sounds come from the Hilario twins typing and the squawk of seagulls outside.

"I'm lost. What kind of story submission is that, Glenn?" I ask.

We want to see Steven and Julia *outside.* Free from that green room! If Steven gets outside, he can move. If he can move, he can find a place to hide. If he can hide, he can escape. That's his skill."

I pat Glenn on the shoulder. "You are good, Major Ward."

"Why would he ever let Steven and Julia outside?" Trishelle asks.

"Those green screen scenes take a lot of time to create, and they get old, fast. Viewers want reality after too much computer generation. If he wants to keep making money, Bushnell must bring the game up to the next level. We will define that level, with gamers demanding that Steven and Julia be let out to face real adversity."

"They could be in a warehouse in Downtown LA, thirty miles from here," I say. "If that's the case, he'd never let them outside."

"They are in a remote location. That's Bushnell's modus operandi. A remote cay in the Bahamas. A yacht in the South China Sea. An airstrip in Mexico. They're always far from civilization, so Bushnell can control the environment."

Trishelle shakes her head. "But the moment our game drops, Bushnell will know what we're trying to accomplish, and just pull the plug. And then he'll kill them."

Glenn smiles. "He won't quit. It would be admitting defeat. He'll want to play us."

"Trishelle crosses her arms. "What makes you so sure? We're playing with their lives, Glenn."

"I know this man. I found him. I studied him. I wrote the only dossier that exists on him. I know how he thinks. But he doesn't know anything about me. He doesn't even know that we know his name. He thinks he's safe."

Glenn's right. Finding Tina Swig's identity was easy because she worked with Robert Snow at Velodrome. But Bushnell believes we only know him as Boss Man. That might make him cocky.

Glenn points at me. "Bushnell owned a casino in Macao. He's a gambler. He likes to bet big and win big. It's his nature. And every time one of our *Rescue Game* players goes onto *The Danger Game* and pays to make a spoiler story submission, Bushnell makes more money. He'll like the challenge and want to beat us at our own game, while we try to beat him at his. He'll double down and keep playing."

Darna stops typing. "And while he plays, we hunt for Steven and Julia."

Trishelle sighs. "When *The Rescue Game* drops, they'll be looking at Steven and Julia even closer. They may hurt them more, to spoil our spoiler game."

"True. And they'll be searching for us, too, every person in this room," Glenn says. "But it's our best chance. And when Bushnell and Swig try to find *our* servers, we'll lead them on the same internet goose chase they put me through. They won't find us."

"It's all part of the game," Rafael says. "Both games."

I remember the Boston Whaler out in the cove, taking pictures. I have to keep this beach house secure and private. If Bushnell finds out that we know his identity, he'll turn out the overhead lights and kill Steven and Julia on the way out the door.

And they must have already known we were closing in on Tina Swig. That's how she got away. The sick feeling in my gut about Mendoza and Marsh gets worse.

Darna pushes her chair back from the table. "Major Ass Burger, sir?"

Glenn doesn't even turn to face them. "You cricket-eaters have an update?"

"I don't appreciate your racist comment, Major Ass Burger, sir. I don't accuse your Thai grandma of eating rats in Chang Mai."

"Then stop calling me Ass Burger, Corporal. Please proceed."

"We can have a version of the game up and running in fourteen hours. We can push it on Reddit in all the gamer subreddit communities. We'll recruit the best players for leadership roles. Then, we can hit social media for our foot soldiers," Darna says.

Glenn turns back to me. "Master Sergeant Webb, we just need your go-ahead."

"Go for it."

"We're going to need to be paid. Three thousand dollars a day."

"What? How do you all deserve three thousand a day?"

"That's for *each of us*. When we're on leave, we play video games and earn game credits, which we sell to other players online, through a blockchain cryptocurrency we created for video gaming. Each of us makes that much a day, easily. All we want is what we usually make gaming. And we're not playing. We're building the game."

Trishelle smiles and shrugs. "They have us over a barrel, handsome."

"Done."

Rafael claps his hands. "Yes! Our game is a laser burning right through their hot garbage."

The three Army geeks lean over their keyboards like they're driving Ferraris. Their fingers accelerate as the energy rises in the room. I feel a rush that starts at my heels and goes right up through the top of my skull. This is the feeling I used to get prepping for a mission. Glenn looks at me with a diamond glint in his eye. He gets the feeling too when he's doing his cyber ops. It's a heightened awareness, an excitement with an intense focus.

Trishelle crooks her finger, calling me into the kitchen.

I follow her over to the sink. "What's up?"

"If *The Rescue Game* drops in fourteen hours, the producer in me thinks we need to promote this thing." The edge of her mouth twists up in distaste.

"The last time I saw that sour look was when we talked about Larry Naythons."

"He did tell you that we could come back to him when we had something that will grab eyeballs. If he wrote about their horrible game, he should write about ours."

I pull out my phone. "I'll set something up for tonight."

CHAPTER 27

TINA SWIG

Wednesday, March 13, 6:00 p.m. (CET)

Douglas helps me down the ancient stone stairs to the beach on Ustica. I love this island and its history. These rocky steps were carved by ancient Romans.

We reach the sand and walk around the rocky point to a secluded cove, where a formal dining table waits for us. Carlos, the bosun, stands in his uniform, looking half-sailor and half-waiter. Three silver serving wagons are lined up behind him.

Douglas kisses my neck. "Surprise. I wanted something special for our last night at this anchorage." He holds out my chair.

"So, this is what you were doing when you went ashore this earlier today?"

"Of course. What else would I be doing except planning for your happiness?" he asks with a sly wink. My man covers his tracks well.

Carlos fills our glasses with prosecco, and we clink. *Reckoning* is two hundred yards offshore and lit up red and yellow from the setting sun. My beautiful son Devon is on board that yacht, hopefully back to cracking the code for the Hobbs conjecture. I didn't speak to him this afternoon; Douglas and I have been playing tourist for the past few hours, which I regret. I should've checked on him.

"I'm glad we took a break," Douglas whispers. "The game is going well."

"It is. We're close to two hundred and fifty million dollars in a little more than three days, and we've only had two episodes. I'm sure we'll crack three hundred million by midnight," I say. I don't like episode three, which we just finished, but stay quiet.

"When episode three drops, we'll reach half a billion."

"I have no doubt."

"Yet, you have reservations?"

Carlos serves the first course. Delicious grilled cuttlefish with lemon and olive oil on a bed of arugula and tomatoes. It gives me time to dodge the question.

"Where's Rebecca?" I ask. "I expected her to be serving us, not the bosun."

"She needs a day off, and Carlos can do it all. And Min, Ismael, and Eliot are glued to their computers, following your exact instructions."

I wonder what she does on her day off. Is she on Ustica? Or is she still on the ship, maybe leaving more of her perfume on Devon?

Douglas leans close. "Tell me."

I bite into a piece of cuttlefish. "I don't like it when Julia and Steven go off script."

"What do you mean?"

"When Quintana fought back, and we shocked him, and then when Julia Travers shouted those lines from that Greek play. I don't want to include that in the episode."

Douglas sips. "Why not? It's real. It's the premise of the game, and why people buy the app. *Act or die: The Danger Game*."

"They're *too* compelling."

"It's classic over-the-top Julia Travers, howling at the moon. People love it."

"I prefer the silly cartoon scenes. When she speaks as herself, she gains power."

"We kidnapped a movie star for a reason, my love. She grabs eyeballs and makes us money. And we're still destroying them. You, yourself, picked the scene in which he chokes her unconscious. It looks great. And there are twenty scenes of pain after that."

I can't admit it to him, but torturing Julia bothered me. It reminded me of my stepfather's violence toward my mother and his abuse of my sister. And when Julia goes off script and fights back, she shows courage, which my mother and sister lacked. Julia Travers, that little performing monkey, makes me *feel something* with her acting. I resent that her talent is powerful enough to get inside my head.

"Just take out the lines where she's ad-libbing."

"Darling, that ship has sailed. The episode is ready."

"It's risky."

"Not anymore. Your second episode was such well-produced comic book foolishness that fickle Hollywood considers *The Danger Game* a trifle. No one believes they've been kidnapped. Because of you, we're safe to make easy money, and the more money we make, the more freedom we will enjoy. Savor this."

Carlos removes our appetizer plates and brings us grilled lamb and couscous next, my favorite, which Douglas remembered. I saw off a piece and taste the meat. It's rare, seasoned with salt, pepper, and a hint of honey and tarragon. I want to savor this moment. But am I really free? Like Douglas?

"What will you do with total freedom, my love?"

He swallows his lamb and closes his eyes. "We will invent new identities. We will travel the world and mix with artists, scientists, and world leaders. And we will use our wealth and power to make a difference."

"In what way?"

"There are more people alive right now than in all of human history. We have a population crisis, a food crisis, a water crisis, and an education crisis."

"I've never heard you talk this way."

"Our survival requires finding a needle in a haystack. We need another Einstein, another Darwin, another Curie to find solutions. People like us."

"You think you can find those people?"

"I think we can find more than one. If Einstein is one in a billion, there are six or seven Einsteins alive right now."

"Devon could be one of them."

"I believe that already. How is he doing, by the way?"

"He's still frustrated."

"I'll get him on a jet ski. Going fifty miles an hour on the water will give him a thrill."

"Sounds dangerous." I sip my prosecco.

Douglas sips, mirroring me, which he does when he's trying to convince me of something. "You're worried about something else. Say it."

"Quintana is blinking in episode three. There could be a message in there."

"Elliot can't see a pattern, but I've already farmed it out to a foreign intelligence specialist. If there's some hidden message there, we'll find it. And he won't do it in this next episode. We're going to cut him off quick."

"I just want the game to be over."

"When we reach a billion dollars. But I wouldn't mind making more than a billion." Douglas is gloating when he should be shoring up our defenses.

I touch his hand. "The attacks will come. Hollywood thinks we're silly, but we're popular. People will try to hack the game. Interpol, the FBI, and then the CIA may start investigating. That will definitely happen if they find Mendoza and Marsh before Sunday."

"But they haven't, because everything is proceeding like you planned. And for them to do any damage to us, they have to find us. And me. Do you think I would risk this?" He gestures to our feast, and our yacht in the distance, lit up by the last rays of sunset.

Trishelle Hobbs and Carl Webb are up to something."

"Of course, they are. They're engaged in a vain attempt to locate their friends and convince the world that Julia and Steven really were kidnapped three days ago."

I carve my lamb into bite-size pieces but avoid eating. "I hired someone in Los Angeles to follow them."

Douglas raises an eyebrow. "What else have you been doing behind my back?"

"My love, please understand. You shouldn't have to micromanage every detail of the show. This is me being a good producer."

"How have you been talking to this person?"

"Every discussion has been encrypted on secure lines."

"What is his name?"

"Walter Lemming. He's my dog. I know enough of his secrets to destroy him."

"Good. And what has he learned?"

"Trishelle Hobbes and Carl Webb are holed up in Julia Travers's beach house with the drapes closed. Two military cars drove through the gate and haven't left. He believes three more people are inside."

Douglas laughs. "It's sweet that you're worried. Carl Webb runs a security company and relies on his military connections for work. If all he can muster are three people in uniform to help him, we're fine." Douglas touches my short hair, giving it a tiny tug. "And I will try to forgive you for going behind my back."

"They ruined *Six Passengers, Five Parachutes.* They and Julia Travers were the ones who learned my identity and tracked me down."

Douglas kisses my cheek. "So many worries! What can I do to make it better?"

"No more episodes with so much acting and ad-libbing. Julia Travers is too good, and Quintana is too terrible. It's better to have episodes with over-the-top scenes with computer graphics."

"I haven't lined up a new set of computer graphic companies. We burned out the last group doing episode two. But if you grant me one more episode with acting, I promise you nothing after that but cartoon silliness where we all laugh at their pain. Then, it'll be a tumbling rush to the series finale."

I nod because I can't argue with him. I'm the series creator, but he's the TV network.

A low throb starts. A helicopter flies over our heads and out over the water. It hovers over *Reckoning,* then lands on the helipad on top of the ship's bridge. The wind from the chopper blades flutters the ship's flags and flattens the water below.

"The captain is restocking our supplies. We'll be at sea the next few days."

If the helicopter is arriving with supplies now, that means Rebecca is still onboard to receive them, even on her day off, along with the captain and first mate.

I touch his face. "Thank you for this life. Devon and I are grateful."

He kisses me. "You're welcome."

"Would you like to make love now?"

Douglas turns to Carlos, standing ten yards away. "Would you please round the bend and make sure no one comes around those rocks for the next hour? I appreciate it."

140

Carlos nods and walks down the beach. I kiss Douglas long and hard, and he more than meets me halfway. That billion dollars can't come fast enough.

CHAPTER 28

STEVEN QUINTANA

Kidnapped 68 hours ago

The car accelerates. Julia is in the seat next to me, yelling to drive faster. We've escaped, and we're speeding down a mountain road. Suddenly, we're on a Los Angeles street, and a truck drives in front of us. We smash—and I jolt awake.

Julia and I lie on a bare mattress in the dark. One red LED light shines high above us. A camera. Probably infrared. They're watching, even in blackness. I close my eyes.

It's warm, even with no covers. They gave us cotton sweatsuits to sleep in since they don't trust us under a blanket. They want to see everything we do now.

I slept only an hour, maybe two, after ten hours of work. We're fading.

Julia snores lightly. She needs rest. I hurt her today. Many times. I strangled her unconscious. I burned her arms with a cigarette. I cut her legs with a knife. I whipped her with a leather belt. I hate myself, which Heyman enjoys.

My guilt only lifted when they made her do the same to me. She tied me to a chair and beat me with a rubber hose across my back, hit me in the head with a phone book, and shocked me with a Taser. It felt like penance.

Her snoring stops. She reaches back with her hand and finds mine. I drape my arm over her, spooning her, and grab her hand. We sigh and go back to sleep.

Or pretend to sleep. Our hands move fast with tiny squeezes, tapping out the letters as fast as we can go. Her first line kills me.

Sorry I hurt you. I love you.

Of course, she'd worry about me first. I squeeze back. *Hurt you worse. Hate them.*

She squeezes. *People pay to watch us. Obey them and we live. No games.*

I squeeze back. *Me, no game. Have plan. Trust.*

Julia lies still, not responding. She's afraid to give me control. She doubts me, which may go all the way back to that interrogation room. I must win her confidence back.

We are in Mexico.

She squeezes fast. *Sure?*

They wear black shoes from Tijuana. I called one coward in Mexican slang. Got mad.

Us where?

Maybe desert. Warm at night. No moisture. Heard seagull. Water close.

Must get out.

My job. You distract. Keep eyes on you.

Tell plan.

No. Be ready.

CHAPTER 29

CARL WEBB

Wednesday, March 13, 9:00 p.m. (PST)

Trishelle and I pace the lobby of Shutters on the Beach, a posh hotel just off the boardwalk in Santa Monica. Outside the window, the crowded circus of California nuts moves past. Walkers, bikers, skateboarders, body-builders, and fitness freaks fill the walkway and the bike path, even late at night.

"I hate that we have to meet him here. It's so public," Trishelle says. "We hid in the backseat of Glenn's car to escape the house, then took two rideshares to get here, and now we're out in the open?"

"He insisted. I requested the meeting, so I don't have much choice."

"I hope he comes," she says. "I hate him, but we need him."

"He doesn't love us either, but he loves a good story. He'll come."

The sofa next to us begins to speak. "I couldn't agree more." Larry pops his head up from behind a couch cushion. He stands to greet us. "We don't have to like each other to help each other."

"How long have you been there?" I ask.

"A bit. I like the highbacked sofas. Good for eavesdropping. Would you like to watch episode three of *The Danger Game?* I have to write a review for tomorrow's posting." Larry drops back onto the sofa. He takes out his smartphone and pats the cushion next to him, inviting us to join him.

I walk around the sofa and sit next to him, sinking into the plushness. Trishelle purses her lips in distaste and sits on his other side. A roaring fire blazes in front of us, warming my face. I wish I could enjoy it, but nothing is enjoyable right now. Larry hits *The Danger Game* app on his screen and holds his phone up so we can see it.

That dumb intro comes on again, showing infrared images of Steven and Julia being punched and kicked in the darkness. Heyman's voice comes on: *"Previously on The Danger Game…a ruthless cartel kidnapped and imprisoned Steven and Julia, with plans to torture them unless they perform for the world's amusement. How much can they endure?"* A rapid montage shows them bound and gagged, tossed into a dark room, then kicked and poked with electric prods. We hear Peter Heyman's voice: *"Act or die."* There's a big symphonic hit as titles fill the screen: *"You write the story. The Danger Game."*

Yesterday, they were battling puppets in space. Today's episode has actual acting, with scenes set in a New York apartment. Julia is good, but Steven sucks. In the first scene, Julia shoots him for cheating, which is lame. Then, in the second scene, for no reason, Steven strangles Julia until she collapses unconscious. It looks fake.

Trishelle still gets up and paces in front of the fire, clenching her fists. She glances at me, asking me if it's okay to come back.

I shake my head.

They want him to strangle her again, and when Steven refuses, they shock him some more. He lies on the floor as Julia holds his head. Steven blinks, fighting to stay conscious, but he mumbles nonsense.

That's it for me. I join Trishelle at the fireplace, fighting to keep the bile down. We're still close enough to hear the movie music mixed with human pain coming from Larry's phone. He finally turns it off and slides it into his pocket. "I get the idea."

"It was disgusting," I say, sitting down again.

Trishelle joins me, but on my side. She doesn't want to be close to Larry.

"The script was forgettable until they fought back. Then, it got interesting. Very meta. Self-aware. *Au courant,*" Larry says.

"Do you speak French?" Trishelle laughs. "Va te faire foutre, cul merdeux."

"What?"

A waiter appears, dressed in his white apron, looking more like a butcher than a booze slinger. "Would any of you like a cocktail? We specialize in tequila drinks."

"Three margaritas with salt. You can put all that on my card," Larry says, and hands over his plastic. "And put them in cups we can take out by the pool, please."

Trishelle leans in and whispers, "They're not acting self-aware, Larry. It's really happening to them."

"Can you prove it? Maybe you coming here is just a sophisticated ploy to help Steven and Julia promote their game."

"You act like you're doing us a favor," Trishelle says.

"I am. No other news outlet is writing about *The Danger Game* because everyone else thinks Julia is just committing career suicide. I need *news.*"

The waiter returns with three drinks. Larry signs fast and tips large.

"Thank you," the waiter says, lingering.

We all stare at him until he goes.

"We have something new. Tell him, Carl."

No one else is in the lobby bar. The waiter is with the bartender, looking at the basketball game on the TV above the bar. It feels safe. "Trishelle and I are launching our own free storytelling app: *The Rescue Game*. We will recruit players to watch *The Danger Game*, and help Julia and Steven to escape."

Larry perks up, curious. "Your own game to challenge theirs? I can work with that." He leans back against the couch cushion. "To play *your* game, I pay for their app and play *their* game? How does that work?"

Trishelle smiles, shifting from caustic to charming. "People watching *The Danger Game* are submitting story ideas about humiliation, torture, and pain. Our players will flood their platform with story ideas in which Steven and Julia will not only be given a chance to live—they'll also get a chance to escape."

I chime in. "While also looking for clues that can help us find them."

"What makes you think people want to help them escape?"

Trishelle points at his phone. "You said the best part was watching them fight back. They're underdogs. And our stories of survival and escape are going to make Bushnell and Swig so much money that they won't be able to resist playing along for the profit."

Larry shrugs. "Maybe for a little while. But not forever."

"We don't need forever. Just long enough to find them."

"Can you give me an example?" Larry asks.

"You'll have to play the game and see," Trishelle says, and winks.

Larry smiles, appreciating her coy approach. "How do I know that your game isn't just a big promotion for their game?"

"You don't, but you have a story either way. If Steven and Julia are masterminding everything, then Julia is a marketing genius, which makes it a story. But, if it's real, then it's an even bigger story, and you could be helping save two lives."

Larry picks up his margarita. "Grab your drinks. I like eavesdropping, but I don't like people eavesdropping on me."

We grab our glasses and follow him out of the lobby to the second-floor pool overlooking the boardwalk and beach. The ocean is a black streak past the gray sand.

Larry leans against the wooden railing. The human parade below is still going strong. The original Muscle Beach is five hundred yards away, with pull-up bars and rings on the sand where people are still working out.

"When does *The Rescue Game* drop?"

"Midnight. We hope you can write an article for us like you did for their game."

"There's something you should know. When I spoke to Julia and Steven on Sunday, or whoever was *pretending* to be Steven and Julia, they offered me two hundred thousand dollars to run that article."

"And now you want the same from us? Is this a shakedown?" I ask.

Larry shakes his finger. "Careful. You need me, Mr. Webb. The people on the phone *insisted* that I accept it. But I never take the money. I don't need to."

"So, you'll run our story?" Trishelle asks. We stand with our drinks in our hands, waiting for an answer. I feel like a dumb kid at a nightclub again, hoping the girl will say "yes" to a dance.

Larry sips his drink and stares at the beach. "You call me names, and now you want me to risk my life for you. Because if what you're saying is true, that's what I'd be doing, right?"

"I apologize. We came back to you because you said if we came up with a new angle, you'd publish it. We hope that you can help us."

He sticks his hands in his pockets. The bright lights of the Ferris wheel on the Santa Monica Pier turn behind him, matching the wheels turning in his head. The pause is so long I can hear kids screaming on the roller coaster.

"I like it. I can imagine an article asking what people want to see. Maiming and killing? Or struggle, escape, and triumph? Whichever game wins reveals what we prefer."

"We believe in our better angels. Escape and triumph will win," I say.

"But I can't publish it. I'd rather not deal with the wrath of an international criminal cartel. But, I will feed the story to a rival. I'll even write it."

"Which rival?" Trishelle asks.

"You don't get to choose."

"I don't get it. What's in it for you?" I ask.

"Half their ad money for any click-throughs for that story on their site. I just embed a tracking pixel. We do it all the time. And, if 'Steven and Julia' contact me again to run another story contradicting yours, I may run that article too. We can get a story war going in rival publications. Get you even more eyeballs."

"And you'll make even more money," Trishelle says.

"And even more people playing. That's why you came to me, isn't it?"

"I have an entire security company that will protect you," I tell him.

"I can take care of myself, Mr. Webb. But, just in case we're being watched, when we go back into the lobby, I'm going to laugh out loud and say that I refuse to ever work with either of you. You're going to threaten me, and then I'll hit you in the face. Then I'm going to storm out."

"You're serious."

"If Bushnell and Swig are as powerful as you say, they could have people watching me 24/7. I need to protect myself." He grins and sips his drink and grins.

"Okay, drama queen. I can take a punch from you."

He turns to Trishelle. "And then I'll throw the rest of my drink on you. That would be good for effect."

"This shirt is silk. Can you aim for the pants?"

"I'll try. Now that I feel safe, tell me everything about *The Rescue Game* so I can write the best article possible for you."

CHAPTER 30

JULIA TRAVERS

Kidnapped 79 hours ago

I wake up in the dark. My shoulders hurt. My breasts hurt. My legs hurt. Steven exhales in his sleep; he's coming out of his last dream. He'll be awake soon.

I smell the air. And salt. Or it could be dust. It's warm and dry, like he said. A tiny bit of light is sneaking in from somewhere, probably dawn's first light. I listen and hear birds far away—a seagull squawking followed by a sweep of birds chirping. We're not in Los Angeles.

The sounds remind me of running through the underbrush with Steven at dawn on Elysian Cay, in the Bahamas. I heard birds then, too, and we were fighting for our lives just like today. That was the most scared I'd ever been. Until now.

But he was right about the air. And the seagulls. Maybe there is hope.

Steven jerks awake, then lies still, pretending to fall back asleep. I squeeze his hand three times, and our morning conversation starts. *1, 2, 3.*

Love. Sleep?

Need more. Sore.

Hate myself.

Don't. Get us out.

I will.

How?

People watching is good.

But Heyman, Swig, and Bushnell are watching, too, and Steven is no actor.

The overhead lights blast on. *"Wakey wakey eggs and bakey."*

Heyman's silhouette moves on the catwalk. Two buckets descend from the ceiling. One has water and food, the other toilet paper.

"You go first, I'll eat," Steven says, and pops off the mattress ready to run a marathon. He pulls a sandwich and water out of the bucket and eats facing the wall. I grab the piss bucket, plop it down in the corner, yank down my sweatpants, and empty my bladder. There's blood in my urine and blood on the toilet paper when I dab myself. I want to look at all my bruises, but don't dare.

"Done." I yank up my sweats and stride away, fighting not to show pain. I eat my turkey sandwich and drain a plastic water bottle while Steven empties his bladder.

"Done," Steven says, and the cord holding the bucket retracts back up.

His stare is angry. He saw the blood.

Fluid moves inside me. I hope it's the water I just drank, and not blood flowing out of my kidneys into my abdominal cavity.

We trade looks again. My eyes are calm, telling him to behave the same way. He gives me a micro-nod, asking *me* to trust. Quid pro quo. Agreed.

"Heads up." Two more scripts drop down from the rafters and hit the floor.

"Get busy memorizing."

Steven and I pick up our scripts. It's one hundred pages, which means more dialogue until we drop from exhaustion. I preferred the silly scenes—dangling from mountains and leaping lava streams. They were only physically exhausting. This script has more scenes with me speaking than getting punched, which is a relief. I may survive the day.

I shout at the ceiling. "Two days of talking in a row? What gives?"

"People like your mouth. It makes the producers money."

"That means people want to watch me fight more than watch me suffer."

"I don't."

"That's because I beat you once before. And I will again."

"No, you won't."

"You shoot everything we do. I dare you to put what I just said in the next episode. If you don't, it will be proof that I do scare you."

"I'm already scared."

I read. Me yelling spontaneous lines from Shakespeare and Euripides must have hit a nerve with the internet audience because now I fight back.

A wife berates her husband, a femme fatale tempts a hapless suitor, a queen sentences a criminal to death, a witch casts a spell.... I can tell they're from different authors. Two of them are from women. My character is smart, and I challenge Steven as an equal. In the *femme fatale* scene, however, I must wear high heels, red lipstick, a red dress, and I must offer Steven great sex as long as he promises to kill my husband. Obvious alert: a man wrote that one.

Time disappears. Pain fades. Having a script with lines to study is an escape. Even the bad scenes are worth it, as I try to find a way to make them real.

Whatever I'm doing must be making them a profit because we're still alive. I'm doing my job. Is Steven really doing his?

I look over. He's on the last page already, and his face is white. Of course, he's already on the last page; he's got a freak memory and knows all his lines already. But, what's so scary? A monologue? I go to the last page. There it is in bold: *Steven cuts off Julia's left pinkie finger with garden shears.*

My heart pounds in my chest. The end game starts here.

"You're sick, Heyman!" Steven screams at the ceiling.

"Don't blame me. The producers know you're up to something. This is your punishment."

"I won't do it!"

"Drop five."

The lights go out. The ninjas drop and poke Steven with their cattle prods. Sparks flash each time they jab him, and I can see him fighting them in the strobing light. The shocks overwhelm him, and he hits the floor.

The ninjas fly up as the lights turn on. Steven has bad burns on his face and hands. I kneel and hold his head in my lap. "He'll do it. Just don't shock him again."

Steven forces his upper body off the floor and props himself on an elbow. "No."

"We expected that. I will give you another option."

Steve pushes himself onto his knees and spits blood on the floor. "I have an option? That's funny."

"Quintana must do a good job acting. No more blinking. Travers must behave. No backtalk. Accomplish this and the final scene will be Travers cutting off Quintana's finger instead."

Steven's eyes widen as the color drains from his face. My skin feels clammy, and the room tilts. He grabs my hand, steadying me. He squeezes out the message: *you can do it.*

"The producers want a guarantee that you will deliver good work."

"So, I'm supposed to bleed to death? Is that it?"

"You will be given alcohol and bandages."

"What about his pain?" I ask.

"He's trained to withstand pain. Your mental pain will be worse, and we'll have a dozen cameras on you. Accept or reject this option now. We start filming scene one in five minutes."

Steven heaves himself into a sitting position and hugs me. I hug him back, not caring who in the world is watching this. He pulls away. His face is stern, without fear. "Only if we get a shower and clean clothes."

"So be it."

The ninjas drop and corner Steven, as the small door in the wall magically opens. I go through and follow the maze of wooden walls to the bathroom and shower. There's a breeze coming from where the ceiling should be. Above me are the dark catwalks and bright lights and the eyes that are always watching.

The shower feels good and gives me time to prepare. Can Steven handle this? Can I? I drive away the fear of what is coming and focus on the first two pages of dialogue.

"Julia," someone whispers.

I jump so fast, I bang my skull on the showerhead. There's a tiny speaker embedded in the tile. They're filming me in here, too.

"Don't trust him. He planted the bombs for money, because he was jealous of your success, and then we turned the tables on him."

"I don't believe you."

"Betray him. Stab him. Kill him. Do something…and you live."

My mind wants to scream, but my body resists. My face goes blank as my arms and legs put on the clothes laid out for me. No emotion for them. Not until I'm acting.

I walk back. The little door opens. I hunch over and step back into the green room. Steven is already there, clean and showered and wearing fresh clothes.

He gives me a thin smile. "Let's do this."

CHAPTER 31

TINA SWIG

Thursday, March 14, 7:00 p.m. (CET)

The captain dropped anchor an hour ago, and *Reckoning* now floats in flat warm water, baking in the sun, a half-mile offshore from a city that was founded in 580 BC. That should be intriguing enough for any teenager as smart as Devon to enjoy.

"I don't want to," his Paul Newman voice says through the closed door.

"It'll be fun. I want some mother-son time."

"I can't," he says.

"Devon, unlock the door. It's demeaning to talk to you through a piece of wood." That's the agreement we have. I respect his privacy, but we always speak face-to-face. He triggers the automatic lock via computer, and the door opens. He backs up his cherry-red wheelchair into the middle of the room.

The shades are drawn, which he also controls electronically from his wheelchair. It's too dark, even for a sullen teenager. I yank the curtains open, revealing Porto Empedocle and Agrigento in the distance. The town is yellow, with green trees and the water is as flat and blue as the sky.

"It's beautiful out there. Come on. It'll be an adventure."

He spins his wheelchair so he's facing away.

Rebecca's perfume hovers in the air. Maybe she's still here, hiding in his bathroom. I look out the window instead. "This part of Sicily is so ancient and wonderful. We can even drive inland. There's a fortress town, Enna, which has castles."

"Castles? I'm not five, Mom. And I'm making progress on the Hodge conjecture."

"That's wonderful. Tell me about it."

"It's complicated, Mom, you wouldn't understand."

"You get your math genes from me. Try me."

"I believe that by using more than three projective lines—x, y, and z—all intersecting the complex shapes of a geometric cycle, we can predict the details of any geometric shape, assuming the factors x and y and z are numbers that can be complex, rational, or irrational but not imaginary. This requires creating an algorithm that will use variations of three unknowns, but all together will predict shapes of any three-dimensional object of unending complexity. I'm halfway through writing the code for the algorithm."

"I like the idea. Almost like satellite triangulation for determining location, but over an infinite number of points so that it can reveal shape and form, like a multi-variable vector calculus equation."

"Show off."

"How long do you think it will take?"

"Rebecca showed me an email from Professor Carlton, saying my approach is solid, but we need to crunch a lot of numbers. We have to work backward from simple shapes we can actually determine. We can start running our first tests in a few days."

"I'll tell Douglas that you want to send more emails to Professor Carlton so that Rebecca and the crew are ready to encrypt and send them for you."

"Thank you."

Calculations fill his computer screens. This is a better use of his time, and less risky than cruising the internet. "I feel an advanced degree coming. Do you need anything?"

He smiles. "Lots of pizza," he says with his Paul Newman voice.

"I'll tell Rebecca to tell the chef. We'll keep the pies coming, my wonderful son." I kiss him on the forehead and leave.

"How is he?" Douglas asks as I step out on the sundeck. He walks away from his view at the railing to meet me at the breakfast table. A light wind ripples his silk shirt.

"He's making progress. One of the planet's Einsteins may be onboard this yacht."

"Good. It's one less thing to worry about," he says with a sharpness he's never used with me before. He pushes his electronic tablet across the table, between the croissants. "This article dropped ten hours ago." On his tablet is a news article in *Variety Premier:*

The Rescue Game Challenges *The Danger Game*
Written by Evelyn Bouchey

Julia Travers and Steven Quintana's interactive story-telling app, Tales by Travers, *with their series,* The Danger Game, *is the fastest growing app for mobile devices since it dropped Monday, March 10, with projected profit from both the app and the story submissions topping a half-billion dollars in less than a week. But a rival app,* The Rescue Game, *designed to be a "game spoiler," quietly dropped today, and is already getting half as many daily downloads as* The Danger Game, *with no marketing efforts on any platform or in any media. It's also free, which may explain its quick surge in popularity . . . . It is not clear who is behind* The Rescue Game. *Jeanne Riley, who writes for* OnLineGamer.com, *says there is online chatter that Julia Travers and Steven Quintana are behind this game as well. Since both games encourage purchasing and playing* The Danger Game, *Quintana and Travers will continue to profit as long as both games remain popular.*

Trishelle Hobbes, Julia Travers's producing partner, and The Griffin Agency all declined to comment for this article.

Douglas shoots me a suspicious look. He thinks I'm involved.

"Is Naythons behind this article?" I ask.

"If he is, he'll regret it."

"We should have insisted that he take the money."

"Too late now. What about Hobbes and Webb? Are they behind this game?"

"The last I heard from Walter, they were still holed up in Malibu."

Douglas strokes his chin, with a faraway look in his eye. "Interesting."

Let's pull the plug now. I'm happy with half a billion," I say. "Heyman thinks he can mindfuck Julia Travers into killing Quintana herself. That would be a great ending."

He smiles and shakes his head. "I'd rather keep playing."

"Why risk it?"

"Because we're making money faster than ever."

"I'd rather disappear and build a new game. Or find Einsteins in the Third World."

"I never leave money on the table. I also never fold when I have decent cards until I can tell if my opponent is bluffing or has a better hand than me."

The swell from a passing cargo ship makes *Reckoning* rise and fall, and Douglas widens his stance to maintain his balance, but doesn't uncross his arms.

I shrug. "Let's go ask the boys then. We'll see how much money is on the table."

We go inside.

"Talk to me, boys," Douglas says.

Min, in the first chair, spins to face us. "The game dropped four days and three hours ago, and we just passed the eight-hundred-million-dollar mark. Downloads are way up. We're going to hit a billion dollars in just downloads within a day."

Douglas points at Ismael, who sits up straight. "What about story submissions?"

They're up two hundred percent over yesterday." He turns to his monitor. "Ten percent of submissions suggest castration, dismemberment, and torture. However, ninety percent want us to move them outside. Players want to see them running between real trees, wading through real water. Comments on the message boards say that players are tired of the green screen room and want to see them battle real elements."

"Elliot? What kind of chatter is out there? Any serious threats?" Douglas asks.

Elliot shrugs. "No. Some people chase their own submissions, trying to get inside, but I ping them around the world."

"Douglas shakes his head. "Tina, fill them in, please."

The boys listen to my explanation of *The Rescue Game*, then each of them reads the article from *Variety Premier*. Douglas eyes me the entire time.

"Crazy. Is this our game too?" Min asks.

"No, it's not our game too!" Douglas shouts.

Min twists his face up like a bad dog who just shit the rug.

Douglas points at Elliot. "You. You're head of security. Examine *The Rescue Game*. Get inside."

"Yes, sir." It takes Elliot ten seconds to find *The Rescue Game* online and download it onto his computer. He scrolls through it. "It's a basic site. It encourages you to submit clues about their location, which they will go through. They also ask you to submit spoiler stories to *The Danger Game* and to alert them, which they also don't list. They promise rewards for the best spoilers, but they don't say how that works either."

"That's it?" Douglas asks Min. "That can create millions of submissions?"

Min shrugs. "Yes. Thus, we have to assume any story submission that's about survival and escape is a spoiler submission from *A Rescue Game* player. And that's now already most of our submissions."

"That's a huge jump. Can we find these spoilers?"

The boys look scared.

Elliot answers, "We would have to compare their email list to ours. They may be attracting defectors from *The Danger Game*. Even then, their site insists people create new email addresses for each submission, to avoid detection."

"Get inside their game. Find out what they know."

"Yes, sir," they all say.

"Gentlemen, I have a question," I say, and it takes a second for all of them to look at me, Douglas included.

"What about Quintana blinking in the last episode? Any progress?"

Elliot shakes his head. "It seems to be Morse code, but it's random. There could be a deeper pattern, but I'm not a forensic math expert," Elliot says. "It's nonsense unless we can find a definitive start point within the randomness."

"Just running the game keeps us super busy," Min says.

"Episode three dropped yesterday," Ismael says. "We never leave the consoles."

"If millions are playing *The Rescue Game*, they may spot a pattern first," I say.

Douglas shrugs. "What could Quintana share? That he's been kidnapped? And Heyman is planting doubt. If they betray each other, that'll be a better story than any submission. Until then, every submission makes me money. I'll know when to fold."

I cross my fingers that they turn on each other. I want this game to end.

CHAPTER 32

CARL WEBB

Thursday, March 14, 12:00 p.m. (PST)

The gray Pacific Ocean is still outside the kitchen window. I need to get back to the Atlantic, which is a real blue. A squadron of six pelicans drop down from the sky and fly in single file formation right over the surface of the water, riding the air between the swells. The Pacific still doesn't care about Steven or Julia or Mendoza and Marsh.

Trishelle touches my face, breaking my gaze. "You're a good man, Carl Webb."

"I hate feeling helpless." I glance over at our trio of military cyber-experts, typing in the dining room. "They could be playing solitaire in there."

"Any news from Wisconsin?" she asks.

"We're still rolling calls. There are sixty rivers and hundreds of motels in Wisconsin."

We stare at each other. Besides some meditation music coming out of Darna's portable Wi-Fi speaker, there's no noise in the house except their typing.

"Touchdown!" Glenn yells, which is followed by a round of applause.

We rush back into the dining room.

Darna raises her fist. "A *Rescue Game* player cracked the code. Steven is sending us messages in episode three. He's using the Fibonacci sequence to hide it."

"Fibonacci sequence?" Trishelle asks.

"It's a sequence of numbers, where the next number is the sum of the previous two numbers," Darna says.

"0, 1, 1, 2, 3, 5, 8, 13, 21, 34, 55, 89," Glenn recites.

"It's a sequence often found in nature, in everything from the number of leaves on a twig to whorls in a seashell. It's always a Fibonacci. The ratio of two consecutive Fibonacci numbers tends to the golden ratio as the sequence increases," Rafael explains.

"Wonderful. So what?"

"Look at this," Glenn says. He turns his monitor towards Trishelle and me, and then scrolls to the start of the third episode.

"Start? Do I start?"

"Action means start, moron! It's your third day!"

Wait, stop. I can't remember! I have to start over!"

"Then do it, idiot."

They included Steven's bad start, complete with cartoon music, just to make him look stupid, which makes me hate them more.

"Did you notice the blinking?" Glenn asks.

"Guys, I've seen the episode. He blinks through the whole damn thing. He's nervous because he can't remember his lines, he just said so."

Glenn shakes his head. "Steven Quintana remembers everything."

Damn, he's right. My heart picks up.

Glenn smiles. "After Steven says the word *start,* he blinks Morse code for 0,1,1,2,3,5."

"And then he says the word *stop*," Darna says. "That's his first message. He's telling us to watch for Fibonacci numbers."

Trishelle and I both lean on the table, crowding five heads around one monitor. "This is his second message," Rafael says, and hits the space bar, starting the video.

"The things we did have never ever been worth anything. Let's not kid ourselves that we can change. I have napped through my life like a sleepwalker. But I'm awake now. Nothing can rescue us."

Steven blinks throughout. I shrug. "Rafa, I just see blinking."

Rafael takes it back to the beginning. "Watch his hands right here," Rafael says, and he pauses the screen. Steve twists his finger into the palm of his other hand. "That gesture means 'start' in American Sign Language."

"Fantastique," Trishelle says.

"Start what?" I ask.

Glenn takes over. "Start paying attention. Steven blinks after the third word, and then after the fifth word, then after words eight, thirteen, and thirty-four. All Fibonacci numbers." Glenn points at his second monitor. "I did some fast editing to include only those words." He starts the video again.

Steven moves in jump cuts onscreen. *"We-have-been-kid-napped-rescue."*

Trishelle grabs my arm so hard her fingernails dig into my flesh through my shirt.

"Now watch this," Glenn says and fast-forwards to when the Peter Pan idiots descend and zap Steven until he collapses. Julia cradles Steven's head. Steven speaks: *"We...we are trapped...we're somewhere in hell. South of hell. No...it's of...no...below hell. Worse than hell. No border. No door. No way to escape. No way out."*

"He looks like he's having a seizure," I say.

Glenn clicks on the cursor and takes it back to the beginning of the scene. "This is his third message. Look right there." Steven twists his finger into his open palm of the opposite hand. "That means *start.* He then blinks after the words that are in the Fibonacci sequence." Glenn points at the monitor. "Again, I did some editing for you."

He hits *play.*

"We-are-trapped-somewhere-south-of-border."

Glenn grins. "They're in Mexico."

Trishelle claps her hands and bearhugs Glenn. He cringes. She heads for Rafael next; he's already recoiling. Darna stands up and winces, knowing she's next. Trishelle lifts her off the floor. Darna pats her on the back, like a wrestler tapping out in a fight. Trishelle puts her down and wipes tears from her eyes. "How did you do it?"

Glenn shrugs. "It wasn't us. We have ten million players, and someone named *Too Cool for School* sent in the solution hours ago, and we've been analyzing it to confirm."

"Larry Naython's article paid off. Ten million people playing *The Rescue Game*—that's good," I say.

"And more keep joining. The Army of Light is strong," Darna says.

"How did you find this solution out of ten million submissions?" Rafael and Darna hold their hands up. "We plead the fifth."

Glenn coughs and shifts in his chair. "We're using some of the NSA computers at the Utah Data Center. We have friends there who play *Nightstream* with us. They helped us data crunch the submissions. *Too Cool for School* seems to be our man."

"Or woman," Darna adds.

"Later in the episode, he tells us he hears gulls. They're close to saltwater, too."

"How much do Bushnell and Swig know?" I ask.

"We don't publish results. They have no idea how much we know," Darna says.

Glenn nods. "And now our players are flooding their game with requests to give Steven and Julia a fighting chance."

"—To get them out of that green room. So they can be outside," I interrupt.

"Yes. And they're making a lot of money from our submissions. If they want to please their audience, they'll pick a storyline that the players are demanding."

"Or he could just kill them," Trishelle says. "That's what I'm afraid of."

"That won't happen, Ms. Trishelle. Bushnell will keep playing. It's in his nature to want to win. He wants to beat us, both at his game and ours."

"Has he figured out Steven's code within a code?"

"Not yet. But people are forming subgroups on Reddit and different gaming sites and posting about both games. With this many people playing, it's only a matter of time before everything comes out."

"Especially if *Too Cool for School* goes online and brags," Rafael asks.

"Can we find *Too Cool for School* ourselves?" I ask. "Maybe we can keep him quiet. Even hire him to be part of our team."

Glenn tilts his head. "Or he could turn around and go to *The Danger Game* and offer to sell them everything he knows."

Darna raises her fist again. "We still need to find him. If he brags, it could be a death sentence for him and Steven and Julia."

Rafael chimes in. "We'll scour social media. If he makes noises, we'll find him."

"I use a special ops force from Brazil when I do rescue work in Mexico. I'll call them in and get them prepped. If Steven gives us enough details, I can swoop in."

"Can you just do that? Invade Mexico?" Trishelle asks.

"Hopefully, we'll have time to go through the proper channels. But if they're someplace remote, the rule of law may not apply, or can be purchased."

"Can't we get U.S. law enforcement to help now? These clues he's sending up are solid," Darna says.

On cue, my phone buzzes with a text from the office: *Found a motel on the Pine River with a female guest who doesn't want to be disturbed until Sunday. Manager hasn't seen her come out of her room.*

I haven't spoken to Mendoza in five and a half days. I can fly to Milwaukee and drive through the snow to the Pine River and be banging on that motel door before dawn, but I'm afraid of what I'll find.

I show Trishelle the text. "Looks like I'm going to Wisconsin."

CHAPTER 33

JULIA TRAVERS

Kidnapped 88 hours ago

The day happened. I felt apart from it, and stayed floating deep inside my brain, watching myself and Steven perform our lines. The work must have been adequate since we weren't punished. Steven didn't change any words. Nothing kicked me out of the zone. Heyman's offer that I betray Steven doesn't earn a second thought.

We survive. Then, we are done.

Metal falls from the ceiling and hits the cement floor, taking out a green chip as it bounces. It's a pair of black garden shears for pruning roses. A bucket descends next.

Steven moves fast. He pulls out towels, medical tape, an elastic bandage, alcohol, and long strips of gauze. Once empty, it rises fast back up into the rafters.

Steven lays out a towel on the floor and arranges the bandages and the alcohol and gauze on the terrycloth like he's prepping for surgery. I remember that he's a trained Ranger medic, and flash back to Elysian Cay when we removed a bullet from Carl's thigh and saved his life.

Steven pours alcohol on his hands and on the garden shears, and then rubs them clean with another towel. He nods at me, but my body stays frozen in place.

"Remember my offer, Julia."

"Screw him," Steven whispers. "Do it."

I fall to my knees on the other side of the towel. He grabs my hand and forces it onto the garden shears, and then pushes his pinkie fingers in between the blades.

"From this moment, only one of you will survive. You choose."

"He wants me to betray you."

"He made me the same offer. Snip fast, then hand me a towel."

"I love you." I press hard and feel it crunch through.

He screams.

CHAPTER 34

STEVEN QUINTANA

Kidnapped 112 hours ago

My finger flips in the air and lands on the towel, like a twig snipped from a tree. Nausea hits me as electric pain rushes up my arm. My mouth screams, but it's like my mind is viewing the moment through a long, cardboard tube.

My finger lies there on the white towel like a piece of raw turkey with the bone still in it. My left hand has three fingers and a thumb, not four. I stare; it's weird that my hands are no longer symmetrical. Then, a stream of blood squirts out of the hole and shoots four feet across the green floor. It squirts again and again in time with my pulse.

Julia tosses the garden shears, sending them skittering. She clamps a towel over my wounded hand, rubbing exposed nerves, giving me yet another pain I've never experienced before.

I grab the towel from her and wrap it tight around my left hand. All my previous injuries flash through my brain. I've been shot, punched, kicked, stabbed, had my teeth knocked in, been burned…none come close to the pain I feel right now.

"Pour on the alcohol."

She pours half the bottle over the towel, soaking it. The alcohol reaches my wound with a searing sting.

The pulsing is still happening. I don't want to bleed to death. "Send down one of your men!"

"*Why?*"

"I need the cattle prod on my hand to cauterize the wound."

"*I like you bleeding.*"

"The cauterizing will burn me. You can torture me even more."

"*Drop five. Four to hold him, one to burn him.*"

Julia backs away as five pajama boys in black drop from the rafters, one with a cattle prod. Four of them slam me against the green wall. The fifth one rips off the towel, exposing my bloody left hand. He pushes my wrist against the cement. The wound spurts again, in time with my heartbeat. He jams his electric cattle prod against the raw stump where my finger used to be. A blue, electric spark jumps from the tip. The pain moves through me like ocean waves now, rippling every muscle.

My mind separates from my body, floating above the scene, intrigued by how much pain my body can endure.

The smell of burning flesh brings me back.

Two of them snicker.

"¿Te gustan las perras gays follarte en tus pijamas? Te gusta meter esas cosas en el culo de cada uno, eh? Putas." *You guys like to fuck each other in your pajamas? You like to stick those things up each other's asses, eh? Whores.*"

One slams my head against the cement while another knees me in the balls, giving me two new waves of pain, which I welcome. The new pain helps override the first.

The fifth one drops his cattle prod and falls to his knees, twisting and screaming. Julia has plunged the garden shears into his back. She puts her foot on his shoulder and yanks hard on the shears, prying them out. Blood squirts out of him in a fountain bigger than the one from my finger, and she plunges it back down again. He howls and falls on his face, clawing at his back, trying to reach it. The other four release me and rush her.

"Julia!"

She sweeps up the loose cattle prod and does a round-house kick that catches the first guy right in the mouth. Some of his teeth go flying.

Julia kicked me in the teeth once, and my mouth remembers the power that her long, muscular legs can generate. He drops, unconscious. She jams the prod into the next guy's crotch, and his eyes jiggle as she delivers 20,000 volts. The last two guys corner her. Two more cattle prods fall from the rafters. They grab them and poke at her, shocking her.

The electric winch whines so much it hurts my ears, and Kidney Boy, the Toothless Wonder, and Jiggly Eyes fly back up into the rafters, their blood raining down on us and staining the floor. More will come, once they re-harness, so I have just seconds.

My left hand is cauterized and no longer spurting blood. I scoop up the elastic bandage waiting on the white towel. I shake out the roll, grab an end with each hand, and run across the room. I flip it around the neck of one of the last two Pajama Boys from behind. I yank it tight and roll him back onto the floor, turning him into a choking, flailing crab. My wound opens up again, and blood gushes all over his face.

"¿Dónde estamos?" I whisper in his ear. *Where are we?*

He shakes his head, and I make sure my blood flows into his mouth. "¿Dónde en México?" *Where in Mexico?*

The whine of winches starts again, and three new Pajama Boys with cattle prods descend. They surround Julia first, poking her, but she fights back. I tighten my grip on the elastic bandage. "Dilo, y te dejo respirar." *Say it and I'll let you breathe.*

Julia goes down. They poke her again and again, sending up little sparks until she convulses on the ground. They'll turn to me next. I tighten the bandage, then let it loose just enough for him to breathe. "Dilo." *Say it.*

He gasps, and then exhales a word that is almost all air. "Baja…"

I let him go as the Pajama Boys surround me. One pokes me in the kidney, and I contract so hard my knees hit my forehead.

He jams one in my crotch next.

But I know where we are—Baja.

CHAPTER 35

TINA SWIG

Friday, March 15, 7:00 a.m. (CET)

Min, Elliot, and Ismael work their monitors while Douglas paces behind them. We've been up all night. The boys are in their nerd zone, living on Red Bull and getting up only to pee. I'm bored, but Douglas is energized like he's playing online poker or running a drone assault in Pakistan.

His smartphone vibrates, and he holds it up. "Peter Heyman is texting that episode four is ready for download. Min, please check your inbox and upload it to *The Danger Game* site. We can all watch together at the same time as our fans."

Min taps on his keyboard, and the monitor, recessed into the mahogany cabinet above their monitors, emerges and turns on.

Episode four is decent, but not great. The mixture of new material and scenes from the classics feels fake. Julia and Steven do a decent job with *Taming of the Shrew*, but I wouldn't pay for it. They've rendered them into a Renaissance garden, and Steven Quintana in Shakespearean costume looks stupid. Julia Travers, as usual, pulls it all off. Heyman stopped Quintana's blinking, thank God, and Travers is behaving.

The computer animation drops away, and Julia and Steven are in the green room, pacing the floor between scenes. Julia Travers yells up at the cameras in the rafters.

Heyman yells down. *"People like your mouth."*

"Maybe people want to watch me fight more than watch me suffer," she responds.

"I don't."

"That's because I beat you once before. And I will again."

"No, you won't."

"You shoot everything we do. I dare you to put what I just said in the next episode. If you don't, it will be proof that I do scare you."

"I'm already scared."

My gut drops. When this footage came in, I reminded Douglas of his promise not to use any ad-libbing in the episode. He not only used it, he's making it a centerpiece, with rapid cutting and camera moves. But, I don't dare complain. He already has suspicions about me, both from *The Rescue Game*, and from my using Walter as a resource.

The rest of the episode is good. Then the finale comes. It's color-corrected with a fantastic soundtrack. Julia snips off Steven's left pinky finger with garden shears, which is horrible but oh, so watchable, like watching a car crash happen next to you on the freeway. With drums pounding, five of Heyman's tribe members descend to cauterize Quintana's blood-spurting hand with an electric cattle prod. Julia somehow stabs one with the garden shears, then both Steven and Julia kick and punch their attackers until five more tribe members descend and shock them into submission.

The music crescendos over the scene fading to black, and we hear Steven's voice: *"The Danger Game. You write the script."*

Then Julia's voice comes next: *"We perform...or we die."*

Everyone stares at the black screen, frozen, as the music fades away.

Douglas turns the monitor off and the boys come back to life.

"That was crazier than a snuff film on the Dark Web," Min says.

"It was sick. And I mean sick-sick, not good-sick," Elliot says. His face is white.

"The close-up of the garden shears going in. That was so real," Ismael says.

"That's because it was," Douglas says. "But only we know that."

The boys laugh with high-pitched nervousness. At this point, they'd probably rather play *The Rescue Game*, but they're stuck with us until it's *game over*.

"Talk to me, Min," Douglas says. "Tell me we're making money."

"Episode four dropped thirty minutes ago and we're now making fifty thousand dollars every ten minutes. Best numbers yet!"

Ismael looks at his screen. "Same with submissions. They're way up too. A few are pro-torture and death, but most are pro-survival."

Elliot holds up his hand. "People on social media are saying that the last five minutes, when they fight back, is the best part. That may be driving the downloads."

Douglas peers over Min's shoulder and sees the downloads increasing. He nods, rubbing his hands together. "Perfect. We'll listen to our fans. We'll give Steven and Julia a fighting chance for the final episodes, stretch out their struggle, and then end it. We'll win at our game while beating them at theirs."

The boys fake more awkward laughter. Douglas shoots me his smug, closed-mouthed smile. I fake a smile back at him. He's making a mistake. We should do just the episodes like I planned, kill them, and disappear. But he can't resist a challenge.

"Is everything all right, my love?" Douglas asks.

"I do like making money, but I want them dead more."

Douglas pretends he didn't hear me. "We need to talk to Peter Heyman in the warehouse. See how we can make these survival requests compelling."

"*Short* and compelling."

Douglas closes his eyes and exhales his frustration. "I have been in these situations more than you have, my love."

He may know gambling, but I know how to tell a story. And the more we show them fighting for survival, the more people will like them, which can't be tolerated. We want people to hate them, so it will be a pleasure to watch them die.

"My love. One suggestion," I whisper.

"What?"

"They are at the breaking point. When we talk to Heyman, let's push harder on getting them to betray each other. That way, we both get what we want. One survives, one dies, and our numbers go up."

"You're so good." He kisses my hand, which is the first display of affection he's ever given me in front of staff. But he's changing my game, and I hate that.

CHAPTER 36

CARL WEBB

Friday, March 15, Midnight (CST)
Wisconsin

The gray-haired woman in the pink robe behind the counter shakes her head. "She doesn't want to be disturbed until she checks out on Saturday, and I never bother my guests. It's the key to our success."

I glance around the "successful" motel office lobby. It's got fake veneer walls and shag carpet throw rugs, glass and brass lamps, a rocking chair, and a hundred small ceramic cows crowded onto every flat surface. There are also four mounted photographs of different fly-fishermen holding up massive trout in mid-stream. "A lot of cows and fish around here?"

"We're in Wisconsin." She crosses her arms. Jimmy Kimmel is on the TV in her apartment, which is just beyond the office door behind her. She's missing her show and she's pissed—that must be it.

I push my LA sheriff's deputy badge across the Formica top. "I flew from Los Angeles and drove from Milwaukee. Two men who work for me are missing."

"I know. Major Glenn told me you were coming. But, unless you've got a warrant, I can't open the door." She's got that unassailable Midwestern integrity that's baked into the people around here. She follows the rules just like her parents and grandparents did. She's also patient with me, not slamming doors and throwing me out, which is what would happen in California or New York or Florida. "I knocked for you, and there was no answer, Deputy Webb. That's the best I can do."

My phone dings with a text from Glenn: *Try this*. There's a photo attached. I touch it and bring it full screen. It's Tina Swig's ID card from when she worked at Velodrome International producing TV. How did Glenn dig that up? He's the best.

I set my phone in front of her. "This is her, right? See, Tina Swig."

She sees the name and the face. Her nostrils flare and she exhales like an angry Wisconsin bull. "She said her name was Frida Kahlo. That's what she wrote on the register." She flops open her book. "I remember because she's our only guest."

"Frida Kahlo is a famous Mexican painter and artist. Also, a dead one." I enter *Kahlo* into the search engine on my phone and show her Frida's photo.

"So, she's a liar."

"And worse, she may be a criminal. May I ask your name, ma'am?"

"Vanessa Hughes. I'm the owner and manager."

"Ms. Hughes, will you help me out and open the door to the room?"

She tugs on snow boots and pulls a parka over her pink, terrycloth robe and bangs out the front door. I follow, and almost slip on the icy walk in my Italian loafers.

She bangs hard on Room Number Three. "I'm coming in!" She jams her pass key into the lock, swings open the door and clicks on the light.

"Sinners!" Vanessa runs out of the room.

I step through the door into the weak light. The room is freezing. One bloated body lies on the bed, with his pants down. Another lies on the floor surrounded by a hardened pool of blood. My heart pounds. My mind flashes back to the ten times I had to look at my dead brothers: Colombia. Afghanistan. Iraq. Mexico. Bosnia. All images remain vivid, and now I must add two more.

Taylor is on the bed. He looks surprised. Mendoza is on the floor. He looks asleep. Taylor has a service weapon in hand. Mendoza's shirt front is brown with dried blood. I remember Taylor's parents and Mendoza's wife and young daughter.

My phone buzzes with a text from Trishelle: *Episode 4 just dropped. Julia cut off Steven's finger. We need you.*

Taylor and Mendoza. How can I leave them?

I walk gingerly on the ice back to the motel lobby and try the doorknob, but Vanessa has locked the door. "Mrs. Hughes? Can you open the door, please?"

She wails an answer that's impossible to understand.

"Please, we have to call the police."

"Go away!" She goes back to sobbing.

There's no time for this. I can't stay to answer questions and explain this double homicide to the Wisconsin sheriff. I must get back to Los Angeles where I can make a difference; otherwise, Mendoza and Taylor died for nothing.

I go back to the motel room and say a prayer for my men. I find McCusker's and Gum's cards in my wallet and set them on the desk. They'll find me soon enough.

I skate across the icy parking lot in my loafers, pop into the rental car, and out onto the road, passing the sheriff's car with lights flashing coming the other way. No sirens are wailing, though, so they have no sense of urgency.

I'll be back in Milwaukee in two hours. I'll catch a 6:00 a.m. flight back to Los Angeles. A curtain has been lifted in my brain and my thoughts turn from red to cool blue. My breathing slows. I will command my body to sleep on the plane. My dead comrades again flash through my brain. There are now two more, frozen back in that room. I am in warrior mode now, and I'm fucking pissed. I will find Bushnell and Swig on my own, without the law, and kill them both. I hit the gas.

CHAPTER 37

TINA SWIG

Friday, March 15, 1:00 p.m. (CET)

Devon spins, tilts, and pogoes in his red chair, timing his movements to the beat of electronic music blasting from the speakers. He programmed his computer screens to pulse with colored lights, which makes his suite feel like an Ibiza disco.

"Are you celebrating?"

He stops, stares at me, then slowly puts his mouthpiece in. "I'm dancing, Mom," he says in his evil alien voice as the music drops in volume. He really can do a lot with that mouthpiece, which makes me grateful again for Douglas, even though he is frustrating me right now.

"I know, I heard the music. We used to dance together all the time, remember? You would choreograph dances for us to perform together."

"I was five."

"You're never too old to dance with your mother. Come on."

I take his left hand in my right, which is how we always did it, so he can use his right hand on the toggle and lead us. He puts his mouth over his mouth piece and stares at his computer screen, which fills and magically scrolls with a music list. He picks a soft Austrian waltz, then rises up in his chair so we are face to face.

I hold up his hand and curtsy. "Lovely choice, my Lord."

He leads, moving his chair is a perfect three-four time, adding just the right amount of sway. I whisper. "You really are good, you know."

"Stop."

We rotate as we dance, and he leads us past his bed and sofa without brushing either. "I mean it. You could choreograph for a company that features dancers with disabilities. Music is math, and dance is geometry."

He stops. His eyes get big. "Nice, Mom. I like that idea."

I kiss him on the cheek. Rebecca's scent is barely there. We lock eyes. "I'm glad you're growing up. But don't grow up too fast."

"I won't." He raises the volume and we dance again.

"But you are celebrating something."

He smiles and spins me faster. "Yes. It's almost done."

I squeeze his hand. "The Hodge conjecture? Show me."

"When we get off this boat. That could be tonight if you want."

"One more day. I promise. We're almost done."

"And then you can explain the secret project you two have been working on?"

"Maybe someday. But, for now, just know we're making enough money that we can live on a yacht, on a mountain, in a skyscraper, or floating in space if you want."

"I like that idea."

The intercom crackles. "And so do I," Douglas says. Our heads turn to the speaker/intercom mounted over the suite door. Each suite has one. It's for safety in an emergency and we never use it, so we forget that it's there, which means that we also forget that he can listen in on us at any moment. He probably sees us, too.

"Do you need me, my love?" I ask the air. I feel like I'm beholden to a capricious god.

"Can you come to the master suite? I have Peter Heyman on screen."

"Coming, my love."

Devon's eyes are wide with fear. Smart as he is, he does not understand power yet, but he will learn it all from me. "Us against the world," I whisper, and his face relaxes. He still trusts me. Needs me.

Peter Heyman's shiny bullet head fills the huge screen on the wall of the master suite. "Hello, Peter. How are things on your end? You're our boots on the ground."

Peter grins, and the skin on his face widens, revealing even more of the surgical steel he inserted under his cheek. It glints, making him look like a wounded robot. "I'm grateful that you and Snow found me and the tribe. I'm even more grateful that you couldn't sell a TV show about us. This job suits us much better."

"You have three injured men," Douglas says. "How are they?"

"They are getting medical treatment. No one will die. They all receive hazard pay, and your bonuses for their injuries are appreciated."

"How many are your tribe members, and how many are locals?" I ask.

"Two are locals. Julia stabbed Panther, a tribe member, so he's actually proud of his battle injuries. The tribe will sing songs about him."

Douglas sits on the edge of the bed. I stand next to his right shoulder. "We are almost done. Your tribe will receive all the pay you deserve, and you can start fresh."

"Thank you, Boss Man." Peter closes his eyes and bows his head. Douglas raises an eyebrow at me, gesturing to proceed. He wants me

189

to run this meeting? That's bold but I get it. By making me tell Peter what Douglas wants, it becomes my idea as well.

"Peter, our audience is demanding that Steven and Julia get a fighting chance."

"I've heard."

"Do you think you could find a creative way to do that? While also guaranteeing that you remain in complete control?"

"Yes, ma'am. Like a cat playing with two captured mice."

"If they were allowed outside, you'd be going live. Can you handle that? You'd need a lot of cameras."

"I have drones, helmet cams, and mounted cams ready to go."

I remember the elaborate car crash videos that his tribe created, which is what first drew Robert Snow to his underground video work years ago. "What about switching?"

Peter smiles and moves the camera, so we can see the room he's in instead of his face. It looks like a cross between a TV control room and an air traffic control tower. "You let me build what I wanted, so I did. I can switch between thirty cameras. We can broadcast a moon landing from here."

"If this happens, you may incur more injuries. Quintana fights."

"Honu, the turtle, is a worthy adversary. I expect nothing less from him." I remember that Heyman tattooed Quintana to look like a turtle during our last adventure together.

Douglas gets off the bed. "How long will you need to kill them—if we let them out?"

"On demand. In three minutes, three hours, or a day. Your choice."

"It will be more than three hours but less than a day. But only when I say."

"Yes, Boss Man."

"Proceed."

CHAPTER 38

JULIA TRAVERS

Kidnapped 131 hours ago

S teven and I will die today.

That's my only thought, over and over, as we lie on this cement floor in the pitch black, waiting for them to blind us with the bright lights again. My mind goes to a dark place. Could Steven have planted those bombs? Did they trick him?

It's my fault. I forced my wolf into a cage, trying to make our lives perfect instead of admitting that we were broken. I refused to listen to him, and now we're going to die.

My spleen is bleeding, or my intestines, or even my uterus. The bruise on my belly spread down my hips, past where Steven punched me. My skin is tender and swollen everywhere. I need a doctor. I need rest. I need more water. I need to eat.

Steven lies next to me. We're both on our right sides, lying under the one thin, wool blanket they threw down from the metal rafters. He balances his wounded bandaged hand on my hip. He hasn't budged in hours, which makes me afraid to move. I think he's in a coma until he exhales on my back. His warm breath gives me a glint of hope.

Steven shifts. His fingers touch my neck. We roll onto our backs and hold hands.

A weak, yellow light ekes through the dirty skylights high above. It's past dawn. Metal creaks. Someone is on the catwalk above us. We're being watched. Let them. I tell myself to fall asleep, and I almost do, until Steven squeezes my hand. *I love you.*

That's the message I needed. I pray it's true. *I love you.*

We're in Baja. Close to water.

How do we get out?

Working.

How is hand?

Pain. Must change bandage. Infection.

After they shocked Steven unconscious, I used the rest of the alcohol to clean the wound, then wrapped it with gauze and an elastic bandage. He woke up for part of it, then passed out again. Maybe the bandage is too tight and cutting off his blood supply.

Sure about Baja?

Yes. Others will learn. Find us.

"*Wakey-wakey eggs and bakey,*" Heyman says through his loudspeaker.

Lights snap on. Steven and I roll onto our knees and look up. The silhouettes of four men move on the catwalk above us like dark ghosts.

Two buckets descend from the ceiling on ropes. One is full of food: warm chicken sandwiches, oranges, apples, cheese, and cooked vegetables. I unwrap the sandwiches and peel the fruit, so Steven doesn't have to use his left hand. We devour it all. The other bucket has bottles of water, chocolate protein drinks, and ibuprofen tablets, which we wolf down. Why so much food? Maybe they want us to heal. Or, maybe they want to build us up, so they can just torture us and break us down again.

"Quintana, stay put. Travers, go to the small door and wait. When it opens, follow the maze to your bathroom and shower."

I look at Steven. "Go," he says. "I'll be fine."

I kiss his lips then his wounded hand and go to the racquetball door. It opens, and I follow a new path through the wooden maze. The black shadows still hover on the metal catwalk above me. The bathroom is new and warm with white tile everywhere.

There's a real toilet instead of a bucket, which I use right away. I don't care who's watching. The shower is the best part. I strip down and step in and let the hot water pound onto my neck and shoulders. It hurts when it hits my belly. The black bruise has spread down my thighs and up to my breasts. Maybe a hot shower makes it worse.

A huge warm terrycloth towel waits for me on the wooden bench along with new clothes: running shoes, tiny socks, new underwear, new bra, green track pants, a long-sleeved T-shirt, and green track jacket. It feels good to put them all on. Combine that with the warm feeling in my belly from the food, and it's a like a rush.

"Feel good?"

"Only because you've taken so much away."

"You look happy in your close-ups. We got plenty of angles of you in the shower and getting dressed."

"I'm not going to thank you for it."

"You earned it. My employers are pleased with your performance. You still have fight. That makes them money."

"I'll fight you all, until you kill me."

"There may be a way out for you."

"Don't say it."

"Betray Quintana. The offer still stands."

"Never."

"Then back to your cell. But the opportunity is coming."

The bathroom door unlocks. The maze leads me back to the tiny racquetball door, which opens on its own. I crawl through on my hands and knees. Steven sits on the floor on the opposite side of the room next to a new bucket.

I rush to him. The bucket has a first aid kit inside. Scissors. More gauze. Neosporin. Surgical tape. Another elastic bandage. Steven's bandages are damp. His hair is wet, too, and he's wearing new track clothes like me, except his are blue.

"They let you shower and clean up too."

"Yes. But I need help changing the bandage."

I grit my teeth and help unwind the elastic around his hand. It falls away, revealing a thick layer of burgundy-colored gauze stuck to the gash where his pinky finger used to be. It's dried and crusted over and his whole hand is black and blue. He moves his fingers and winces. The color leaves his face.

"I have to move them or I'll lose mobility." A fresh splash of red appears on the dried gauze stuck to the scab.

"You're bleeding again. Don't overdo it." I open a packet and add another piece of sterile gauze to the hardened tower that's already there.

He laughs a bit. "Don't overdo it. That's funny."

He holds the gauze in place while I attach surgical tape. My hands shake. Not too tight and not too loose. None of it matters, though, if they're just going to make me cut off his next finger. "How's that?"

He hands me the new elastic bandage. "Good. Wrap it so I can still use my thumb and first two fingers." I wrap it around his hand, while looking at his eyes. He nods that it's good. I lock it into place. He smiles. I hold his right hand and squeeze.

Love.

Same.

They say betray you.

Fuck them.

This will only get worse.

Steven smiles and kisses me on the cheek, which is amazing. He's been shot, beaten, stabbed, burned, drugged, and tattooed because of me. I even cut off his finger. He props up his aching left hand like he's holding an invisible ice cream cone.

"How can you smile right now?"

"It's amazing what a hot shower and a meal can do."

We look up at the rafters. Is there a new script coming? This feeling of calm only exists because the punishment has stopped. They let us sleep, bathe, drink, eat, they gave us new clothes, medicine, and first aid kits for a reason. But, why?

"This is like combat. Waiting for the inevitable. At a certain point I just want their shit to start so I can deal with it."

"The next choice is here."

An explosion shakes the building. The green cement wall to our left collapses, sending cinderblocks tumbling around us like fifty-pound Lego bricks. Steven throws himself on top of me. Green dust gets into my ears and eyes.

There's a breeze. Steven feels it, too; he rolls off me and jumps to his feet. There's a gap in the cement green wall, like a huge rat hole with twisting rebar metal coming out of it. Blue skies, clouds, and trees are just outside. I breathe in the clean air, which smells like freshly cut grass.

"People want us to give you a chance."

Steven stares at the hole, then looks up at the black silhouettes in the rafters. "How do I know you won't just shoot us?"

"We will. Viewers estimate that we will kill you in three hours."

"Why not kill us now? Isn't that what people want to see?"

"Yes, but the longer you live, the more money we make."

195

"And you'll broadcast all of it, you metal-face scum!"

"If you both run, you both die. Julia, if you stay, you must act, but you will live. No one cares about you, Quintana, so go. Julia, your fans want you alive."

An air horn blares.

"Your hour head start begins now. Decide."

Steven runs to the opening. I can't get off my knees. Steven looks back at me. His brow furrows, confused. Then he walks back to me and offers me his hand.

"He's injured. He will fail you."

Our eyes meet. He blinks three times. I take his hand and he squeezes—*Trust.*

I sob but can't move. Steven grabs me by the wrist and flings me toward the hole.

I run to the opening and climb through the twisted metal into bright sunshine, with Steven right behind me. We are on a packed dirt road that circles a massive warehouse in a sunken canyon. The hills are dotted with cactus, big green thorny trees, and brush.

Machine noise hits my ears—above us are four hovering drones. Steven grabs my left hand with his right and whispers. "Now we run."

And he takes off. I'm only four steps behind him.

CHAPTER 39

STEVEN QUINTANA

Friday, March 15, Noon (PST)
Baja California

I run down the dirt road alongside the warehouse. Julia falls into place behind me. We're too exposed. My eyes search for a trail in the thick brush and rock. There's a narrow path that goes up between white rocks and I follow it, pulling myself up between granite boulders. Pain from my left hand shoots up my arm and into my brain.

Julia was right; they fed and clothed us for a reason…so that we'd be strong enough to hunt. We reach flat ground and find an animal trail. Our legs run faster now. The thick brush, cacti, and palo verde branches whip my arms. Julia's breathing and her footfalls are right behind me. The sound is steady. She is keeping pace. I remember how tough she is. We did this four years ago on Elysian Cay, through trees, grass, and brush in the middle of the night. She'll keep up. Hell, she'll do better than me.

We're in Baja, California for sure. Those are big cardøn cacti all around us. What do I know about Baja? It's dry. Blazing hot in the daytime. Freezing cold at night. It has mountains. Desert. It's a whole goddamn state in Mexico. No, *two* states. Hundreds of miles long, almost the length of California in the United States. How wide? Twenty-five miles in some places? A hundred? And we could be anywhere in it.

We need water. We need to get out of the sun. We need shelter. We need better clothes. We need hats. We need to hide. I need to get a message to Carl. We need to be rescued. I need a strategy.

A noise from above spooks me. A drone camera hovers fifteen yards above our heads, floating in front of us as we run toward it. Someone controls it remotely, like an Air Force drone pilot that bombs targets from a flight center in Arizona.

We're on a narrow trail of crushed white rock. We run through a forest of giant cardón, darting between sharp ocotillo bushes and spiny acacia. It's decent cover for hiding on the ground, but the drones can see us easily from above. Plus, we're wearing brightly colored track suits. Shit, that's why they gave us new clothes.

The hill slopes up. A cool breeze comes down. It's a strong enough wind that those hills may lead up to mountains on our right. We're too close to know how high they go.

"Water," Julia says. "Look left."

Past the trees and rocks and across a long, flat, empty plain is a sliver of blue. It could be five miles away or fifteen. I can't tell. Is it the ocean to the west? Or, is it the Sea of Cortez to the east? Are we closer to Tijuana or Cabo?

It's late winter, almost spring. It feels like it's noon. The sun can help me figure out where we are. A damn drone whirs ten feet above. I can't sit and watch the sun move for fifteen minutes and get my bearings. We run.

"There's a ship. We have to get there," Julia says.

There's a break in the trail with a fork heading down toward a dry plain and a thin line of water in the distance. There are no roads in sight just this trail. Should we take it?

I stop under a huge cardøn that's over two stories tall, surrounded by bushes. We hide under the thick, twiggy branches. Our feet slip on the crumbly hillside.

How do I remember the names of these plants? Photos flash in my brain. My parents took my brother Anthony and me on a camping trip to Baja when we were kids, and we had a guide book. We swam with turtles in the ocean.

The drone hovers outside the branches. Then two more. I look between the branches and see water in the distance again.

She's right, there's a ship down there. It's just a dark shape. It could be a small cruise ship or a fishing boat or the Mexican coast guard or Bushnell's yacht.

Julia tugs me toward the new trail. "Come on. It's this way."

My gut won't let me move.

Look. Analyze. Strategize.

A black raven flies overhead and, higher up, a seagull flies the other way. Down at my feet, I see a scorpion, a hole for an animal that won't come out until tonight, and dried, white scat marks, where some coyote shit weeks ago. If they can live out here, so can we. I grab her hand and squeeze. *Too open. They want us to choose that.*

You don't know.

My training says we stay high. Get above them.

But drones.

We can make it.

I tug her arm. She resists, pulling back. I come close and whisper. "You did your job, let me do mine." She blinks, scared. She has no reason to believe; she hasn't had the same training. She finally nods.

We head off the trail and up the hillside. I want to get inside the big rocks above us, where they can't see us. We crawl on our hands and knees through spiny chuparosa bushes with bright red flowers like hummingbirds. The sand and rock hillside crumbles under us as we move, and we slide back three feet for every six we climb.

Can you get water out of these cacti? Some don't have a lot of spines. The glass shards are still in my socks. I can cut one open....

My left hand brushes a small cactus, and the spines go right through my bandage. I grit my teeth to keep from screaming.

The steepness increases, which leaves us more exposed, but the climbing is easier. My hand is on fire. My pulse pounds inside the tight bandage as my hand swells to grapefruit size. Blood comes through the dirty bandage. Will I lose my hand?

Julia passes me, taking the lead up the rock. She should. She has better balance. Lower center of gravity. Women are better climbers. She'll pick the route.

A buzzing sends a shiver up my neck. The drone is less than a yard away, over my left shoulder. I swing at it with my stumpy hand, but it rises out of range.

"There's a break in the rock. Up and to the right," she whispers.

The hillside tilts. My throat tightens. Asthma. Those cactus spines are doing a number on me. They must have toxins. My hand is in a dark tunnel like I'm looking at it on an old TV. It's missing a finger. How did that happen?

Julia tugs on my shoulder. She's saying something because her lips are moving. I smile. I love her. She pinches me hard, pulling my skin off my forearm.

"Focus!" she yells, from some faraway place.

She points at a break in the rock. Can we fit in there? It's higher up.

Remember the drill. Get your toe on the rock. Twist in. Push up. If it's a big as a quarter, you can climb. Right hand grabs hold. Forefingers dig in. Skin tears away. Left toe next. Jam it in, twist, and push. My left hand is worthless; I use it like a climbing stick, jamming it against the rock, and forcing myself up.

Julia is up ahead. She looks down at me, panting. Her eyes say it all: *Come on.*

Move right hand. Move right foot. Climb. Move left foot. Jam in left hand. Climb. A bird with a red-crested head flies by my nose. I'm by her nest and she's dive-bombing me. That wakes me up. Julia is only ten yards ahead of me now. She gets to the ledge where there is a split in the rock. A drone hovers right above her head. She squeezes between the rock and disappears.

My feet slip. My fingers bleed. I make it the ledge. Two drones hover just above me. The other two ascend and disappear over the top of the hill. Are they following Julia? I can't fit inside the slot where she disappeared. She's tall and skinny, and I'm thicker.

Julia's voice comes from behind the rocks. "Get low. Come through this way."

Down on my hands and knees, the slot widens. I reach out with my hands and shimmy through the dusty hole like a rat crawling into a sewer.

"You're halfway through. Come on."

My right foot gets stuck in the slot in the rock behind me. How did Julia get her whole body through? My shoe comes off. Shit. My shoulders and hips force their way into the dark hole. I need my shoe, but the cave is too narrow to turn around.

I'm failing her.

Julia's butt is in front of me. She inches forward deeper into the cave. "Come on. There's light above us and ahead of us."

A jagged line of light is far above us. We're not in a cave. We're in a narrow slot, about as wide as our shoulders, with air above us and steep walls on either side. Either these rocks fell on each other or water carved it. Machines whine as shadows pass over. The drones are up there.

The slot between the rocks widens. We pick up speed. Soft cool sand is under my hands. Is there moisture? Keep moving. The light gets brighter. Julia reaches the opening on the other side. She crawled right through the hill.

"Shit. We're fucked."

I reach her and stand up. We're three hundred feet above the trail we left on an exposed ledge. We haven't come very far, but we did get high. A half-mile away is the trench dug into the hills where the warehouse sits, our prison for the last four days. It's long, tin roof is painted in desert camouflage to blend into the hillside. There are no power lines, just dozens of solar panels. Four all-terrain Humvees and a row of off-road motorcycles are parked on the dirt road encircling the warehouse.

There is no road. No fresh water. No way out. The high-pitched whine returns. Three of the four drones descend from above and stop, floating ten yards in front of us.

"I'm sure one's getting the wide shot and the other two are getting our close-ups. You fuckers!" Julia says, and flips them the double bird.

Another whine starts. I look down. Motorcycles. Four of them. They're on the trail below, the one that we were on. That means we've been outside exactly one hour, and the hunt has begun.

A thought screams in my cloudy brain: *this was a stupid choice.*

CHAPTER 40

TINA SWIG

Friday, March 15, 10:00 p.m. (CET)
Sicily

I like a glass of wine on the aft deck in the late evening. A warm, light breeze blows, sending ripples through the water. The moon is waxing full, and Mars is a tiny, red, solid spot close by. I like that about the planets. Their light is unwavering. No twinkling light emanates from the ancient gods as they follow their own patterns across the sky. Venus is the brightest light in the night sky, but she will show up closer to dawn.

When Venus rises before dawn, her light will be brighter than the mighty Mars. What does that say about power? Douglas is making brazen choices just like Mars, but he's winging it now. Always have a plan, I say, and waiting to see what cards your opponent plays next is not a plan.

We made love right after dinner in the master suite. While we were both climaxing, I screamed that he was the best lover ever and I couldn't live without him. With the endorphins coursing through our veins, we stayed quiet, staring at the walnut ceiling with the gold inlay, listening to the slosh of water against the ship's hull.

Then it arrived—his long sigh of contentment. That was my opening. I asked for his advice and reassurance, which he gave me. My ideas became his ideas, and he then convinced me that he *does* want to end the game, sooner than later.

The rabbits were released from their cage an hour ago. I thought Julia would've stayed, so she's an idiot. The show is just a live sporting event now, and we're cutting between different remote cameras. We will hunt them down, lingering for drama just before the kill, and then we disappear with all the money.

Already we are erasing our tracks, eliminating all our digital fingerprints with computer animators and rendering experts around the globe. Then, we will live our amazing lives as we become global influencers and finders of hidden Einsteins.

While I showered and changed clothes, Douglas bounded out of bed like a teenager, hit the weight room, switched between his cold thermogenesis chamber and his infrared sauna, and ended his workout with a green smoothie laced with NAD+. Now, he's ready to play and win *The Danger Game*, like a card shark in the championship round.

He will win fast. We have enough drones and motorcycles chasing them that it may be over already. All the better. I'll enjoy their final demise in endless replay.

The lights of Agrigento are a thin, golden line. Even the street lights seem soothing here. In the United States, they're ugly, hot, white sodium lights.

I sip the last of my wine when a familiar whirring starts. I turn on my heel just as Devon zooms up. He pushes his toggle, raising his chair so we're eye level.

"You shouldn't sneak up on people."

"Is sneaking up on people bad?"

"Only when they catch you at it."

"Then I'll make sure I never get caught. I want you to take me to Agrigento tomorrow. You could show me the temples and lecture me on Greek and Roman history. I bet you'd love that."

"If you're trying to get on my good side, it's working. I'd love to go ashore with you. But I thought you were working on the Hodge conjecture."

"I need to take a break, then come back and review."

"Review? Does that mean you're done?"

He shrugs and smiles, afraid to say. Douglas leaves the lounge, steps through the glass, and joins us on the aft deck.

"My son isn't sharing, but I believe he's finished the Hodge conjecture."

Douglas touches Devon's shoulder. "I'm not surprised. We're all on the upswing, just like we planned. Remember the five Ps."

"Proper planning prevents piss-poor performance," Devon says, this time with the voice of Bugs Bunny.

"I'm taking him to see the ruins of Agrigento tomorrow morning. We'll ask for the blessing of the gods, so he can finish his work."

"Good. Then we'll pull anchor. We're almost done here."

"And I'll be off this boat!" Devon hits something on his keyboard and a Sousa victory march plays along with the sound of fireworks exploding. Devon motors backward through the open lounge door, music still playing, showing off. Rebecca appears behind him in the doorway and hits the button on the elevator, which will take him up one level to his teenage cave. Red-haired Rebecca, always perfect in her starched ship's uniform, holds the elevator door open as he spins in his wheelchair one more time before heading in. She gives me a tiny wave, and I wave back.

"I admit it, she's good for him." I could say more, but I let that say everything.

"I know."

When the elevator door completely closes, he turns to me, his face in shadow. The yellow lights from the shore give his smooth head a halo. "We have a problem."

My heart races. "Yes?"

"The local news in Milwaukee is reporting a murder-suicide of two men in a motel on the Pine River. Police discovered them twelve hours ago."

A breeze gives me goosebumps. "We knew they would. Have they identified them?"

"Not yet." Douglas steps an inch closer, and his eyes come into a shaft of light coming from the upper deck. "But in your production schedule—the media isn't supposed to know about the deaths until well into Sunday. The media may catch on to us while the game is still in play."

My heart races. I feel like I'm back in production at Velodrome, killing myself to make a billion dollars for the company while Gil Koresh complained I wasn't reaching his arbitrary quota of hit shows in the Monday meeting. I swallow to push my fear down. "How much money have we made, my love?"

"We just crossed a billion. And, it's *The Rescue Game* that did it." He says it with just enough of a demeaning tone to suggest that I should have known about it.

"It's still a billion. Let's pull the plug and disappear."

"Quintana and Travers can't be allowed to survive to argue anything different than our version of the truth. But they're running through the desert now because we let them out." Now he's rewriting history and blaming me? Because someone opened the motel room door two days early?

"Take the show offline at least. Send in a cartel to shoot it up. Hire the Mexican Air Force to bomb that rock pile they're hiding in.

Heyman can dump their bodies in the Sea of Cortez for the sharks and the squid, and we can be in Malta by morning."

Douglas shakes his head. "No. We finish *The Danger Game* as planned. They will die in the final episode, just like the app promises. Then, the story that Naythons published will become official truth."

"Once they identify the bodies, it may not matter. That could happen in four hours or twenty-four. I think we should be gone by then."

Douglas smiles. "We will keep monitoring the situation and play as long as we can."

"Why?"

"I never leave money on the table when I can turn my cards into a winning hand."

A passing yacht sends a bow wave that makes our ship rise and fall. The red buoys in the channel clang. I exhale and count to ten.

"It's your game, my love. Play it as you wish." I touch his arm. "Shall we play now?"

He shoots me his power glance. That was bad, like I was the granting him permission. He turns fast and goes into the main salon with me at his heels.

"Talk to me, boys!"

Elliot and Ismael stare at their computer monitors and at the broadcast on the big monitor above them. Min turns in his seat. "This is almost live. With 5,000 uploads, there's a delay, so this happened about thirty minutes ago."

Julia Travers is stuck in an A-shaped rock cave opening, thirty yards high. Steven Quintana limps up behind her, blinks in the sunlight, and holds up his bloody hand. It looks like a huge, swollen red grapefruit wrapped in bloody, brown, butcher paper. A microphone on a drone gets her voice: *I'm sure one's getting the wide shot and the other two are getting our close-ups. You fuckers!"* She shoots both middle fingers to the cameras.

All three boys laugh and cheer. "She's awesome," Min says.

"Not as awesome as watching her in the shower."

"TMI, dude," Ismael says.

I clap at them. "You're disgusting. Shut up and do your jobs."

The video cuts to a team of four motorcycles riding through the desert hills on a path right below the ledge where Quintana and Travers are standing. Thank God, they're trapped. It will be over soon.

"So, where are they? Arizona? New Mexico?" Min asks.

"And, who's doing the live switching?" Elliot asks. "We've got more cameras

than Monday Night Football."

They're in Baja, twenty miles from the ocean. Peter Heyman runs the broadcast through a fiber optic cable that one of Douglas's companies buried years ago, before our last production. But they will never know that.

"None of your business," Douglas says. "And asking proves that you have too much spare time. Min. What are the download numbers?"

Min looks at his screen. "Climbing way past a billion, Boss Man. Sales took off once they got outside."

Maybe people don't want to see them suffer. Or, maybe they prefer giving spoiled movie stars and their lazy boyfriends a fighting chance. Or, maybe *The Rescue Game* is more fun to play. It doesn't matter anymore. I just want it to be over.

"Law enforcement is coming. But we pull the plug only when I say. Understand?"

"Yes, Boss Man," they all chant.

"Elliot, monitor the app and make sure there's no way outsiders can get in."

"Yes, Boss Man."

"Ismael, story submissions are over. Dump everything. Erase any trace of any link or portal or even a hub or transfer point. Then, focus on *The Rescue Game*. Get inside. Find out who's playing. I want names before this is over."

Ismael twists in his red leather chair. "We've tried. They ping us around the globe."

"Search social media and the gaming sites. Whoever is playing *The Rescue Game* will brag. Engage them. Track them and see where it leads you. That means all of you."

I point at the big screen. Everyone looks. The motorcycles are closing in. Steven Quintana looks down, sees them coming, and pulls Julia Travers back inside the rocks. This is the first time that I can't see what they're doing, and I don't like it.

"This game is getting exciting," Douglas says. "But I have a few cards to play that they don't know about."

I have a card left, too. I still have Trishelle Hobbes's phone number.

CHAPTER 41

CARL WEBB

Friday, March 15, 1:00 p.m. (PST)
California

I spend an hour writing a detailed email about everything that happened in Wisconsin and send it to Detectives Gum and McCusker, and Tim Neavins, a field officer at the FBI with whom I've worked in the past. No response. The sheriff found Mendoza and Marsh over twelve hours ago. Why aren't they calling me?

"Any luck?" Trishelle asks as I walk back into the dining room.

"Nada. Either something big is happening or nothing at all is happening."

"So, we're still on our own. We have to find them ourselves."

"There it is. Let's proceed."

We print out documents and tape the pages to the white walls lining the hallway. We stare at the evidence, looking for patterns, and then write on the walls with Sharpies, linking one paragraph to another.

"That's quite an evidence board," Darna says, looking up from her computer.

"It hasn't helped much," I say.

We then watch the most recent episode of *The Danger Game* nine times in a row, pausing at every bush, tree, and cactus that Julia and Steven run past. A few minutes after they disappeared back into the slot in the rocks, they ended that episode with *New Live Download Soon!* printed across the screen.

"Steven messaged they were in Mexico. That looks like parts of it," Rafael says.

"It also looks like Arizona," Trishelle says. "Those look like saguaro cactuses."

"The plural of cactus is cacti," Glenn says, and none of us tells him to shut it.

"They've been locked inside, how could he know where they are?" Darna asks.

We watch them scramble up the hill and disappear into the rocks. The episode cuts to the POV shots from the helmet cams of their pursuers. The drones catch Steven and Julia emerging onto a tiny ledge halfway up the hill. Darna turns up the volume so we can hear Julia: *You fuckers!* Julia flips off the cameras.

"Freeze it," Trishelle says.

Darna stops the playback on Julia with both middle fingers extended, a twisted grimace on her face.

"What's Steven doing?" Trishelle asks.

I look closer at Steven for the first time. "He's propping up his hurt left hand with his right. He's stumbling. He looks like he's about to fall down."

"His right hand. The one holding the elbow. It's moving."

Darna backs up ten seconds and plays it again and again. I spot it now. He's moving the fingers of his right hand, against his left elbow. Darna zooms in on the image.

"Is that sign language?" Glenn asks, and he brings up the American Sign Language alphabet for A through Z on his screen. We all stare at his screen. He zooms in on the image and we stare at the close-up video of Steven and his moving hand.

"A, J, A, B, A, J, A, B, A, J, A … "

"Baja! They're in Baja!" Rafael says.

Darna attacks her keyboards. "Messages are coming in from *The Rescue Game*. The huge cacti are bigger than saguaro. They're cardøn, found only in Baja."

Trishelle grabs my forearm so hard that her nails dig into my flesh through my dress shirt, but I don't mind. Those nails mean she has hope.

"He's damn good," Rafael says.

"Baja is four hundred miles long," I explain.

"Can we get satellite pictures?" Trishelle asks. "Maps?"

"We don't need to!" Darna yells. "We have the Army of Light!"

"She's right," Glenn says. "We know where Steven is because *Too Cool for School* interpreted the clues. We ask our gamers for help."

Trishelle's phone rings on the living room coffee table. She holds up the screen. It says *No Caller ID*. "Should I answer it?"

We nod. She puts it on speaker phone and answers "Hello?"

"Trishelle? This is Larry Naythons. Can you talk about *The Rescue Game?*"

We all shake our heads, and she hangs up and tosses it back down.

"Keep going," I tell Glenn.

"With a half-million players, some know Baja. Others, with deeper Mexican connections than us, may already be working on it. We just have to alert the players."

"We can't reveal too much. Otherwise, it will endanger Steven and Julia."

We move into the hallway with our Sharpies and stare at the black markings on the white walls. Only Darna stays with the computers in the dining room, still staring at the live feed of *The Danger Game,* waiting for something new and horrible to happen.

Under the heading *Sources,* I underline *Too Cool for School.*

"He's our one in a million," Rafael agrees.

"One in a billion," Glenn says.

"Can we find him? Get him involved directly?" I ask.

"We can post messages on gaming sites, asking him to contact us. We can trace his email, see which server and IP address his submissions are coming from," Rafael says.

Under *Suspects* are three names: *Douglas Bushnell, Tina Swig,* and *Peter Heyman.*

"What about them?" I ask. "If we can find Bushnell and Swig, that may be as good as finding Steven and Julia."

"Cut off the head of the snake. End the threat," Glenn agrees.

"We ask *Rescue Game* players to also search for Bushnell and Swig." Rafael says.

"Too risky," I say. "We can't reveal that we know his name or even that we think they're on a yacht."

Glenn nods. "That would spook him. We have to do that search ourselves too. When are your NRO contacts sending us their pile of harbor photos?"

"Today. Until then, we're looking for *Too Cool for School* and Steven and Julia."

"Oh, we're on it. And when we find something, you must be ready, Sergeant Webb."

I get why Major Glenn Ward is pulling rank on me. If we find them—*when* we find them—it'll be my job to rescue them.

Trishelle stares at me. "What's your plan?"

"The Rey brothers."

The Rey brothers are Brazilian ex-Navy bad asses with their own security company, and they do proof-of-life rescues in Brazil, Central

America, and Mexico. I called them this morning on the way back from Wisconsin. They're going to charge me a fortune, but they can be ready in twenty-four hours.

"They're live again!" Darna yells from the dining room. We rush to her monitors. Three men have left their motorcycles and are climbing the canyon walls to the ledge where we last saw Steven and Julia before they crawled back inside. Three camera drones hover there, one for each man. The images cut from the helmet cams of the men, to the drones—and then cuts to the other side of the hill, where the fourth drone hovers above the slot entrance where Steven and Julia first went in. Two more men climb the slope and crawl inside.

"How long has it been since Julia flipped off the cameras?" I ask.

"An hour. And I don't see any way for them to get out of there."

Everyone stares at the broadcast on the monitors, riveted. I walk into the living room. Trishelle's phone is lit up on the coffee table. I power it off, then step out on the balcony and call Lucas Rey from my phone. He needs to be ready, and we need to be lucky.

CHAPTER 42

JULIA TRAVERS

Friday, March 15, 2:00 p.m. (PST)
Baja California

Steven crawls on his hands and knees with me right behind him, my nose banging into his butt. We scurry in the dry dirt, moving in the narrow sliver at the bottom of two towering sandstone rocks. He grunts in pain. His hand must be killing him. I look up; this slot between the rocks is so narrow we can't even stand, but at the top of the slot is a thin line of blue sky. And hovering there are the three fucking drones.

Voices echo off the rocks. The motorcycle men are inside. It won't take them long to follow our tracks in this maze. They laugh and hoot, knowing that we hear them.

My hand hits Steven's right foot. There's no shoe, just a sock. When did his shoe come off? An idea cuts through my brain. I grab Steven's left foot and try to yank off his shoe. He tries to scurry forward, so I yank harder.

"What are you doing?"

"There's something in the clothes they gave us. Our shoes. A tracker. That's how the drones can follow us. There were four drones, now there are only three."

He turns over and sits up, banging his head. A tiny cloud of sandstone rains down on us. We kick off our shoes. "Good call. Bury yours. That's how the motorcycle guys are tracking us. Save the laces."

I yank out my shoelaces and stick them in my pants pocket, then dig two holes in the dry sand. It's too dark to see. I drop my shoes in and push sand over them. Steven hasn't buried his; instead, he holds his shoe in the one thin shaft of light coming down from the slice of sky above us. "Hold this steady for me." He hands me the shoe.

"What the hell, Steven."

I hold it steady. He pulls out the insole and yanks out the laces. The men whistle. They're close. Steven motions for silence. He feels the fabric and bends it back and forth. There's something in the toe. He pulls out a sliver of sharp glass from inside his sock.

How long has he been hiding that?

He saws at the tip of the shoe, but he's cutting his fingers more than slicing the fabric.

"Come out, come out, wherever you are!" Men laugh.

The hairs on my neck stand up. I want to run but can't.

"They went this way!"

"Down that hole? What are they? Rats?"

He gets the fabric off the toe of the shoe. A dime-sized silver disk shines in the light. Steven puts the tracker under his tongue, then paws at the dirt with his right hand. I help dig the hole. We toss in his shoe and cover it. He lies down, rolls over, and crawls.

Thank you, Lord, we're moving.

There's no more grunting, just silence. He worms his way down the narrow passage so fast, I scrape my hands and knees trying to keep up. The passage widens, and there's another rock passage.

"Don't move," he whispers, then heads down the passage on the left. He's gone for a minute, then shimmies back. He nods at me and we shimmy down the narrower passage to right. He can't know where he's going; he's just guessing now.

We move in total darkness. The passage turns into a tunnel that's so small Steven's chest gets stuck and I have to push on his butt checks to help him through. Voices are close.

The passageway widens, and there's cool air to our left and right. Is there space there? My hands reach out and feel an overhanging of rock on either side. He moves his mouth next to my ear. "Wedge in deep," he whispers, and pushes me.

Steven rolls under the right overhang and I roll under the left.

My head hits a rock and white light flashes in my brain. I bite my lip to keep from screaming then push myself deep into the wedge. Sharp rocks dig into my side and back.

Something moves against my back, then four things, then six! Rats! Their squeaking is so high-pitched it hurts my ears. Now they're flapping in my face.

They're not rats, they're bats. I lie back on the soft, wet sand and force myself rigid as dozens of flying mice flap against my face and their little claws rip into my shirt.

Our pursuers yell, "Shit! Fuck!"

The bats must be flying past them and out of the cave.

"One flew in my mouth!"

"Shut up!"

The bats buy us time. I wedge myself deeper under the ledge, squeezing into wet mud. It must be bat shit. Yuck.

We lie still. Steven is silent, but he's there. I want to pee, but I'm afraid that they can smell it like tracking dogs. The whispering voices come close.

"Fuck, there's no more signal."

"Maybe it's the rocks."

"This handheld tracker is a piece of shit."

219

"These cameras aren't working either. We're broadcasting nothing right now."

Did you hear Heyman on the radio? He's pissed."

"Keep looking."

"No one could fit down here."

"Push through. I'll hand you the flashlight."

"What if there are more fucking bats down there?"

"Just do it."

I slow my breathing. A hand brushes the sand an inch from my foot. I choose a sense memory—a spot of total stillness. The rock fifty yards offshore our family's lake house on Lake Shebandowan in Northern Ontario. My childhood returns. The warm sun dries the cold lake water on my back. I hold my breath and body so still that the dragonflies rise off the lake after laying their eggs and land on my forearms to dry their wings. How many dragonflies will trust me? Two. Four. Six.

The men grunt. "Are you through?"

My mind sends me back to my rock in the lake. Safe and warm. I become the rock. Are the men there? It doesn't matter. The dragonfly on my wrist opens its wings. They are like clear panes of glass that shimmer with color in the sunlight.

Three puffs of air touch my face. Steven's breath. He's an inch away. My hand finds his. *Are they gone?*

Don't know. Wait for dark.

Can I pee?

Yes.

Thirsty.

Find water outside. Sleep. I wake you.

I love you.

I love you.

He pulls his hand away and rolls under his ledge.

CHAPTER 43

STEVEN QUINTANA

Friday, March 15, 3:00 p.m. (PST)
Baja, California

S *leep. I wake you.*
     I love you.
     I love you.

My hand pounds. It's a throbbing stump. Crawling around in sand mixed with a thousand years of animal shit didn't help it. My finger is gone. Those fuckers took my finger. If I don't get medical help, I'll lose my whole goddam hand.

Can I kill a man with one hand? I've never killed anyone hand to hand. Ranger training from over a decade ago doesn't count.

Carl can. I've watched him do it when he saved me. He moves fast without thinking, and can do the deed without wrinkling his suit.

That's it—channel Carl. Let him talk to me. Be my sage, Carl.

Don't worry about what I can do that you can't. Concentrate on what you can do.

Thank you, Carl, you're right. What can I do? I can survive. Stay hidden. Watch and find weaknesses. Opportunities.

I can trust Julia to not freak out. My girl's got grit. We're a team. She'll go down scratching and biting.

Or can I? She hesitated before running outside.

Don't go there. Fear has no logic. She trusts you. Trust that.

Thank you, Carl. Focus. Water is out there, not in here. It'll be a half-moon tonight. Enough darkness to stay hidden, and maybe enough light to find animal tracks. Piñon pines have edible seeds in their cones. Find piñon pines.

You're moving too fast. Assess.

Thanks, Carl. Slow down. What do I have? Nothing. Not even shoes, for fuck sake.

Get a grip. What do you have? Not what you don't have. Make your lists. Figure it out.

Thank you, Carl. Shoelaces. We can tie things. Three glass shards. We can cut things open. We can cut our clothes and use the fabric. I have a piece of tinfoil wrapping from the sandwiches stuck in my pocket. We have our urine, still in our bodies.

The world is silent. Just the wind. A light breeze flows between the rocks. Maybe that's the way out. Or not. My eyes get heavy. I tell my body to sleep more than eight hours but less than twelve. The Army trained my body to do that, too, and it listens. Then, we'll have the cover of night.

I sleep a long time, then dream that I'm surfing off Zuma beach. I can't paddle out no matter how hard my arms pull. My left hand comes out of the water. It's a stump.

Fear jolts me awake. It's black. Where am I? I remember.

One thing at a time. First, find water.

I roll out from under the ledge and listen. There is no noise except for a light wind high up between the towering rocks. The thin line of blue sky that was there during the day is now a dark black streak dotted with stars.

Time to move. I roll under the opposite ledge and locate Julia's breathing. I put my hand on her chest, so she doesn't sit up fast and smash her skull. Still, she tries, then calms down. Our hands touch, and we squeeze 1,2,3.

It's time.

I crawl. Julia follows. It's a labyrinth. We could be in here for days if I'm not careful. And what if I find another exit? If they're smart (and they are), they have a man at every rabbit hole coming out of this warren. I make right turns with Julia touching my socks to let me know she's there. I make left turns. What am I doing? My hand hurts. Assholes.

I'm dizzy, and it's not from banging my head. Feverish. I need something to clear my brain. Nausea. Stop. Exhale. Breathe ten times.

Quintana, you're losing Situational Awareness. They took a part of you. Don't let the pain steal your attention, as well. That is yours. Your mind is yours. Focus.

He's right. It's mental fog. Think. Do we go back? Even if I could, they're waiting.

Julia grabs my right hand and squeezes. *Up.*

What?

Up, chimney climb.

Me one hand.

We met one-arm surfer in Hawaii. She caught more waves than you.

Ouch. Between Julia's messages and Carl talking in my head, a guy can't slack for a second.

But, she's right; it's the way. My socks go in my pocket. This has to be done barefoot. I then stand up, squeezing my shoulders up into the narrow slot. It's like forcing myself in the space between brick buildings. I reach to my right and Julia grabs my hand.

Red Rock.

That's a nice memory. Red Rock is thirty minutes outside Las Vegas. We spent a long weekend rock climbing a dozen different pitches there, including a chimney shimmy four hundred feet straight up. I squeeze back *yes.*

We start. Knees against the front wall, spines against the back wall, and we slide our backs up. Our hands go out to stabilize, and we slide up our knees. We just climbed two feet. Only one hundred more feet to go.

Julia climbs and waits for me to catch up. She's better at this than I am. She uses her strong legs, not her arms, like wooden beams between two stone walls.

We're halfway up and moonlight shines down from above. Julia is a human shape again in the gray light. The slot widens. Time to turn sideways. We face each other, hands and feet, left and right, on opposite walls. We sink into it so our bones take the weight and not our muscles.

One leg up, opposite hand up, other leg up, other hand up. My left hand is throbbing jelly surrounding a rock of pain.

She's strong enough that she can take her right hand off the wall. She touches my trembling left arm and squeezes. *Good job, Surfer Boy.*

She leans in, so I can whisper. "You, too, movie star."

My legs are cramping. The slice of sky is bigger. Almost here. Foot up, hand up, other foot, other—

My foot slips. I throw myself against the wall. My left cheek grinds against the sandstone as I slide ten feet before stopping. The rock gives my face road rash and jars my dental implant loose. Again? It's the same dental implant I got after Julia kicked out my tooth four years ago. That was the first time she ever touched me.

Julia climbs down until we're even. She whispers in my ear. "Why are you laughing? Stop fooling around."

I hear Carl in my head. *He doesn't need tough love right now, Julia.*

Tell her, Carl. "I'm missing a finger remember?" I whisper back.

224

She climbs like a spider. Screw her for making it look so easy. Glancing up, Julia's black silhouette in the weak moonlight is a perfect Da Vinci man of outstretched arms and legs. Nice. I've still got enough mojo to notice that. Another good sign.

I prop my thighs on either rock wall and chimney climb back up. My quads and hamstrings are so flooded with ureic acid that they knot in front and back.

Rest. Climb. Rest. Climb.

The slot widens and footholds appear. I am just below Julia. The moonlight turns her silhouette to shades of gray now. I reach for a handhold and touch water in a tiny sandstone ledge. Yes! It's late winter and still cool enough that rainwater trapped in the shade doesn't evaporate. It could be half-full of bat shit and I'd still drink it.

Julia knows I found something and descends until we are just inches apart. I pull out a sock from by pocket, jam it in until it's soaked, then hand it up to her.

Julia sets her legs, grabs it, and wrings the filthy cotton sock into her mouth. "That's gross going down, but it feels good once it's inside."

I do it again with my other sock and suck every last drop out of it. My throat loosens. My legs regain strength. It's amazing what one cup of water will do. We repeat the process four times until there's nothing left.

"I found tiny eggs," Julia whispers. "A bird's nest in the rock."

"Good eyes. Crack them into your mouth."

"What if there's a chick inside?"

"Even better. Hand me one."

She hands me an egg the size of my thumb and I drop the whole thing in my mouth. I bite, letting the warm fluid flood my mouth. I chew, and let the shells dribble from my mouth, then swallow the warm goop. It tastes wonderful.

"That tastes so good," Julia whispers.

Desperation heightens our senses. Dirt would taste good right now. I climb up and pass her, ignoring the pain in my hand.

"Show-off," she whispers, and climbs parallel to me, two feet away.

I reach the lip and peek over. Nothing. I crawl out and lie flat. Julia climbs out and lies next to me. I hear only wind, but they are out there. The moon is low on the horizon. It will set soon, which will give us an hour of darkness before dawn starts. Our hands touch. She squeezes first. *Are they out there?*

Yes. Wait for total darkness. Then move. No noise.

Hungry and thirsty.

Me too. I find more.

I hope I can. My mind and body are failing.

I drift into fever sleep. She squeezes me hard. *Plan?*

Been sending Carl signals.

What if they don't see it?

Trust. Do what I say when time comes.

CHAPTER 44

CARL WEBB

Saturday, March 16, 4:00 a.m. (PST)
California

T he motel room is cold. The FBI is supposed to call, but my phone doesn't work.
    Someone taps my shoulder.
Mendoza and Marsh are standing, frozen and dead.
"Do something," Mendoza says.
"You should have stayed," Marsh says.

I jolt awake for the fifth time from the same horrible dream. Sleeping in twenty-minute increments doesn't work. And this fancy couch hurts my back.

I need to be on a plane. I'd sleep on a plane, because I'd be on the way to where I can make a difference. Something has to happen soon.

I check my Omega. It's 4:00 a.m. It's 6:00 a.m. in Wisconsin. Vanessa and I discovered the bodies of Mendoza and Marsh at midnight yesterday, which was thirty hours ago. If the bodies were taken to Milwaukee, the county coroner may not have examined them until yesterday afternoon. Gum or McCusker will call me today.

They must. Otherwise, I'll get my office to call them nonstop until someone calls me back.

It's quiet except for the sound of waves hitting the beach outside. The house is dark. I peek over the edge of the couch. Glenn is the only one still at his station. Darna and Rafael had the good sense to shower and crawl into the guest bed to rest. Only Glenn keeps going. Always on point, he only gets up from his chair to go to the bathroom.

I get up and walk behind him. *The Danger Game* app is on one monitor. The title on the screen says *Watch our previous episodes! New live show coming!* On another monitor, he scrolls through *Rescue Game* clue submissions, while, on a third monitor, black-and-white aerial images of yachts in harbors click past, one by one.

"You're breathing on me."

"Sorry."

"I wrote a program. The computer is scanning five thousand photos for yacht hulls similar to the hull on *Clairvoyance* and *Second Sight.*"

"Anything?"

"I would have told you."

A machine noise starts on the other side of the house. It leads me to the garage.

Trishelle pulls clothes out of the dryer.

"That's a smart distraction."

"This house has a mighty strong stank, so I grabbed Darna and Rafael's uniforms after they crashed. How are you?"

"Waiting for McCusker and Gum to call us and give us help. Waiting for more clues. Waiting for the show to go live again."

She shakes out their warm clothes and folds them faster than a Macy's sales clerk, which she probably was once. "At least Steven and Julia are alive."

"Yes." Marsh and Mendoza, however, are not.

She hands me the folded clothes along with a terrycloth robe. "Put Darna and Rafa's clothes next to their beds, then tell Glenn to strip and put the robe on. I need to wash his clothes too. He smells like gym socks mixed with a cheese factory."

I put the Hilario kids' clothes by the guest bedroom door, then go into the dining room and stick the robe in Glenn's face. "Put this on and give me your clothes."

He surprises me by standing up, stripping nude in front of me and putting on the plush robe. His eyes never leave his monitors. "You should get the paper jumpsuits that the house painters wear. I like to wear those on cyber missions. Disposable."

I jam his toxic waste into a trash bag. "So, this craziness is par for the course for you?"

"It's no worse than being a programming drone for a startup in Silicon Valley."

I go back to the garage and hand the bag of poisoned clothes to Trishelle, then retreat. By the time I get back to the dining room, Darna and Rafael are in there, buttoning up their clean uniforms. They sit back down at their computers on either side of Glenn.

"Nice robe, Hef," Rafael says, and they both snicker.

Glenn frowns. "Just do your jobs, Dog Eaters."

"Please keep the racist comments to a minimum, Major Ass Burger."

"Point taken. *The Danger Game* is live again, but this is all you see."

I step behind them and look at their monitors. The broadcast of *The Danger Game* is just a shaky green image of warm desert rocks emitting heat in the cool blackness of night, probably from somebody's helmet cam.

Rafael types on his computer. *"The Rescue Game* players are quiet. We need more game play to get more clues."

Glenn tightens his robe. "You sleepers can help me figure out how to find Bushnell then."

Darna's typing speeds up. "There are six hundred new luxury mega-yachts built every year. Assuming they're on a yacht less than five years old, that's only three thousand yachts to track."

Their typing grows to sharp staccato. The tension is thick. We've been at it for days—and a shower, clean clothes, and a power nap can't fix it.

Trishelle flips open her guitar case, pulls out her smooth lacquered instrument of magic, and strums her latest song. Our three cyber warriors smile and their fingers slow on the keyboards. They may only fight in cyberspace, but they have the same commitment and camaraderie as any Ranger team that I've fought alongside.

The washing machine buzzer goes off, and I follow Trishelle back into the garage. "Have you heard from the Rey brothers?"

"They're waiting for intel from me about where we are going."

Trishelle leans against the sloshing washing machine. "They're in remote Baja close enough to water. That's something."

"Baja California is as big as Northern California, Trish."

"We could get helicopters from the Mexican Army. Planes."

"We need the LAPD and the FBI for that," My voice breaks, which I turn into a cough as fast as I can.

She pauses with damp underwear in her hands. "I'm sorry about your men."

I can't bust a gut crying right now. "I have work to do," I say, and head out the front door. I move my car out the front gate and onto the shoulder of Pacific Coast Highway. The four-lane road is empty at four in the morning. A cool fog hugs the coast. All the homes are dark except ours, and the Santa Monica Mountains rise up fast on the other side of the road. This stretch of asphalt goes all the way down to Cabo San Lucas. Steven may even be able to see it in the distance.

Hang on, Steven. Keep sending messages. I'll find you.

Time to get ready. I go through the trunk of my car. I have my black camo gear. A bulletproof vest. Combat boots. Food rations. A full water bottle. A compass. Remote tracker. Spare socks. Survival knife. Fire starter kit. First aid kit. All I need are weapons, which the Rey brothers will have.

Should I go to Mexico now? Wait and hope the LAPD calls? I could call Warren Wu, a buddy who flies out of Brown Field, the southernmost municipal airport in San Diego County. I could drive there. He has a beautiful, red, two-seater plane that can land on remote beaches. But, fly where?

Not yet. I have to trust that the Reys will be ready when the time comes.

Back in the dining room, Darna, Rafael, and Glenn hunch over their computers while Trishelle stands behind them. They scroll through aerial images of crowded harbors, hoping to spot a yacht like Bushnell's.

What no one says, but we all understand, is that finding Bushnell this way may take weeks.

Trishelle hands Glenn a thumb drive. "That's more music."

Darna takes it. "I'll upload it and play it through my monitors."

The sound of lilting guitar fills the dining room. Trishelle and I head into the kitchen to make yet another pot of coffee. It's black outside the kitchen window. The sun will rise in about two hours. Then, *The Danger Game's* final hunt begins.

"What about Julia's parents? Maybe the Canadians can help us."

"I talked to Julia's parents. They're freaking out. The CSIS interviewed them in Thunder Bay, but that's all I know. I also want to get Anthony down here. When *The Danger Game* goes live again, maybe he can spot something."

Steven's older brother, Anthony, is a high school chemistry teacher in San Francisco. He knows Steven better than I do. "I'll call him."

"What do you think Steven will do next?"

Survive. He did it in the Afghan Mountains in winter with Taliban fighters chasing him. He did it in the jungles of Colombia. He can do it in Baja, for both of them."

"How?"

"He's looking for food and water. A way to stay warm, and a safe place to hide. He's also looking for an extraction point."

"What's that?"

"A place where I can get them out, like a mountain or a plateau or he may move closer to water. He will avoid roads and people."

"But he has to figure out where he is and tell us."

"Or, we hope that *The Rescue Game* players will figure it out."

We look at each other. That may be as impossible as finding Bushnell's yacht.

CHAPTER 45

STEVEN QUINTANA

Saturday, March 16, 5:00 a.m. (PST)
Baja, California

Julia and I lie against the sandstone, absorbing the last bit of heat from the rocks and waiting for the moon to set. She shakes, stifling her tears. Does she regret following me? Maybe she's calculating our odds. That would make me cry too.

The desert sky reveals more stars, which helps with direction. Orion's Belt is low in the sky, so the sun will rise to our right, in the East.

Strategize. What do you have?

The shards of glass are still in my socks. If I tie a glass shard to the end of a stick with a shoelace, it's a tool. A weapon. But can I fight with one hand? The fear returns.

You're better at hiding. Gather. Wait for your moment.

Julia grabs my hand and squeezes. *First thing to eat when we're safe?*

That's my girl, staying positive. *Mom's lemon chicken and rice.*

I want pie.

Kind?

Rhubarb. And chips.

Canadian? Like ketchup chips?

Yes. Parents' lake house, this summer. Chips, chicken and pie. And beer. That's a vision worth fighting for. I squeeze back. *Deal. Time to go.*

The moon disappears, leaving us in close to total darkness. I crawl to the edge of the sandstone rock and peer over. There's no noise. I turn on my belly and climb down it like it's a ladder. My bare feet are cold. They land on a narrow ledge. My toes search for the edge. It's about two feet wide. Julia joins me thirty seconds later, and we stand side-by-side with our backs against the sandstone.

A dark shape looms across from us. It's another huge set of rocks five hundred yards away. Water may sometimes flow between these sets of rocks. Maybe there's an arroyo below where I can dig for water.

When the sun rises, we'll know compass points. What's the date? The explosions in Malibu seem like a decade ago. My brain counts. Today is Saturday, just before dawn on March 16. The spring equinox will be in five days. On that day, the sun will be halfway up in the sky at twelve noon, between 40 and 50 degrees. That's in Los Angeles. We're in Baja, a lower latitude, where the sun will be higher in the sky at noon. How much depends on how far south we are on this damn peninsula.

Julia elbows me. A noise. She heard it first.

A giggle, from below us. Then a whisper. "We can see you. Time to die."

CHAPTER 46

CARL WEBB

Darna shouts. "They're out of the rocks!"

We rush back into the room.

Glenn taps his keyboard. "Recording to *Rescue Game* site now."

The feed cuts between two cameras. A drone floating above them, and someone watching from below. The images are green. It's heat-sensing night vision, and two figures stand on a rock ledge in the dark, not moving. You can barely see their heat outlines against the rock, they are so still.

"Not much is happening," Trishelle says.

Steven know he's being watched, so there's no reason to move until they do. The clocks say it's five in the morning. "He must move before the sun rises, which is in another two hours."

They could shoot them now but they want to play with their prey, the sick fucks. But they won't wait until dawn. Something is going to happen soon, but I don't tell them that.

CHAPTER 47

TINA SWIG

Saturday, March 16, 2:00 p.m. (CET)
Sicily

Min, Ismael, and Elliot stare at the big monitor. Plants and rocks, lit up green in the dark, swing back and forth. Some idiot is climbing around in the dark with a night vision camera mounted on his helmet. Elliot adds more luminance on the monitor, making the grainy image brighter.

"This image is giving me motion sickness," I say.

"I'll message Heyman to stabilize it," Min says.

Then, Steven Quintana appears in the corner of the screen on a rock ledge. Julia stands next to him. It cuts to a night vision drone that floats about fifty yards above them.

Douglas laughs and moves closer. "There they are. Let's go live again."

"We've been live the whole time, Boss Man," Min says.

"What the fuck? You mean we've been broadcasting that shaky shit all night?"

Min, Ismael, and Elliot look at each other and then at me, confused. "Heyman controls the broadcast. We just do the app, sir," Min says.

"Fucking morons. You should have told him to go dark."

Douglas is blaming. My perfect man is fallible, and I don't like it.

I rehearse a speech in my head:

We have over a billion. Kill them. Pay Min, Elliot, and Ishmael and send them to Club Med.

I opt for something shorter. "Let's call in a sniper. End this thing."

Douglas tosses me a sideways glance. "You want to cash out now? Min, how many downloads are we getting?"

Min scrolls through his screen. "We're making five thousand dollars a minute with new subscribers."

Douglas is thinking like a gambler on Macau, so he's not hedging his bets.

"We've achieved everything we set out to do, my love."

"We can also make a quarter billion more in the next few hours. And I'll give all of it to Devon. How does that sound?"

He's tossing choices on the table like it's a negotiation, which it isn't.

He glares at Ismael. "Have you gotten inside *The Rescue Game?*"

"No, sir, I haven't. They ping me around when I try to get in. I've been on the gaming sites, on the subreddits, and on Stack. If people are figuring out where they are, they're not sharing it on social media. No one is bragging about knowing where they are."

Douglas squints. "That may be good for us then. Message Heyman. Tell him to keep the shot from the night vision drone up there so we don't have to look at this shaky helmet shit. He screwed up once already with the locators in their clothes."

Ismael types an instant message. The image on the monitor switches to a high shot from a flying drone. The sandstone rocks are lit up dark green against black, still emitting the heat they absorbed yesterday. It's almost beautiful. And, there, on a ledge halfway down a rock wall, are two brighter figures, Quintana and Travers, emitting just a bit more heat than the rocks behind them. They stand so still they almost blend in.

"Why aren't they moving?" Min asks.

"It's too dark? We can see them but they can't see us," Ismael says.

The drone floats. It's as still as a painting.

"This is boring," Elliot complains.

"It's like watching bank surveillance footage," Ismael says.

"Shut the fuck up," Douglas says.

Min scans his computer. "Traffic is dropping. People are signing off."

I can't hold back. "Then get a rifle out there with night vision and laser sighting and shoot them in the head. Give our fans what they want!"

Douglas glowers at me. "Our fans expect a show, my love. We wait to kill them in daylight, up close and personal. That's the climax. This is playtime."

I shoot his own look back at him and walk onto the deck.

The winter sun is blazing hot in the middle of the day and the light off the water is silver white. I need my sunglasses but I'm not going back in there.

Reckoning is the only yacht anchored outside the harbor right now, which is one more risk we're taking. Too many eyes are drawn to us.

When the ship rises on the swell, you can spot the ruins of the ancient temple of Concordia. Devon and I are supposed to be there right now, enjoying our victory before disappearing. Instead we've been up all night. My son must hate me.

Always have a plan.

This can't turn into another *Six Passengers, Five Parachutes*. It's time for my insurance policy. I park myself on a corner cushion under a sun awning, and speed dial Walter.

"Hello, Tina."

"Don't call me that. Not even on an encrypted line."

"How about 'Muffin?' That's what I called you for the two months we dated. Me, a lowly tech nerd in the IT department, and you, head of reality casting."

"Stop it. I need information. That's why I'm paying you."

"Wire another ten thousand dollars into my account. Now."

"Now? Really, Walter?"

"I'm waiting."

I can't believe this guy. He was lucky he got close to me for even two days. Two months was an eternity. But he continues to serve his purpose. My thumbs attack the banking app on my phone, and another ten thousand dollars goes into his account.

I put the phone back up to my ear. "Happy?"

"For now."

"We are connected, Walter. If I go down so will you, so be nice."

"Yes, ma'am." He adds a dash of snark, but I let it slide.

"Did she answer the phone when you called?"

"She did. But she did not believe that I was Larry Naythons. Your deep fake software wasn't deep enough."

Or, Walter talked like an IT nerd instead of the senior editor of one of the largest entertainment news sites in the world. Jackass. "No, you blew it, Walter."

"Hold up. She didn't turn her phone off. She just hung up. So, I was able to run my spy software and keep the phone alive. There was a lot of ocean noise and dishes banging in the kitchen, but I did hear some interesting things."

My mouth dries up like cotton. "Talk. And don't ask for another ten thousand or I'll have you castrated."

"They have three computer programmers there. They're the ones designing *The Rescue Game*."

Trishelle Hobbes and Carl Webb are smart enough to create *The Rescue Game*? That wasn't something I anticipated.

"Muffin? They also said your name. And the name Douglas Bushnell. And they're looking at yachts."

My skin flushes hot. I look around, convinced someone is watching me.

"Who's Douglas Bushnell?" he asks.

"What else did you hear?"

"Someone online is helping them. Someone named *Too Cool for School*. Sounds like a Twitter handle or Instagram or Snapchat. He found something in Baja. Then, the phone went dead."

My game is failing. Douglas will scream and throw accusations at me.

"Muffin? Are you still there?"

"Walter. Listen carefully. Find *Too Cool for School*."

"That's even more work. It will cost you."

"Did you hear any police officers, FBI agents, or detectives in the room?"

"Nothing. They complained about it. You're in luck there."

"Good. You're the tech genius. Go find *Too Cool for School*." I hang up.

No cops means that we're still in luck. We're going to kill Julia Travers and Steven Quintana before noon, anyway, and then disappear.

But, if we don't, I must tell Douglas everything I know.

CHAPTER 48

JULIA TRAVERS

Saturday, March 16, 5:00 a.m. (PST)
Baja, California

I grab Steven's hand. *You hear?*
Three below. Look up.
I do. A red LED light hovers. The drone whirrs like a fan.
Don't move. Let them come to us.

He lets go of my hand. He's digging in his pockets.

My torso aches from my breasts down to my thighs. And, standing so still makes me cold. And scared. I want to run run run, but he says not to move, so I don't. I'm doing my job, this is his. Listen. Trust. But it's hard.

He grabs my hand, pries open my fingers and places a long shard of glass in between my forefinger and middle finger. He then closes my hand and makes a fist. How is that going to work? He then takes the glass away and squeezes a message: *Put it in my right hand. Same way.*

Then what?

Shoelaces. Wrap around my fingers. Then fist. Tie around wrist. Tight.

Boxers wrap strips of cloth around their wrists—I get it. I put the long shard in between his first two fingers and then wrap the shoelaces around his hand, turning his hand into a spear.

"Tighter," he whispers.

A man laughs below. It's so quiet, he heard Steven.

I finish. Steven whispers. "Do it to your right hand. Two shards are in my pocket."

His left hand is a swollen bloody softball and his right hand is a spear, so he can't help. My fingers find his pocket and the sharp glass. Am I going to hurt someone? My mind flashes back to the Bahamas. I shot a man in the shoulder. Steven shot a man in the chest and killed him, and we swam past his dead body in the sinkhole. Those memories don't go away.

I wrap my hand around the glass shard and pull the knot tight with my teeth. My hand throbs from the tight shoelaces. Our hands touch. *Done.*

He taps back. *Act scared. They'll drop guard. Go for throat. Ears. Eyes.*

My heart pounds up my chest, through my throat, and into my ears. Why is he making me do this?

A rock moves below. I can hear breathing sounds moving closer. He's climbing up next to me, not Steven. He perceives me as weaker; that's why.

"Puta."

My hands go up. "Don't hurt me!"

He laughs and grabs my shirt front. From his breath on my face, a mental picture of his size and height pops in my mind. I stab hard where his throat should be.

The glass goes in, deep. He gurgles as he screams, and warm fluid spills onto my hand. He grabs my arm with both hands. My wrist is connected to his neck, and I twist and saw with the glass, drenching myself with his blood. It smells like a butcher shop. He releases one hand and leans back, trying to pulling me off the ledge. A gun barrel touches my stomach. I twist away as it goes off.

BAM! My backs slams into the stone behind me as a searing heat stabs the flesh above my hip. My hand comes out of his throat.

I'm shot. Steven gets shot. I'm not supposed to get shot.

Steven kicks him. The man lets go of my shirt. Steven must be punching and stabbing him. The man falls and cries out as he hits the rock below.

My side is bleeding, but the bullet didn't hit bone. It went through flesh and muscle, thank God, but now I'm bleeding both outside and inside.

"Put these on," Steven whispers. Goggles hit me in the chest. He got the man's goggles? I slide them over my face, careful not to stab myself in the eye with my glass shard.

Green images appear. We are up high. There are rocks across from us, a canyon between, and a tumble of rocks below. A drone flies three feet above our heads. Steven looks like a haggard green alien, and he's cradling something in the crook of his right arm—a gun. He got the man's gun, too?

He gestures for me to take it. It smells like burning metal mixed with firecrackers. It's heavier than a prop gun, and hot in my hand.

"Fast. Hit the drone, then the men below. I hear three of them."

I hold up my laced-up right hand as if he could see it. "I'm right-handed."

"You're a lefty today. Brace against me." He sticks his right arm in front of my face. My grandfather trained me how to aim and shoot a rifle on our duck hunting trips, and his lessons come back to me. The gun fits in my left hand, I brace it with my right and rest my wrists across his rigid forearm.

"Up two inches," I whisper.

He raises his arm.

I must hold my breath and squeeze. *BAM.* I hit the drone as it retreats.

The man who we wounded groans below us. I wish we could help him, until I see three moving shapes on the rocks. *BAM-BAM-BAM.* They retreat.

Steven gestures with his elbow to put the gun back in the cradle of his arm. "Take off the shoelaces," he whispers. "Put the glass in my pocket, keep the laces in yours."

My teeth and my left hand unwind my weapon. I slip the shards into his pocket and the laces into mine. My hand tingles with pins and needles as the blood flows into my fingers again.

He holds up his right hand. "Now me."

My fingers tremble.

"Are you bleeding?" he whispers.

"Just my love handles."

"Stick the wet socks against it." He jams his wet socks into my hand and I tuck them into my underwear, along with my own.

"Why don't they just shoot us? Don't they want us dead?"

"They're lingering. Our suffering is their entertainment," he whispers, then slaps the gun in my hand. "Someone below us. Five o'clock."

His heat outline is clear in the night goggles. I aim. *BAM.* He grunts and tumbles behind a rock.

Did I kill him? My stomach drops. I hate that Steven is making me do this. My muscles tremble again as I barf the raw egg and dirty water back into my mouth. Was that fear? Or am I bleeding to death?

"Put the goggles on my head. I'll guide you down."

"I can't climb blind."

"You must."

I put the goggles on his head, and the dark night returns.

"Give me the gun back and your shoelaces," he asks, and I gladly do. He looks over the edge, then leans against the rock next to me. "There's a ledge twenty feet down, and then we can jump from there another six feet to the ground. I'll guide you, and I'll shoot anybody who comes close to you. Then, I'll lower the gun down."

"How?"

"Shoelaces and my elastic bandage. Then you do the same for me."

My hand finds his in the dark. I squeeze three times.

"Sidestep four steps to your left. Reach down with both hands. You'll feel a pointed rock. That's the top of your ladder. Grab it and scoot yourself off the edge and turn around so both feet land on the rock wall. Prop your legs out."

My hands find the pointed rock. Time to climb down the rock ladder. I've done this with Steven at rock climbing gyms, but never in the dark on a strange mountain with people trying to kill me.

I scoot my butt out into thin air and twist my body. My toes land against stone.

"Right foot down two inches."

My right foot moves.

"Right hand down six inches and to your right two feet."

I find the handhold. And another. Steven guides me down fifteen feet.

BAM! Something zings off the rock to my right and dust goes in my eyes. I scream, which makes the men laugh. Steven shoots another bullet. *BAM!*

"Stretch down with your right foot. Far."

I stretch my foot but touch only air. I let go with one hand—and my foot lands on it. Hand, foot, hand, foot and I'm on the ledge!

My legs buckle as pain shoots up my hip and blood squishes from my wound. The socks stuck to my stomach are sticky. Thick gooey stickiness. Maybe that's good. There's a breeze on my face. There's a thin line of light to my right. Dawn is coming, which terrifies me.

Steven whispers. "Stand and reach up with your right hand."

Stretching hurts even worse. The dark makes me dizzy and my fingers touch only air. I hear wood cracking and gravel moving below me. The men are close.

"It's there. Reach higher."

My hand brushes the stone wall, but my fingers touch nothing. It's like I'm clearing invisible cobwebs from an imaginary ceiling.

"Take two steps to your right."

Someone is breathing close to me. Warm metal lands in my hand.

A hand grabs my arm and an image of the man forms instantly in my brain. I spin, aim for his chest, and shoot twice. The explosions push me back. My head hits rock, sending a white flash of pain through my whole body. The man grunts as he falls and hits the rocks, then I hear nothing. I crouch and get sick again. Did I kill him?

"Incoming." The long elastic bandage and the shoelaces still attached to the gun land on my head. Thanks, Steven.

A moment later, he's beside me. We untie everything. "You did great."

No, I didn't. I hurt more people. The shoelaces and elastic go back into our pockets.

"Hold my pants from behind. When I exhale, we jump."

I aim the gun to the side to avoid shooting him or myself. My hand finds the back of his sweatpants and grabs tight.

He exhales, and we jump into blackness. We land in loose gravel, pitch forward onto our faces, and tumble down a rocky hillside.

We jump up and run, sprinting barefooted across rocks as sharp as glass. Bushes scratch me on both sides and whip my face. There's enough light that the rocks are now gray shapes that we can dodge. The voices chase us but they can't keep up. My eyes glance up and spot red LED lights. Another drone, but it's not overhead. Maybe it hasn't spotted us. We dive headfirst into tangled bushes. We're hidden by thick brambles now. We crawl deep inside, and he pushes against the twisting twigs and branches, uncovering some kind of animal trail. We get on our hands and knees again. It's like crawling through a tunnel of razor-sharp toothpicks. My front is so soaked with blood that my sweatpants stick to me.

Steven grunts with every movement. His hand must be killing him.

He stops. We're inside a larger space. He moves to the left and I follow him. My hands touch soft sand. He taps code on my back. *Dig. Bury.*

I put the gun down and dig. He taps again. *Grave deep.* Yuck, Steven, is that some kind of dumb Ranger humor?

We dig six inches down and lie in it, side by side, our arm and legs intertwining, then scoop the sand back on top of ourselves.

He squeezes my hand. *Hold gun* and hands it back to me. Why does he make me hold it? I push my arms and legs deeper into the sand, trying to hide. We both stink. Can they find us by our smell?

Steven freezes, which is my signal to do the same. We did this before, in the Bahamas. He can stay still like this for hours. Cracking noises surround us. Can they see our heat in their goggles? Can the drones? Maybe we're too deep in the brambles and the sand to be spotted. Or maybe we look like a coyote.

Minutes pass. Are the men gone? There's more light from dawn now. Steven pushes out of the sand and rolls onto his back. The brambles are six inches above our faces. He takes the gun back and lays it on the sand, then pulls the shoestrings and elastic bandage from his pocket.

He taps on my leg. *Dress wound.*

It hurts to pull my arms and legs out from the sand. He hovers over me. Thankfully, he's a medic too. He touches the sticky wet socks but doesn't move them. I'm bleeding right through them, but they're stopping a creek from turning into a river.

He squeezes my hand. *Tap me when tight enough. Lift hips.*

I set my heels and lift my hips. A wave of electric raw pain flows right up my spine. I bite my tongue to keep from screaming. He wraps the bandage around my hips and across the wet socks two times, then tightens.

Tight.

He stops. My hips touch sand again. My side throbs. My bare feet feel like cold stumps, and they have a million cuts on them. The cold makes my brain cloudy. Or is that the blood that I've lost?

I grab his hand. *How bad?*

Bad. Rest now.

We lie very still.

A week ago, we were in Malibu, stressing about the start of production, anxious about finding the time to get married, and worried about whether our love was strong enough to raise a family.

I'd give anything to have those worries back again.

CHAPTER 49

STEVEN QUINTANA

Saturday, March 16, 9:00 a.m. (PST)
Baja, California

Being cold helps when you're bleeding. Everything slows down. But, good turns bad when hypothermia sets in. Being terrified helps. Fear keeps the system moving. But we can't lie here much longer.

Julia's tough. She can run and climb faster than I can. She must. I'm the gimp.

My hand is infected. He took my finger. It's not hurting as much, which is a bad sign. Once blood poisoning sets in, I have two days. Then I'll lose the hand for sure. I may get sepsis and die. That makes my heart pound. Fear wakes me up.

I squeeze her hand. *Time.*

Plan?

Find water. Get warm.

Then?

Talk to Carl.

We roll onto our hands and knees and push through the prickly bushes. We reach hard sand. Light comes in from above. Brambles cut our faces. Spines jam into our arms and legs. My hand is a swollen stump.

We listen but hear nothing. But they are out there, looking for us.

Dried scat is next to my hand, bleached white—coyote shit. That's a good sign. Things live out here and find water.

More yellow light. The sun is up. It rose on our right, which means we're crawling north. The water to our left is the ocean, not the Sea of Cortez. It looks to be about five miles away, so, by the law of threes, it's probably fifteen miles away. We're at the base of a small mountain, about a thousand feet high.

I try to remember the call sheet for the press conference from last Saturday. My eidetic memory trick fades fast. I put myself back on the bluff in Malibu and see the paper in my mind's eye. My thumb moves to the four quadrants as my eyes scan the writing. Sunrise on March 9 was at 7:11. Or was it 7:21? The sun rises a minute earlier each morning. That means today, March 16, it rose about 7:02 a.m. Or 7:12. I think.

The Army also trained me to know my internal clock. It feels like it's been two hours since the sun rose, so it's now 9:00 a.m. The sun will be at its highest point in three hours. I remind myself again that during the spring equinox, the sun is between 40 and 45 degrees high in the sky in the northern hemisphere, depending upon where you are. I need to find bare, flat ground to figure how high the sun will be exactly.

Julia tugs at my ankle and squeezes. *Listen.*

We hear talking, but far behind us. Let's hope they stay noisy, so we avoid them.

Our hands touch. *Water next.*

Animal trails lead to water. Animals stick to them no matter how many predators are around, because they have the best success rate over time, even if your babies get picked off once in a while.

We come out of the prickly tunnel in a sand gulley, half in sun and half in shade. High rocks are to our right, and there's cardøn and candelabra cacti to our left. This is an arroyo, a dry river bed that fills with water maybe once a year. But there's water underneath.

We crawl forward, staying on our knees. Against the rock embankment on the other side of the arroyo, I spot tracks. I see no scat but spot a dry hole in the sand. I reach back and grab her hand. *Dig here for water.*

Why?

Animals did.

Julia digs fast, scooping out handfuls of dry sand. We're lucky it's March. In August, we'd overheat and die of dehydration. She digs, alternating hands, and soon she's forearm deep. I try to help, but she pushes my arm away. She points at me, at the gun in my hand, then at her eyes, then points at our surroundings.

She's right; I'm the lookout. My brain is cloudy with fever and thirst. I'm losing situational awareness. It's getting worse.

Focus. Assess.

Thank you, Carl. There's no breeze. This arroyo is low, so we are still hidden. But we have to be out in the open if we want to make progress. Then they can see us.

How many bullets do we have? I count back. This gun went off twelve times. The clip holds fifteen bullets. We have three bullets, at most. Fewer if he fired the gun more.

The hole she's digging is shoulder-deep now, and she must put her face against the sand to get another scoopful. The sand she pulls out is dark with moisture. She smiles so big the mud cracks on her face. She's found it. Water.

She motions for me to peer into the hole. At the bottom is a black mirror with the silhouette of my head moving in and out of the light. We trade grins. I pull off my jacket and try to yank my shirt off, over my head.

The fabric brushes my stump, which feels like sandpaper on raw flesh. The pain makes me dizzy and nauseated, and I stagger on my knees with my head still stuck in the cotton. Julia pull it off the rest of way. My bare back is frozen in spasm, until a shaft of warm sunlight hits my shoulders. That helps. I ball up my shirt and toss it in the hole, and she presses it the rest of the way down.

She pulls her hand out and squeezes mine. *Is water clean?*

Sand is clean. So yes.

But muddy.

I love mud. Squeeze it into my mouth.

I roll onto my back, making sure the weapon is secure in my right hand. She pulls out my shirt like a rag out of a bucket, with water dripping off the bottom. She squeezes a glorious stream of muddy water into my mouth. It tastes earthy and sweet. She fills me up three times, then I wave for her to stop. Too much water and my stomach will cramp. We squeeze. *Your turn. Three. No more.*

She lies down. I drop in the shirt and pull it out sopping wet. There's no way my lame hands can squeeze as well as she can, so a third of the water goes onto her hair and down her blood-soaked shirt, but she doesn't care. She grins as the water fills her mouth, then motions with her hand to stop. I repeat the process three times.

We roll onto our knees. Our hands touch. *Shirt back on.*

She squeezes out the excess water and helps me pull the wet shirt onto my torso. It's cool and clammy at first, but the sun warms me up. She helps me zip up my jacket next, like I'm a little boy on the playground. A little boy with a stump for a left hand and a black pistol in my right, shaking from cold.

Assess the environment. What do you have?

My eyes spot a plant with clumpy stems that look like thin, green straws. That's ephedra, also called Mormon tea. Chewing it gives you a rush of energy.

I squeeze her hand—*break some plant*—then, point to it, and then my mouth. She glances around, then reaches up, and grabs a handful. I put down the pistol, take the stems, jam them into my mouth, and chew. She watches me, then chews just tiny piece. It will give us a rush like caffeine, maybe enough to push us through.

My hand finds her. *It gets rough now.*

She looks around, listening. She squeezes back. *No choice.*

I put on the safety and tuck the gun deep into my right pocket. Julia takes out the elastic bandage and wraps it around my waist, tying the weapon against my hip so it won't fall out.

Her face is filthy, her hair is matted, she smells like a latrine, but damn, she's still beautiful.

Energy returns to my legs. It must be the ephedra. We smile…and run.

We dart to the other side of the arroyo and onto the rocks. She falls into place behind me. The full sun hits us, warming us enough to remind us how cold we are. But now we're out in the open. We're at risk.

I climb. She follows. There's a path between the rocks. It becomes a steep trail. The Pacific Ocean, flat and blue, appears in the distance. Civilization is there, but that's where they want us to go. For my plan to work, we can't go there yet.

Someone shouts from behind, but they're far away. We've been spotted. Time to zigzag. We head west for four hundred yards, trying to put distance between us and them. I want them to think I'm heading west, toward the ocean.

Julia pants behind me, right on my heels. My left hand throbs, shooting pain up my arm. A thick vein bulges out on my forearm, heading up to my biceps. Blood poisoning. Not good.

After four hundred yards, we cut back and go higher. A break appears in the rocks—a way up the steep hill. We climb. We're still exposed, but now in shade and hopefully they'll think we're still heading toward the ocean.

The water in my belly sloshes and I burp dirt and ephedra into my mouth. Coyotes can digest mud but not me. Maybe in my next life.

You can hide and survive like a coyote. Concentrate on that.

Voices come from below. I force myself against the rocks. Julia stops four feet below me. We're in shadow. She asks me with her eyes: *Why are we stopping?*

A hundred yards below, four motorcycles tear by with two drones in close pursuit above them. They think we're headed west, and they missed us.

After thirty seconds, we climb again, and keep climbing. And climbing. Ten minutes more. And five minutes…. I must keep track of time….

We reach a plateau. There's a flat section of open ground, surrounded by thick brush before the hill rises again. One tall, lone cactus stands about eighteen feet high on one side. Perfect.

The ocean is in the distance, blue and calm. On the other side of this mountain range is the Sea of Cortez. We can't get there, but we have to get as high as we can.

But not yet. We have less than two hours until noon.

"What happens now?"

"We send Carl a message."

CHAPTER 50

TINA SWIG

Saturday, March 16, 7:00 p.m. (CET)
Sicily

Devon races his wheelchair across his suite and slams it into the plate glass window, shaking nothing except for his chair and his monitor. His speakers crank out the sound of a screaming toddler at high volume. He knows I hate that sound more than any other in the world. He's trying to torture me.

"Talk to me, Devon."

He bangs his chair against the window twice more, then spins and talks to me in the threatening voice of an Italian gangster. "I want internet access. Professor Carlton must give me feedback before I can finish my paper on the Hodge conjecture."

"Finish it on your own and we'll send it in a few days. Tell him it's a first draft. If there are mistakes, he'll understand."

He spins in his chair and plays funeral dirge music. The computer screens on his desk are full of equations. I recognize the symbols for e, pi, and phi, but nothing else.

"That's a waste of my time," he whines in the voice of a little girl.

"Stop that. Be an adult. Your childhood is over."

He reverts back to his Paul Newman voice. "The final ideas are still coming. I must bounce them off Professor Carlton to keep the flow going. I can't lose momentum."

"You'll get it back."

"No, I won't! And I won't get the Fields Medal before I'm thirty!"

"You're not even eighteen yet. You have time. Einstein did his thought experiments while riding on a public bus. You can do yours while cruising on a luxury yacht."

"I need to finish now!"

"We're pulling anchor soon. When we drop anchor again, all communication comes back. Until then we communicate with the outside world with semaphore flags and nothing else."

"You're a terrible mother."

"And I struggle with that truth every day, my wonderful son."

"You said we'd go to Agrigento again before we left."

"We'll come back."

"I also want to see Enna. And the place with all the mosaics, Piazza Armerina."

"Now you want to see Sicily? As we're leaving Sicily? You're such a teenager."

"I hate you."

"I love you. And I'm giving you the best possible life I can. And we will change the world, I promise, but not for another few days."

I leave and head down the side staircase. Where's Rebecca when I need her? Some loving attention from an attractive redhead would save me a lot of headache right now.

She exits the galley right on cue. "May I be of service, Miss T?"

"Rebecca, yes. Devon is being…a disruptive teenager. Your employer and I have a lot to accomplish in the next twenty-four hours. Please keep Devon occupied."

"Yes. I'll do everything in my power, Miss T."

"Thank you." I say no more. A mother doesn't need to know the details.

Douglas is next. This will be the harder talk. I find him in the main lounge pacing behind Ismael, Elliot, and Min. The boys stare at the big screen and their monitors, fretting like option traders on Wall Street on a down day. On the big screen, the transmission switches between a drone shot of the motorcycles from above, roaring through the Baja desert hills, to the GoPro cameras mounted on the riders' helmets. Steven Quintana and Julia Travers are nowhere to be seen.

"I can watch better motorcycle riding on YouTube," Elliot complains.

"People are leaving the site," Ismael says.

"Is anyone buying in?" Douglas asks.

Min checks his monitor. "Not really. About a hundred new people an hour, most looking at older episodes."

"What's our profit?"

Ismael stares at his monitor. "We're at a 1.3 billion right now, I estimate."

"Once we corner them, viewership will jump again. We'll stretch out their demise. I think we can get to one and a half billion. Nothing brings in the bucks like a good splatter ending."

The boys chuckle and elbow each other.

They don't notice me standing here. No one mentions Heyman's three men, who Travers and Quintana almost killed in the green room, or the man they stabbed in the throat, or the two others who Travers shot last night on that mountain while Douglas was "stretching out their demise." It's just more kills in a video game to them.

"Boss Man, my love? May I speak with you? It's important."

Douglas tilts his head. He remains suspicious, which I understand; it's part of his competitive nature. I asked in the right diminutive way, however, so it's hard for him to turn me down. "Keep the app live, men. Let me know when you find something."

He follows me onto the back deck. The lights of Agrigento reflect off the flat water. There's a slight breeze, and a solitary buoy bell rings in the distance. I kiss him long and hard. He more than meets me halfway, which makes me push deeper into his arms.

He finally breaks free. "That was unexpected."

"I'm proud of you. And thankful for everything you've done for me and Devon."

"You're welcome, my love. We're almost there."

A cough interrupts us as Rebecca the steward and Carlos the bosun descend the port side staircase carrying a tray of espressos and small Sicilian candies and cookies. Carlos snaps a white cloth onto a table, and Rebecca sets down the late-night coffee and treats, along with pink napkins and silver stirring spoons. She and I make eye contact, she tilts her chin down in a mini-bow, and they retreat. No wink, no smile, just impeccable service, and they disappear. I'm going to miss her.

"Nice touch," he says.

"Rebecca did it all, not me. But I do have something to tell you."

He crosses his arms and sighs....

I tell him how Walter discovered that Trishelle Hobbs and Carl Webb are the ones running *The Rescue Game* from the Malibu beach house, and how someone named *Too Cool for School* figured out that Steven and Julia are in Baja.

"Anything else?"

"Yes. Walter heard my name and your name, and they suspect we're on a yacht."

Douglas takes a step back. "Was any law officer part of this conversation?

"No. But once they identify the bodies, law enforcement from around the world will be looking for us. The motel door was opened twenty-two hours ago."

He rocks on his heels and smiles at me. "You're a busy little bee. So many secrets."

"You don't trust me."

"Of course, I do. I trust but verify. I'll make my own calls and confirm all this."

"They know our names, love. They're coming."

"We knew they would. Our plan is still to disappear and start over."

"We should leave now. Call in the helicopters and kill them."

"That would draw even more attention. Are you telling me how to play my own game?"

"It's our game. You said so yourself."

"Why not challenge yourself? Isn't that the point, ultimately?" He smiles, calm and stoic. He's playing philosopher right now, instead of dealing with the task at hand.

"I like to declare victory when I'm ahead."

"So, you want *The Rescue Game* to win?"

I sip, giving myself a moment. "No, because I always win."

"Maybe you're winning twice. Maybe you're getting a cut of *The Rescue Game* too."

"That's crazy talk. You're saying that just to see my reaction."

"Maybe. But it would also be a great way to hedge your bets." He pops an amaretto cookie in his mouth, then downs a shot of espresso with a twist of lemon.

My head pounds. We're in the soft light on the back deck so he can't see my skin flush. His face is blank. For a man who may soon have the FBI and Interpol sweeping down on him, he sure is calm.

But this is his zone. He's exactly where he wants to be. He's playing the highest risk game possible, on a global scale, with the highest payout if he wins, and he loses everything if he goes bust.

I touch his arm. "I have nothing to do with *The Rescue Game*. Everything I do is for us. And, yes, I do things without telling you, so you can worry less. You do it, too, without telling me."

"I do?"

"You told Rebecca to 'educate' Devon. I smelled her perfume on him. They both dodge my questions. I could complain. After all, he's my son, not yours, and my first concern. I told you that when we first met. But I trust your judgment. I know you love us, so I never question your motives."

Douglas smiles and takes my face in his hands. "Well played."

I kiss him. "We've both played the game well. So have our opponents. It's time to cash in our chips. Erase everything, sink this yacht, and start over."

He hands me a marzipan orange slice. "And let them get away? Steven Quintana? Who invaded your last brilliant game and ruined everything, putting us on the run?"

My anger rushes back, a white heat that fills my whole body. That anger is an old friend who's been at my side for years, pushing me. Douglas is right, walking away from total revenge against Steven Quintana and Julia Travers is hard, but we must. "I don't need to see them die on TV, as long as Heyman kills them. Living well is the best revenge now, and that's what we must do."

Douglas stares at me. He's deciding.

CHAPTER 51

STEVEN QUINTANA

Saturday, March 16, 10:30 a.m. (PST)
Baja, California

The ephedra rush clears my head. "Search the underbrush. Find three sticks, one a foot long, another two feet long, and the last one a yard long. Look for dead cactus. The dried ribs of the cardon cactus are straight enough."

"What if they see us?"

"My infected hand will kill me in less than two days. This is what we do."

Julia goes on her search. I unwrap the bandage and pull the gun from my pocket and manage to hold it with my swollen left hand. I take the clip out of the pistol and check it—only two bullets. Damn. I can't waste them. I put the pistol on the ground and dig out the glass shards from my pocket. I brush clear a large circle in the dirt, six feet in diameter, until it's flat and clean, like an empty plate. I then walk toward the one tall lone cactus on the bluff, pacing out my steps. One hundred feet. Perfect.

She comes out of the brush with three straight cactus ribs—one, two, and three feet long, respectively. "Which one first?"

"The two-footer." I hand her the longest glass shard from my pocket. "Hold this against one end."

She holds the glass shard against the tip of the cactus rib. I wrap a wet shoelace around, tying the glass shard into place like an arrowhead. Once she sees my plan, she takes the stick from me and does it herself, tying the knot tight.

"Impressive."

"I got the Girl Scout badge for knots." She holds up the stick with its new glass blade. "It's not much of a weapon."

"It's a tool. Sharpen the end of the foot-long stick and jam it so it's straight up and down in the middle of the circle."

"What are you going to do?"

"I need to gather small, straight sticks about four inches long."

She grabs the short stick and starts whittling. I walk to the where the slope starts again and find more dried cactus ribs that I break into four shorter pieces.

Julia has already stuck the long stick into the ground in the middle of the circle. It casts a nice straight shadow. I hand her the sticks. "Sharpen these."

"You're making a sundial." She grabs the sticks from me. "Why?"

"If we do this right, we can find exact east and west. Once we do that, I can use this," I say as I pick up the yard-long cactus rib, "to determine our latitude."

"You can figure out where we are?"

"No, but Carl and Trishelle can. If they're watching."

"How do you know they're watching?"

"I don't. But I hope they are."

"So do I." She kneels and sharpens my short sticks. I use my heel to scrape out a large square in the dirt next to the circle.

"What's that?"

"My message board." The dirt is flat, but dry and too hard to write on. We need mud. I unzip and piss on the square, wetting it as much as I can.

"What are you doing?"

"Creating a writing surface."

"Thanks for an image that obliterates all of your remaining physical appeal to me."

"You're hardly red carpet ready, my one-two-three." The square is only half wet. "Your turn. Piss on the rest of this square. Turn the dirt into mud so I can write in it."

She stares at me like I'm insane. I look up. Noon is about an hour away. "Can you just piss, please? We don't have much time."

She huffs. "Look away. No one ever watches me pee."

I face the ocean. Far off in the distance there's a glimmer against the sun. That's a drone, about a mile away. There's no noise from the motorcycles. They're searching and will head back this way soon. "It's nice to know that movie stars pee like the rest of us."

"Shut up."

"You smell like an outhouse."

"Don't make me stab you with the tool I made for you."

"Please don't. You already cut off my finger."

"I'm done. You can turn around."

She ties her sweatpants while fighting back tears. She didn't like my joke.

"You made me hurt those men. I may have killed them."

"I couldn't, so you had to do it. That's how we made it this far." I go to hug her, but she puts her hand up.

"Stop. I'll lose it. You stink too much right now, anyway."

The square is a perfect slab of wet mud. "You peed perfect. Tool, please."

She hands me the stick with the glass shard. The sun is almost halfway between the horizon and its zenith. "While I write, look at the shadow the sticks casts in the circle. Jam the first short stick into the ground at the tip of the shadow. Then every ten minutes, put the next short stick at the tip of where the shadow is by then. We're marking the movement of the sun."

"How will you know it's ten minutes?"

"I'll tell you. It's another weird talent I have."

"Thank God for your weird talents."

I write in the mud. "Too bad I can't make a buck using any of them."

Julia jams her first stick in the ground at the tip of the shadow of the vertical stick.

"First stick is in."

Time passes. I have a lot to write, and the mud dries fast.

"The shadow has moved. Is it ten minutes yet?"

"Yes. Ten minutes."

From my brain to my hand to the mud, it's hard to translate everything. My inner clock dings. "Ten minutes," I say again then keep going. The mud tablet almost dry. Soon you'll have to be right above it to see that anything is even written here.

"Ten minutes."

I'm running out of space. "Ten minutes." And I finish.

Julia steps back. The sticks line up, revealing the sun's movement. I pry the glass shard of the tip and lay my writing stick alongside the four pegs that she's been sticking in the sand over the last forty minutes.

"That's a perfect east-west line. And, at twelve noon, the long vertical stick will cast a shadow perpendicular to it, which will be a perfect north-south line."

"When's that?"

"In about five minutes."

She raises her eyebrows. She looks at my mud tablet. "What are those chicken scratches? It looks like ancient Sumerian."

"Shorthand. Another lost language. But, my brother knows it. Pick up the last stick."

She picks up the last and the longest of the three sticks she found for me. I hand her the last two glass shards from my pocket. "Poke holes in either end of the stick and put in the glass shards, so they are like gun sights."

She proceeds. I hover over her. She holds it up. "How's that, Ranger Rick?"

"Adequate." I hand her the glass shard I pried off the writing tool. "Now, stick this in the middle, but underneath. This longer stick must balance on the vertical stick that's already in the ground."

"Like a T-shape?"

"Yes, but it has to tilt. I need to aim it at the sun at noon."

She pushes in the last glass shard hard enough to draw blood on the sides of her fingers, then walks into the circle and pushes the downward-facing shard into the stick coming out of the ground.

"It's not going to be sturdy enough," she says. "The longer stick will fall off."

"It only has to work for a minute."

Julia pushes the glass in deeper, forming a "T." The cactus wood is soft, so the longer stick tilts just enough. We stand back and admire our work.

"That's different than a regular sundial."

"It's called a gnomon. It's like a sextant."

"Show-off. What now?"

"Noon is a minute away. Tell me when you see the shadows of the glass shards."

267

I tilt the T-stick toward the sun until its shadow gets shorter and shorter, until we see mostly the two, tiny shadows of the glass shards sticking out on each end.

"I see their shadows now. They're thin, but I can see them."

I tilt the T-stick on its hinge and aim it right at the sun. "Tell me when the tiny glass shadows line up and make one shadow."

"Now."

I release the stick. "See that angle of the stick now? That's our angle of latitude."

"How can you measure it?"

"I can't. Not accurately. I'm hoping other people can, when they see it."

She glares at me, confused. "How's that going to happen?"

She glances toward the ocean. She hears the noise before I do—the motorcycles are coming. But I need them here now—not after noon has passed.

"You might want to turn away for this one."

"Why?"

"Don't ask. Just turn away."

She does. I squat, reach into my underwear, and push. Out pops the last tracker beacon that they hid in my shoe. I toss it in the center of the circle.

"You can turn around now."

She recognizes the shiny metal. "You were hiding that? Where?"

"I wrapped it in the tinfoil from the sandwiches they gave us and then shoved it where the sun don't shine."

"That's disgusting, Steven."

"Disgusting will save us. Hide against the rocks. I have to stay standing here."

"Why?"

"So people watching can measure my height. It's all written in your pee mud on the message board. I can't explain more, just do it, Julia."

"The night goggles are still on your forehead. Toss them here."

She's right. We can't let them know what we have. I toss them to her. "I can't believe my girlfriend is giving me shit right now."

"I'm not your girlfriend, I'm your fiancée," she snaps back, and, instead of hiding in the shadows like I asked her, she lies down on the ground on the outside of the circle and splays her hands and legs out like she's hurt.

"What are you doing?"

"Creating a dramatic moment. Aim the gun like you want to shoot me."

I pick up the weapon. A whirring noise arrives. One of the drones that chased us yesterday is back, hovering ten feet above us. The tracking disc is sending its signal and doing its job.

Julia grabs her bloody hip. "Don't shoot me, Steven! I want to live!"

She weeps. The drone rises. I get it now. They're shooting the scene she's creating. I stand still. Julia pounds the ground. "Steven! Steven! Look at me! What's happened to you?!" I hope the shot lasts long enough that people can see all the clues.

The motorcycles are closer. Men yell. I don't want the other drones to find us. Noon has passed. Our window is closing.

I aim the gun at Julia. The drone drops closer to capture the moment. It's now close enough to get the gnomon in its frame and, hopefully, everything written in the mud.

The motorcycles stop. The men are climbing up. I aim at the drone and shoot. *BAM!* It lands on the now dry tablet, raising a cloud of dust. I have one bullet left.

"They heard that."

"Had to. I just hope we got the message out." I pick up the drone and smash it against the ground, then put broken pieces in my pockets. Julia copies me.

"What now?"

"We climb."

She beats me to the rocks. The men's voices are loud below us.

CHAPTER 52

TINA SWIG

Saturday, March 16, 9:00 p.m. (CET)
Sicily

Douglas downs another espresso and stares out over the water. Conceding any kind of defeat is not in his nature, but he has no choice.

Min shouts from the sliding door. "We found them! Drone on the way!"

Douglas's face lights up like a gambling addict at a horse race. "We'll finish them quick. No lingering, I promise." He pops one more cookie into his mouth and heads inside.

All my muscles are shaking. My anger toward Steven Quintana and Julia Travers is gone. I just want out. I step out of the cool night back into the bright lights of our global, floating, crap game.

The boys are hooting it up. "Viewership is jumping! Word is out! We're at eight hundred purchases a minute!"

On the big screen, a drone flies through a narrow canyon in the Baja hills. "This drone is linked to one of the beacons hidden in their clothes. Heyman is texting that it just became active again," Min says.

"They're only a mile away from the warehouse. They haven't traveled very far. I thought for sure Mr. Army Ranger would have made it farther," Elliot says.

"She's shot two of our men and he's stabbed a third. That's better than you clowns could do," Douglas says. The boys flinch, but don't turn from their monitors. Their charming boss is turning on them.

"How did that tracker show up? I thought they kicked off their shoes," I say. No one answers me: the invisible woman in the room. Familiar.

Two small figures come into focus on a tabletop plateau halfway up the dry mountain. Heyman in his control room switches to the shot of motorcycles, which turn around. They've gotten the message that they've spotted Quintana and Travers. Chase music kicks in, adding to the thrill. The riders rev their throttles and tear back the same trail. Heyman switches back to the drone's POV, as it descends close to the mountain. The chase music lowers as the shot stabilizes.

Quintana stands as still as a statue, a pistol in his hand. Twenty feet away, Julia Travers lies on the ground, her legs twisted under her.

"Is she hurt?" Min asks. The fucker sounds like he cares.

"That dude shot her, remember? After she stabbed him in the throat," Elliot says.

"That dude was an idiot," Ismael says.

Douglas claps his hands. "Focus!"

The drone settles into a solid two shot with Quintana and Travers on either side of the frame. Her legs are limp under her. Maybe she's bleeding to death, which gives me a tiny rush.

The drone descends closer. "Don't shoot me, Steven! Please!"

"Whoa, he shot her?" Min asks.

His tone bugs me. Douglas picks up on it, too. "Min, do you have a fucking crush on her? What are the downloads?"

"Downloads are climbing. People are back online."

"I want to see if we can make a million dollars a minute," Douglas says.

"We will if he shoots her again," Elliot says.

"This thing will be over in five minutes," Douglas says.

Quintana stands at the top of a circle he's drawn in the sand. It's got sticks stuck in it. The drone drifts back, revealing a square that's been swept clear of brush and grass, and it's darker with markings on it.

My heart races. "He's sending a message, pull the plug!"

No one hears me.

"Is he going to shoot her or not? He's like a statue," Elliot says.

The drone descends. "That's a sundial! He's sending a message! Pull the plug!"

Quintana aims his pistol at the drone and pulls the trigger. The image goes dark.

"Shit, that sucks," Elliot says.

"Were you recording that? Back it up!"

"What?" they all ask in unison, like I'm the one who turned their TV show off.

I slap Elliot hard across the face. He raises his hand to hit me and I plow my heel into his groin. He falls out of his chair. I point at Ismael, the only one I now trust. "Back it up! Quintana sent out a message!"

Douglas's eyes widen and he starts breathing fast. I've never seen him scared before, but he is now. "Do it," Douglas whispers.

Ismael backs up the recording.

"Freeze! Right there!"

We stare at the image: a circle with sticks, one of them perched on top of the other alongside a square with markings. "That's a sundial," I say.

"We have to figure out what he's saying," Douglas says.

"No, we don't. The FBI, CIA, and Interpol are already doing that. We pull the plug. We tell Heyman to torch the warehouse, and we all disappear. It's time to go."

Douglas blinks like he doesn't understand. For the first time I feel like I'm smarter than he is...and I don't like it. The boys all stare at him, waiting for an answer.

"How much have we made, Min?" he finally asks.

"1.32 billion."

"Good enough. Pull the plug."

We should have pulled the plug ten hours ago, but, no. He put everything at risk for an extra two hundred million dollars. Getting angry won't help us right now. I clap my hands and they all look at me. "Close the sites, shut down the servers, erase your tracks. Then pack your bags. No electronics, not even an MP3 player. No talking to each other. Stay in your rooms. Cameras are watching you. We'll drop each of you off in a different Italian city within the next twenty-four hours. You will each get your promised payouts in bitcoin within forty-eight hours as contracted."

Douglas hits a button on his smart watch and Rebecca and Carlos appear from the galley on the floor above. "Rebecca, these men will be leaving the ship soon. Carlos, notify the captain and first mate that we're pulling anchor immediately. Only maritime short-wave communication is allowed, and only to respond to the harbormaster. Get the tender in the water now and we'll tow it. I want their drop-offs to go smooth."

They nod and leave. The frat boys all stare at him. Elliot finally asks the question. "What about Steven and Julia?"

"Oh, they're still going to die, you just won't be a part of it. Pull the plug."

They sigh and turn back to their monitors. Min shuts his down first.

It's about fucking time.

CHAPTER 53

CARL WEBB

Saturday, March 16, Noon (PST)
California

I 'm standing in the kitchen when Lucas Rey texts me: *Need details. Can't wait forever.*

Shit. He's got his team together, and they're waiting in Ensenada. If we're doing this by land, he'll need Humvees. If we're doing this by sea, we need boats, maybe a barge. We need a helicopter either way. I'm paying through the nose for a half-organized rescue squad that's waiting around for information.

I text him back: *Soon.*

Marsh and Mendoza flash through my brain. We found them thirty-six hours ago. Even if they took them to Milwaukee yesterday morning, why so long? The coroner must have identified them yesterday afternoon.

Anthony Quintana, Steven's brother, arrived thirty minutes ago. He looks just like Steven but with a touch of gray at his temples, ten extra pounds, and a happier face. Probably because he *is* happier. Being a chemistry teacher sure beats this.

He comes in the kitchen and pours more coffee. "You all caught up, older brother?"

"Yup. This shit seems familiar."

Darna shouts. "A high drone sees Steven and Julia!"

Trishelle, Anthony, and I rush in and crowd around our three cyber warriors and their six monitors on the dining room table.

A drone flies through a slot canyon in the rocky hills of Baja, rises up to a plateau, and slows when it spots Steven and Julia. Steven stands ramrod straight, a pistol in his hand, while Julia lies twisted on the ground ten yards in front of him.

"Don't shoot me again, Steven! Please!"

Trishelle scoffs. "This is fake. Steven would never shoot Julia."

Steven points his pistol at her. The drone drops down, almost level with them. Steven turns and shoots the drone. The screen goes black.

"Rewind it!" Anthony says. "Show me that last shot!"

Glenn brings the last shot back on screen. Julia lies on the ground. Steven stands ten yards from her.

"In that square at the bottom of the frame. Those scratches are shorthand. Our mother taught it to us," Anthony says.

My eyes return to Steven and Julia. In between them are sticks—some on the ground, some sticking in the dirt, and two are stuck together, making an angle.

It hits me. "He's trying to show his latitude. That's a sundial."

Rafael points at me. "Yes! Like a sextant!"

Anthony nods. "Yes. We can figure out their angle of latitude to the sun."

"And their location from the angle of that stick," Rafael says. "It's just after twelve. He aimed it at the sun close enough to noon, to get a decent measurement."

Trishelle looks at the frozen image of Steven and Julia on the screen, and the arrangement of sticks between them. She shakes her head. "This drone is aimed down. We're too high up to see the angle. How do we figure it out?"

Glenn types like crazy. "We don't even try. We put it on *The Rescue Game*. We have almost a million online players. Someone will solve this puzzle." He hits return. His screen fills with a moving bar: *MP4 uploading*.

"Maybe *Too Cool for School* will come through for us again," Darna says.

Rafael types. "I can hail him in *The Rescue Game* chat rooms on Reddit."

"FYI, *The Danger Game* is gone," Darna says.

Trishelle hovers behind her. "What do you mean, it's gone?"

She points at her screen, which has a sad emoji face and some script. "See? 'This URL is not available.' They planned for this. They're erasing their tracks."

"Zoom into that square, the one with the shorthand," Anthony says.

Glenn zooms in. The image stays clear, but it's also at an angle that's hard to read. "Can you tilt it?" Anthony asks.

"Done and done," Glenn says. He pushes in on the square, and then tilts it, so it's flat. The lines at the bottom of the image are stretched, but it all fits.

"It looks like faded chicken scratches," I say.

Darna leans in from the other side. "You can enhance it, Major. Turn the image black and white."

Trishelle leans in from behind and touches his shoulder. "She's right. Push the contrast. It will make those lines stand out," she says, pointing at the screen.

Glenn shrugs off her touch and stands up fast. "We're not a six-person bobsled team! Back away!"

"Dang, Glenn. We're all stressing here," Trishelle says.

"I demand four feet of space between me and all of you!"

"The man's on sensory overload. Give him his space," I say.

The Hilario twins snicker but we grant him his half-circle of privacy.

He types at his computer. We wait. He clicks his mouse and smiles.

"Screw it, Glenn, we're bobsledding you," I say, and we crowd him again. On screen, the dirty brown square is now white, and every scratch is a dark, black line.

I shake my head. "It still looks like Assyrian hieroglyphics."

"Shh." Anthony holds up his hand. He moves his mouth, translating the scratches into words. "It says, 'Calculate latitude from the angle of the stick. Adjust image to match measurements. My height is six feet. Circle diameter is twelve feet. Cactus is eighteen feet. Sighting done at noon.'"

Darna peers at her screen. "That transmission was at 12:05. Is that close enough to noon to determine precise latitude?"

Glenn has been typing the whole time. He hits the return key. "*Rescue Game* players are working on it. I just updated the chat rooms and subreddits with Anthony's shorthand translation."

Trishelle taps Anthony on the shoulder. "Did he write anything else?"

"'In Baja, fifteen miles from ocean. Colombia repeat, 8:00 p.m., before moonrise. We have one set of night vision goggles.'"

"Anything else?" I ask.

Anthony turns from the monitors. "Nope. That's it."

Adrenaline surges through me. *Colombia Repeat.* He wants a Ranger exfiltration. Almost a decade ago, Steven and I were trapped at the top of a Colombian mountain, surrounded by FARC rebels. The Colombian Army sent in a helicopter and airlifted us out. Steven was shot and unconscious. I had to lift him in a fireman's carry to a high clearing, and then clip us into long ropes and we were lifted high into the sky while the FARC assholes shot at us. My butt cheek got hit by a random bullet. He wants the same thing again, in less than eight hours. Since he has one set of night vision goggles, we can fly with no lights and he'll be able to see us coming. So will Heyman and his men, but it helps.

But, how am I going to see you, Steven? How do I even find you?

Darna's computer dings and she smiles. Everyone crowds around her computer next. "Damn, he's fast. *Too Cool for School* has come through for us. Check this out."

She brings up four frozen images of Steven and Julia on the plateau. *Too Cool for School* has drawn lines and angles with calculations in the corners.

"He really is too cool for school," Glenn says.

"Someone explain, please?"

"See the degree of this acute angle right here?" Darna points at an arc that *Too Cool for School* has drawn on the sundial, between the stick stuck in the ground and the titled stick pointed at the sun. "The degree of that angle is their degree of latitude. Just like the angle on a school protractor."

"But you can't see it clearly. We're too high up," Trishelle says.

Glenn brings up the next image on screen. *Too Cool for School* has tilted and stretched the image. It now looks like we are on the same level as Steven. Everything is stretched, and the image is grainy, but you can see the sundial.

Darna reads off her screen. "He's adjusted the image so that it roughly matches the heights and lengths Steven gave us in the shorthand, as if we were ground level with him. *Too Cool for School* estimates the angle to be approximately twenty-seven degrees. That means they are twenty-seven degrees north of the equator."

Rafael types fast. "Twenty-seven degrees north latitude, fifteen miles from the Pacific Ocean puts them…here. Give or take twenty miles in any direction, probably."

We all switch and bobsled behind Rafael and his monitor. A map of the Mexican State of Baja, California Sur comes on screen. Rafael draws a circle on the coastal mountains of the El Vizcaíno Biosphere Reserve. They are in wilderness. The closest town is El Juanico, a tiny fishing village on the coast.

A little too big an area, but it will have to do. As I snap a photo of his screen with my smartphone, it rings. We all jump. It's Detective Niall McCusker.

Trishelle sees the screen. "About time."

I put him on speaker phone. "Believe me now, McCusker?"

"Get your butt to Malibu City Hall. Bring a snack, you'll be there a while."

Trishelle looks stunned. Steven and Julia—hiding in the hills fifteen miles east of El Juanico, in the El Vizcaíno Biosphere Reserve—need me in less than eight hours. And now this?

"Webb? Do I have to send a squad car for you?"

I hang up. "I'm going to Mexico."

Glenn screams. "Wait! I can find *Too Cool for School!*"

Darna and Rafael bobsled him, their heads an inch away from his on either side.

"How?" Darna asks.

"He or she was bragging in a subreddit chat room, and I can trace it back! He was using a computer using a cell phone as a hot spot," Glenn says, pointing at his screen.

"Damn, he's using a cell phone for his Wi-Fi?" Rafael asks.

Trishelle's phone rings. She shows me her screen: Niall McCusker, LAPD. He wants her to come in, too. A squad car will be here soon. She mouths one word: *Go.*

I text the photo of the map to Lucas Rey as I slip out the front door. I get through the gate and jog to my car, which is already waiting on the shoulder of the Pacific Coast Highway. My phone dings with his response as I slip behind the wheel: *Downloading topo maps now. Time frame?*

Mission starts at eight pm.

I drive two hundred yards, then get his next text: *You have passport?*

Shit. I pull over, get out, open the trunk, and rifle through my travel bag. My hands search through the pockets while my mind goes over the mission: combat-ready rescue helicopter, pilot, co-pilot. Exfiltration gear. Crew of one: me. Weapons. We can't muster on land. We have to take off and land from the ocean, at least a mile out, and that means some kind of barge. We will need paramedics on the barge, waiting.

I search every pocket again and find it, then text back: *Yes. Where am I going?*

He texts back. *Brown Field, South of San Diego. Three hours from now, Warren will fly you into Mexico. You will land on a private beach close to that latitude.*

Warren will load his homemade, red, two-seater plane with surfboards and beach coolers and tell customs that it's a surf trip. That's the cover.

I text back: *And?*

Response: *Look for a speedboat. Paramedics will drive you out to a barge.*
Chopper type?

Am I hooking up gear inside a French Eurocopter from the Mexican Navy? With no mounted guns? Or is it a Huey from the Mexican Army? Or is it some news helicopter from Tijuana?

He responds: *Working on it.*

Shit. He doesn't have the chopper yet. I text back: *Mounted gun?*

He responds: *No weapons. Not part of deal. Search and Rescue only.*

It's his gig; I'm just hiring him and have no clue who he must grease to make the Mexicans ignore us for eight hours. But I'll get the bill.

I text back: *On my way.*

It's 1:00 p.m. We fly into Mexico at 4:00 p.m. We then have four hours to find and rescue Steven and Julia. This is not the time to ponder my odds.

My butt hits the driver seat and my foot punches the gas.

CHAPTER 54

JULIA TRAVERS

Saturday, March 16, 7:00 p.m. (PST)
Baja, California

I'm in the dark, again. Cold. Alone. Waiting.

At least it's not as cold as this morning. That's because I'm lying in a trench that Steven dug. He covered me with warm sand, until just my face was sticking out, and he covered that with grass and twigs.

And then he left me.

That was hours ago. It was warm at first. My hip felt wet. Bleeding, but the dry heavy sand stopped it, I think. *Apply direct pressure.* More lifesaving info from the Girl Scout Handbook.

I even slept. Then the sun set, and the sand got cold, and some animal creeping by startled me awake. It must have passed because cricket noise came back.

The desert looks barren from far away but, up close, there are brambles everywhere, and under every bush there's a hole for some crawlers, snakes or scorpions. Earlier, when we were lying in the darkness, waiting, two tiny eyes blinked at me from a hole. It must have been an owl, since the eyes were big and round and had lids.

Then Steven buried me.

Face it, Julia; Steven dug a grave, buried you and left. All they have to do is find you and shoot you, toss dirt on your face and walk away. Push out of this sand grave and find him.

That's Doubting Julia, my inner voice. I let Calm and Trusting Julia take over:

Relax, Julia. He's done everything he said he'd do. Yes, he's weak and hungry and making mistakes. But this is where he excels. Stay still until he comes back.

The voices battle while my mind spins. He should have cut off my finger. Then I would have trusted his strength and wouldn't have hesitated when we escaped. He wouldn't have gotten an infection. His mind would be clearer. He would have shot those men instead of me. They may be dead because of me.

A twig breaks. Two men are whispering. They're walking close. Nature's noises—so loud a second ago—disappear. I smell sweat.

"Fuckers can climb," one says. "And hide."

"I wish they'd run. Then we could chase them and kill them. Peter would pay us all, and we could leave."

"I say we firebomb the place. This isn't worth getting shot, even if the idiot only has one gun. Not for some shitty show."

Their voices drop to a whisper. Their footfalls are close enough to send mini-shock waves into my shallow grave. One of them steps on my shin and stands there. I hold my breath to keep from screaming.

"What was that?"

"What?"

"Did you hear an animal?"

"No. But if you're scared, aim at it and shoot."

"Shut up."

Mr. Shut Up steps off my shin and keeps walking. I wait a full minute before breathing again. The smell of sweat is gone, but

Mother Nature stays silent. They are still close. The twigs on my face keep me from seeing anything.

Minutes pass.

Three thumps—*one, two, three*—vibrate the ground, close by. Steven is back. I want to escape this sand grave and hug him. His hand pushes away the twigs and he kisses my forehead. His face is dark. He plunges his hand into the sand and finds mine.

We climb one more time. Fifty yards up.

Men were here.

Carl is coming. Trust.

OK.

You wear goggles. You will see chopper.

OK.

Pack will drop. Put on stuff attached to outside of pack.

What?

Vest with loops for arms and legs. Like climbing harness. Cinch tight.

OK.

Goggles, vest, harness for me are in pack. A weapon will be there. If I say, you must use it.

Memories of the dying men come back. but I can't refuse.

OK.

A line will drop. I will clip you in. He will lift you very high, fast. If you see men below, turn away. The ride will be long.

And you?

If I clip in, I will be below you on the line.

No if. We both go.

You expert in movies. Me this. Trust.

My emotions shift from scared to furious, then to an overwhelming love for him, and then to a deep sadness for us. Why is this when I feel my strongest love for him?

His hand grabs mine again. *Move body, not brain.*

He tugs my hand and I kick my legs and push my arms and pop out of the sand. My throat screams for water. He must see it through his goggles, because he puts the edge of his shirt into my mouth. It's wet. He found water again, but not much. I suck on the tip, pulling out every drop of dirty brown water like its fine wine. My muscles fill with a new rush of energy.

He pulls me up and tugs me into a run. There is just enough light for me to see his shape in front of me. I keep pace. His shape rises. We're going uphill. My side aches and send shooting pain down my legs. I'm squirting blood again.

Rocks move under us. He bends over. He's climbing. My arms reach out and my hands touch rocks, then boulders. We're in a notch in the hill, and we're climbing a rock ladder.

We reach the top and wait. Steven listens. I know this drill now. He tenses next to me. "Listen."

There's a distant throbbing, a familiar sound from Los Angeles. It's the helicopter looking for us.

"I fucked up. They're too far north."

"I could never have done even this much."

He tugs my hand. We run across flat ground in the dark. He's wearing the goggles, so he better not lead me into some prickly bush. He slows, then stops. He kneels and pulls me down next to him.

"Put on the goggles. I need your help sending a signal."

He puts the goggles on my head and pulls them over my eyes. The green light returns. We are almost knocking knees in a shallow depression filled with dry grass. The pistol is next to his right knee, and there's a flat rock next to his left knee. In front of us is a thick, two-inch, brick-shaped thing wrapped in white plastic with wires.

"Is that a battery?"

"From the drone." He shows me a short, sharp stick. He has made another tool with the glass shard at the tip, wrapped tight with a shoelace. He must have done it with his teeth and one good hand. He touches the battery in the dark. "This is a lipo battery. If you stab it hard enough, it catches fire. I'll hold the stick. Take the rock and hit it so the glass goes in. You have to hit it right, like a hammer on top of a nail. It will break into the chemicals inside, there will be a fireball, and it'll light all this grass on fire."

"Won't they see it?"

"Yes, but so will Carl. I didn't want to do this, but now we must."

We can hear men shouting.

Steven holds the sharp glass point against the battery. "Use both hands and smash the rock down hard. But look away as you do it."

I pick up the flat rock slab and feel its weight in my hands.

"The fireball will be big. Roll away the moment you hit the stick. The grass will catch fire. I'll grab you and we'll run north up this hill another five hundred meters."

The voices are close. I hold up the rock. "Here goes nothing." He nods and closes his eyes. The flat rock stays frozen in my hands. What if I miss? This is our only chance.

My eyes stay open. My hands drive the rock down onto the stick.

The battery pops with a white flash, and a hot fire ball engulfs my face. My hair is on fire. I cover my head and roll, remembering the drawing in the Girl Scout manual.

My whole head is on fire. It hurts.

My brain says to roll, but my body says run.

CHAPTER 55

STEVEN QUINTANA

Saturday, March 16, 8:00 p.m. (PST)
Baja, California

I leap on Julia, covering her flaming head with my body. She kicks and punches, trying to get away. The stench of burning hair and skin stings my nostrils. We roll in the dirt smothering the flames. She hits my back and whimpers under me. She can't breathe.

I yank her to her feet as she gasps for air, and I jam the gun in her hand. "Take it."

The fire we started is growing and her face is illuminated from the flames, but not her eyes behind the goggles. She nods. She's back now and fighting.

I throw more grass and dried barrel cactus skeletons that I gathered into the pit. The earth vibrates. Someone is running at us. A shadow appears against the rising fire, a gun raised.

"Steven!" she screams. I drop. Julia shoots and—*BAM!*—hits him. The man flies backward and lands on his side, still. She's a better shot than me. All of that movie training has paid off.

That was the last bullet. Another man pushes through the growing wall of fire. I grab the gun from Julia and throw it hard, beaning him square in the face. He goes down.

Julia staggers. I push her. "Lead the way! Run! Up that rise!"

Julia takes off, and I fall into place behind her. We run a hundred yards in world-record time. Behind us is a barrier of fire now, but we see shadows of men getting through. A line of dead cacti explode into flames like burning giants.

The taste of blood rises in my mouth. My pulse pounds in my temples, my neck, my groin. The hill gets steeper. My legs are empty. The helicopter noise comes closer. We reach flat ground. This is the spot. I grab Julia's shoulder and pull her to a stop.

Gunfire erupts, which sounds like popcorn popping. They are shooting at the chopper, and people on the chopper are shooting back at them.

The helicopter hovers right above us. A line drops and hits the ground two feet away. Julia grabs it.

"Look up!" She looks a second too late. A pack flies down the line, hits her on the shoulder and knocks her to the ground.

"I wanted you to dodge it, not catch it."

"Shut up, it's not funny." She kicks me in the leg, then pulls the pack between us. My hand touches it in the dark, feeling for what's there. Stuck to the outside is a harness with a vest just like I promised her. She pushes my hand away and rips it free from its Velcro straps.

The fire is getting close. The chopper blades push heavy air down on us. The popcorn keeps popping, keeping the men away. I put myself in front of Julia, so kernels won't hit her. *BAM!* Someone punches me in the back with an iron poker. That wasn't a poker; it was a bullet. Thank god for the vest. My adrenaline supercharges me, and my pain disappears.

My hands find the new goggles. I rip them free of their Velcro straps, tug them over my eyes, then pull the rifle out of a webbed sheath on the side of the backpack.

A rush of air goes by my face, followed by a gun crack. That bullet went right past my ear. They're either getting around the fire or they're shooting through it. My bruised back won't let me lift the rifle all the way, but my finger finds the trigger. Bullets fly at the fire-lit silhouettes, hurting my own ears.

"I'm in the harness and the vest! He gave us helmets too!"

I plop my helmet on my skull just as a bullet hits the back of my head. Damn it. I put the rifle down, find the straps on Julia's legs, arms, and chest, and yank them tighter.

"Too tight!"

"You'll live! You better, after what we've been through!" I push the rifle into her hands and wave at her to shoot the shadows coming at us. She squeezes off one shot, which knocks her back, and then she widens her stance and does it again.

I pull on my harness and bullet-proof vest. Julia grunts as a bullet hits her in the chest She retreats three steps, but then comes back angry and shooting.

PING! PING! PING! They're close enough to hit the helicopter hard now. Heavy popping comes from the above.

Carl screams over the noise of the blades.

I cinch my straps tight, grab the drop line, find a carabiner, reach behind Julia's vest, and clip her in. My hand follows the line and finds the next carabiner.

Julia motions for me to take the rifle back.

"You're a better shot!" I wave up at the chopper.

It rises, lifting Julia off the ground. Me next—

Six bullets hit my vest in the chest, and another grazes my cheek. Julia grunts above me. They're hitting her too.

A shape rushes out of the dark and grabs the harness loops around my thighs. I twist and kick but he hangs on tight.

Bald head. It's Peter Heyman. He looks up at me; his face has been altered with a gash of metal through his cheek. He's bright green in my night vision goggles like a grinning ghoul.

"Honu! Time to die!" He plunges a knife into my thigh, so deep that I feel nothing, but an involuntary jerking begins.

The chopper rises, pulling the knife against my leg. Heyman lets go and falls fifteen feet to earth, where he goes into a perfect parachutist roll, popping to his feet like a gymnast. Bastard.

Julia squeezes off five bullets in a row—sending red light from its tip and hurting my ears, but she hits Heyman in the hip. He spins and falls to the ground.

We keep rising. Another bullet rushes past my ear, and then three more punch my chest. Damn it. I already have a knife in my leg. I twist, and three more punches hit my back.

And, then…

The shots no longer reach us. The yelling disappears. The only noise comes from the chopper above us. The knife in my thigh is bad. I'm losing blood.

We are high, at least two thousand feet and we're flying west. There's a sliver of water in the distance. We're heading for that. The ocean. Far below my dangling feet are the brown rocks and valleys of Baja. They look pretty from here.

There's a road. Hell, it's probably Highway 1. Why does that surprise me? A wind comes off the ocean, swinging us like we're on a long trapeze. Julia drops the rifle. Good call, girlfriend.

My body shakes from the cold. Too cold. Am I dying?

We fly into the wind for ten minutes, then head over water. My shaking gets worse. Come on, Carl, land! Are we flying all the way to San Diego?

Then I see it—a barge with lights, floating on the water. We get closer. A man with two long, red lights in his hands waves us in, just like the airport guys at LAX. He crosses his arms, the chopper hovers, and the winch lowers us. They set me down on the barge surface, and, as my feet touch, someone rushes forward and detaches me. I fall to my hands and knees. Men shout in Portuguese. Carl hired the Brazilians. That makes me feel safe. Julia touches down next, a few feet from me. The harsh lights on the barge show the red, raised bubbles on her face and arms—she's burned.

"Eyes up! Man coming down!"

A man dressed in black camouflage flies down the line, the cord hissing. He touches the barge surface. It's Carl in full camo gear. He unclips, waves at the chopper, and it zooms away.

He rushes to Julia first and helps her take off her helmet and goggles. Her hair is charred, and she's got blisters on her scalp, face and arms. She points at me and yells to Carl.

Two more men yelling in Portuguese rush forward and surround her, pushing Carl back. One is carrying a first aid kit. Paramedics. Good.

Carl drops to his knees in front of me next, sending up a splash. We both look down and realize we're in a huge puddle of my own blood. He sees the knife so deep in my thigh, it has to be stuck in my bone.

"Him first!"

The paramedics surround me. "Don't pull the knife out."

Everything goes black.

CHAPTER 56

TINA SWIG

Sunday, March 17, 3:00 p.m. (CET)
Sicily

When we drop anchor, Messina is on the port side. Carlos pulls in the tender that we've been towing and ties it against the bottom swim step for easy boarding. We left Agrigento and made it around the bottom of Sicily and up to its northeastern tip in sixteen hours. We are moving fast, but not fast enough.

We drop off Ismael first. He'll actually appreciate the ancient city of Taormina in the hills. Then, we'll motor north to drop off Min in Amalfi and Elliot in Naples. None of them know this, however. The less they know about our plans, the less damage they could do to us later. The frat boys are packed and waiting below deck, like three Club Med employees who spent a great summer together but will never see each other again.

Whatever is happening in Baja is a mystery. Steven and Julia are supposed to be dead, but Douglas hasn't told me anything. Only he is in contact with Heyman.

Maybe he's tired. We've all been awake more than twenty-four hours. Or maybe we're screwed. I want these fucking kids off this ship.

Douglas calls the boys up from their cabins. They gather around the dining room table on the back deck, their hands jammed deep in their pockets, looking at their feet. Douglas emerges with a dark bottle of spirits and four cordial glasses. "A final drink before the first departure?"

Douglas sets the cordial glasses down on a table and uncorks the Goldschläger. "This is cinnamon flavored schnapps with gold leaf. Drink up, boys."

They pick up their glasses and stare at the gold leaf floating in their clear glasses.

"Is that real gold?" Elliot asks.

"Gold flake. For three hard-working, young men who are soon to be very rich. Cheers." Douglas holds up his glass and they all clink and drink.

"Not bad," Elliot says. "I like drinking gold."

The men stare at their empty cordial glasses and then at Douglas, their eyes wide like deer frozen in the headlights.

"It's not just gold. Each of you just drank a microchip designed to activate itself in the acids in your stomach, and then push through the wall of the small intestine and embed itself, where it will emit a constant signal. I'll always know where you are." They stare at him like shocked raccoons. I could wave my hand in front of their faces, and none of them would blink.

Douglas sets his drink down. It's still full. "Never contact each other again. If you do, I will know, and I will kill you. You can access your money in a few days. Transfer only enough so that you can stay off the grid until September. Enjoy a long spring and summer backpacking through Europe before contacting anyone you know.

Even your parents. No internet cafés, no phones, nothing. That chip will alert me if you do. Do you understand?"

"Yes, Boss Man," they all say in unison.

Douglas hands Ismael his passport. "Enjoy your new life. Now get off my ship."

Ismael picks his bag off the deck and darts down the stairs to the swim deck without making eye contact with any of us. He climbs in the tender, sits on a cushion, then glances down like he's ashamed. Carlos throws off the line and motors away.

Douglas goes into the main cabin, leaving Min and Elliot stunned and silent on the back deck. I follow him inside.

"That was amazing, my love. Are they really carrying embedded microchips?"

"Of course not. But they don't know that." He winks at me.

I kiss him on the lips. "Brilliant. And you made more than a billion dollars in less than a week."

"It was your idea. I just executed it."

"No one could have done it better."

I want to ask if Steven and Julia are still alive, but don't dare. I'll assume they are dead and that he will tell me when we're safe.

Douglas pulls me to him. He slides a hand down the back of my linen drawstring pants and touches my ass cheek. "Would you like to celebrate? In the master suite?"

My hands touch his chest. "Yes, but don't we need to worry about Elliot and Min? It will be several hours before we drop each of them off, and I won't feel completely comfortable until they're both gone."

"Carlos will be back in a few minutes. Once we're under way again, they'll stay on that back deck without moving or speaking."

I smile and kiss him. Nothing will feel comfortable until Devon, Douglas, and I board another yacht and our crew scuttles *Reckoning*, sending it to the bottom of the Mediterranean Sea. Then, we'll go ashore on Malta, where we have citizenship and new identities waiting for us, and our new lives can begin.

"May I speak to Devon first? I haven't spoken to him in hours."

"Of course. We have been neglectful. Both of us."

"Working for his benefit."

"Take your time, my love. I'll be in the master suite doing my final research." He kisses me, then heads off.

The engines rumble up and metal clanging starts as they pull the anchor off the sea floor. Either Carlos made it to shore and back in record time or the tender is going to catch up with the yacht while we're underway. The crew is wasting no time.

The main cabin looks bare. The walnut cabinets that held the computers and monitors are empty now. Douglas already tossed them to the bottom of the sea. No evidence remains of what we accomplished here.

On the other side of the sliding glass doors, Min and Elliot sit on opposite sides of the wide and empty back deck. They face each other without speaking, the wind whipping their hair, with the wake of our speeding yacht framed between them. Douglas is right; they won't speak for the next six hours.

I climb the teak stairs and tap on Devon's door.

"Enter, earthling." He uses his science fiction villain voice.

I enter his teenage lair. "Are you an alien from another world now?"

He motors toward me at a reasonable speed, and smiles. This time he's kind and gentle, which happens once in every six conversations. A mother can't ask for much more from her teenage son. "Yes, I am an alien. I always have been. Look at me."

"Don't say that. You're my son."

"Thinking of myself as an alien helps me survive this world. Somewhere in the galaxy, my planet awaits me."

"Let's start with a country. Pick one."

"What do you mean?"

"Douglas and I want you to pick a country where we can all live for a few years."

"I'd have to think about it."

"What about England?"

"Mom, if we're going to live in England, just say it. Don't pretend that I have a choice."

"I just thought you'd want to be closer to Cambridge and Professor Carlton. You're already a student there. You could finish your studies and get your PhD that much faster."

"I don't need a degree. I'm too cool for school."

Blood rushes to my head. I stop breathing.

"Mom? You look funny."

"What have you done?" I dash into his bathroom, grab a towel, and hang it over the intercom, tugging hard until I feel the terrycloth slip behind the metal. I look around for embedded cameras. Can he see us too?

Devon's zooms toward me. He looks scared. "What is it?"

My fists clench so tight my nails dig into the flesh of my palms. "Are you *Too Cool for School?*"

"Okay, I'll go to Cambridge!"

He moves to get out of the suite, but I pull a chair in front of the door and sit in it.

My eyes close. Inhale. Exhale. My lungs expand and contract ten times.

When they open again, Devon is six inches away, looking even more scared. "Mom. You're freaking me out."

301

Douglas still may be listening. My voice drops to a whisper. "Devon, this is very important. I won't be mad, but I need to know the truth."

"Okay," he whispers back.

"Have you been playing *The Rescue Game* online, and using the hashtag *Too Cool for School*?"

His face flushes to an even darker red. "I was having trouble with the Hodge conjecture. I needed to relax."

"So, the answer is yes?"

"Yes."

I close my eyes and exhale. My own son is *Too Cool for School*. How did this happen? The thought hits me and my eyes fly open. Devon has backed away and turned his chair so he's facing out the window. We are passing through the Strait of Messina, moving at a high speed. We'll be off the Amalfi Coast soon, but not soon enough.

"Look at me, Devon."

"I don't want to. I can answer better if I don't see your face."

The side of his face is wet. He's crying. My heart aches.

"Whispers only, okay? Are you and Rebecca…having an affair?"

"No…I mean, yes…we were—"

"It's not a bad thing."

"She wasn't doing it because she liked me. I mean, she did like me, but not that way. She was doing it because she was afraid."

"Afraid of what?"

"Afraid of Douglas."

It's making sense. So much sense that it digs a hole in my stomach that makes me nauseous. "I'm sorry."

"I do want a girlfriend. I want…"

"What do you want?"

He sighs. His lungs can't actually sigh that well, but his software allows him to choose a computer-generated human response. "I want to go to a planet where I fit in."

"So, she stopped it? Or did you?"

"I did. And I was stuck on the Hodge conjecture and bored, and you wouldn't let me off this boat. Rebecca does like me, too, just not in that way. And she knew she had to keep me happy, that was her job."

"So, what did she do?"

"She gave me the code to the Wi-Fi and told me about *The Rescue Game*."

"She told you about it?"

"She thought I'd like it, and I did. I was good at it. I solved the puzzles right away, and sent them in."

Obedient and perfect Rebecca. So silent. A cypher who I took for granted and ignored. She's known the entire time what we've been doing and betrayed us by telling Devon. Why? Either she hates Douglas or loves Douglas or both. She's been with him for almost a decade.

"Where is Rebecca now?"

"Gone. She said she was going to disappear and reinvent herself. She said you and Douglas would both understand."

My skin flushes hot. *Disappear and reinvent herself.* That's the phrase Douglas and I use with one another. She loves him but hates us both. Is that it?

When did we last have contact? She gave us cookies and espresso last night, before we pulled the plug on the game. She got off the yacht in Agrigento or Messina ....

Was she hiding on the tender that Ismael boarded? Did she swim? Call a water taxi?

It doesn't matter. She's gone now, and since Douglas has been paying her well for the past ten years, she really has disappeared. My teeth clench. "Bitch."

"I liked her, Mom. And she liked me. Just not that way. And it was wrong of Douglas to make her do that with me."

The ship rises and falls on the swells, motoring fast. We've left Sicily behind and we're in the open Tyrrhenian Sea now. We'll be off the Amalfi Coast in three hours, where Min gets dropped next. Douglas is in our master suite doing "research."

On what? On whether Steven and Julia are alive. On who *Too Cool for School* is. He'll know as much as I know—more—and soon.

My butt falls into a chair. *Always have a plan.*

Devon turns his chair and lowers himself so that we're eye to eye. "What is so bad about playing *The Rescue Game?* It was fun. Rebecca and I did it together. That's what I'm supposed to be doing with girls at my age, playing video games."

The ship slams down hard in a wave. My hand flies out and I lock his wheelchair into place.

He scowls. "I can do that electronically now, mother. You don't need to worry about me every minute."

"How long has she been helping you?"

"Since the game launched. She signed into the Wi-Fi, helped me take notes, and then wrote the submissions for me for *The Rescue Game.*"

"After I specifically told you that the internet was off limits, and that only I would send emails for you?"

Devon turns his chair to the window again. "You ignored me. You and Douglas thought if Rebecca gave me blowjobs I'd be happy on this dumb boat."

"That's disgusting. Don't talk that way."

"All I did was go online and play a storytelling app! That's one step below an online escape room."

"Shh. Devon, look at me. This is important. *Us against the world* important."

Devon hears me. *Us against the world* is what we'd say to each other back in my days as a single mom with no money, raising a disabled child.

He turns his wheelchair and faces me again. The whole room rises and falls as the yacht crashes through the swells. "We can tell each other anything. Right?"

"Yes."

"Douglas and I created *The Danger Game*. It's really happening. And you playing *The Rescue Game* has put us in danger."

Devon's eyes widen. "I'm seasick." He gags, then throws up on himself. His stomach problems are back.

I rush to the bathroom, grab a hand towel, and rush back. He pulls away at first, then allows me to wipe him clean. The smell of his bile sends me back a decade, when he'd throw up all the time, when he'd get sores in every chair we got him, when we'd have to clean and disinfect his breathing tubes again and again to keep his lungs and mouth clean from infection, when keeping him alive was a daily struggle.

Our eyes lock. We're back there in an instant—our shared battle. It's a closeness, our closeness, which I didn't think I'd ever miss once we got his health under control, once he found joy within the genius of his own mind.

"I've done terrible things, but for us. Because I know you can change the world."

He blinks at me, confused, then closes his eyes and nods. He puts his lips over his mouthpiece and twists his mouth until the voice of Paul Newman returns again. "And you want to protect me."

"Yes. And that's why you have to tell me everything."

"Okay."

"Have you been going online into chat rooms as *Too Cool for School?*"

"On Stack Exchange and the *Gamers Forever* subreddit. Rebecca did it for me."

"When you were throwing your tantrum yesterday because we shut down all communication, did you then go online again?"

"Rebecca said you changed your mind. She gave me her cell phone, and we used it as a Wi-Fi hot spot. She wanted me to do it. We were still in the harbor at Agrigento."

"Where's her phone now?"

His eyes point at the laptop computer mounted on his chair. The base is raised just enough to slide a cellphone underneath it—my fingers pull out her phone with the pink case. Damn, it's still on.

"Don't leave this room."

I dash down the staircase to the main floor, out on the back deck, and I throw the phone into the moving sea, trying to erase Rebecca and all the damage she's done.

It takes me just five seconds to get up the staircase and back inside his room. "How long did it take you to solve Steven Quintana's message?"

"Thirty minutes," He says, adding a hint of pride to his Paul Newman voice.

"The scribbles, the circle, the sticks...what was it?"

"Their latitude. I calculate it to be twenty-seven degrees north of the equator, plus or minus ten miles."

"How can you be so accurate?"

Devon laughs. "Mom, this is how they measured latitude around the world before computers. This is old school."

"What else do you know?"

"That they're in Baja, California, approximately fifteen miles from the Pacific Ocean. Quintana messaged that using sign language and Morse code."

He hits the return button on his keyboard. A map of a section of Baja comes on the screen on his chair, showing a section of the El Vizcaíno Biosphere Reserve. When Douglas installed the high speed, fiber-optic cable in Baja, he built several hidden warehouses up and down the remote peninsula, and that's damn close to where the warehouse is.

"Erase all of that."

Blue swells rush past the window. Soon, the Amalfi Peninsula will appear on the horizon, with its colorful towns tumbling down steep hillsides. But, I no longer give a shit about Italy. I don't want to stay long enough to even get a slice of fucking pizza. I want to dump Min there, and then Elliot in Naples, and be gone.

Devon comes alongside. "Are you planning?"

"I'm still thinking." If he sent the latitude message out, then they know where Steven and Julia are. Maybe Carl Webb and Trishelle are telling the FBI and LAPD everything. Or not. Peter Heyman should have killed Steven and Julia by now. Or Carl Webb got the message and performed his stupid action hero bit. I do not know.

But Douglas does. He's in the master suite, talking to his people around the world, figuring out exactly what happened, with up-to-the-minute updates about what's happening in Baja.

Figuring out that Rebecca is gone.

And figuring out that Devon is *Too Cool for School.*

Our perfect future is at risk.

Devon looks scared. It's the same scared look he'd give me before he went off to yet another new school, when I was still trying to mainstream him. Whether public or private, both had assholes who went out of their way to torture him. Some were feral losers, others were elitist pigs, but it happened enough the only option was to homeschool him with the best tutors that money could buy. I went out and got that money, and that look of fear went away. Now it's back, worse than ever.

"You'll be fine. I can handle this."

And the look disappears, because he believes me.

The ships intercom dings with a loud bell, right through the towel hanging on it. Douglas's voice comes booming through every speaker on the ship.

"Darling, will you please come to the master suite? I miss you."

Devon stares at me, looking for a "tell." I narrow my eyes and smile, refusing to show him any fear.

CHAPTER 57

CARL WEBB

I pace the fifth-floor visitors lounge of the Naval Medical VA Hospital. There's still no word on Julia or Steven, and we arrived here at 3:00 a.m. Our helicopter landed on the helipad on their roof, the doctors and nurses swept in, and wheeled them away.

The view out the west window is beautiful. The sun is rising, lighting up San Diego with bright gold light and making the edge of every building stand out. And here inside this building, hard-working government employees help veterans with PTSD, drug problems, health crises, and ceaseless pain. They deserve something pretty to look at.

My body and brain are exhausted. In the past twenty hours, I drove to the border, flew into Mexico on a fake surf trip, stopped in San Felipe to gas up and go through customs, crossed the peninsula, landed on a beach, zoomed on a speedboat out to a barge, and climbed into a search and rescue helicopter that the Mexican Navy uses to rescue vaquita porpoises from fishing nets in the Sea of Cortez. At least it had a working winch with a moving arm mounted inside. They gave me a motorcycle helmet to wear, for shit's sake. After begging on the phone, the Reys gave me two semi-automatic rifles before I climbed on board. And the Rey brothers are not cheap. Their bill will cost me—

"Hey, handsome."

Trishelle stands in the entryway, wearing a pink, polka-dotted summer dress, and movie star sunglasses on her forehead. Even after a long nighttime drive from Malibu, she looks great.

"Hello, beautiful. Did you dress that way for me?"

"I know nice clothes make you happy." She kisses me on the lips, then closes her eyes, and lays her head on my chest. We hold each other for a while, feeling our breath fill and empty in our lungs.

She pulls away. "When was the last time you slept?"

"I can nap if I'm moving. I slept in the chopper on the way back."

She pats my cheek, then leaves her hand there. "You done good, Carl Webb. You got them back."

"Don't thank me yet."

"They're alive. I'm thankful."

"So am I."

"Your name has no pull in the lobby, but, when I mentioned Julia, they were all smiles."

"I called from the chopper, and they didn't agree to admit them until I mentioned her. If you get shot, stabbed, tortured and burned, it pays to be a celebrity."

Trishelle stiffens. "Burned? You didn't say she was burned."

My teeth clench. Steven is much worse off than Julia; the knife wound may kill him. He lost buckets of blood.

"How bad is it? Just tell me."

"She has second-degree burns on her scalp, face, and arms."

Her eyes narrow and her nostrils flair. She's about to go off—

"Good morning, Mr. Webb." A woman doctor, barely five feet tall, walks toward us. "I'm Dr. Rao, I'm in charge of Julia and Steven." Her voice has an island lilt. She's probably from Trinidad, and she just saved me from a tongue-lashing.

"Dr. Rao, this is Trishelle Hobbes, Julia's best friend."

Dr. Rao's face brightens. "I read about you!"

"How are they?" Trishelle asks.

"Julia is stable. She was shot in her hip, but the bullet went clean through her fatty tissue. She has deep bruises on her belly and back, but there is no internal bleeding. She has bad lacerations on her hands and feet, which needed careful cleaning and then stitches. She also has second-degree burns on her arms, her right cheek, her forehead, and a lot of her hair burned away."

"Second-degree burns? That's bad, right?" Trishelle asks.

Dr. Rao smiles that calm smile doctors give when they deliver difficult news. "She will heal. She's lucky. This is the best trauma center in California. Veterans with worse burns get treated here all the time."

"And Steven?" I ask.

"He's still in surgery. He lost a lot of blood. The knife nicked but did not sever the major artery in his leg. The medic on the helicopter applied a tourniquet and taped the knife in place. That probably will save his life."

"Probably?"

"His pinky finger was cut off and the wound is infected. Bacteria entered his bloodstream, which led to blood poisoning, and his body has gone into septicemia."

Sepsis is bad. Soldiers got it in Afghanistan when we couldn't close their chest wounds fast enough. Half of them died.

"He and his brother call themselves the cockroaches. He'll make it."

"Once he comes out of surgery, the fight will be up to him."

Trishelle slides herself under my arm and hugs me. "Let's get breakfast."

We're at the door of Old Town Mexican Café as it opens at 8:00 a.m. The waiter looks at me funny. Trishelle looks great in her polka dot dress but I'm still dressed in dirty black camos.

"This place is famous for its shrimp tacos." Trishelle is trying to lighten the mood, but we only order coffee and toast. I spread the orange marmalade, covering every inch of the sourdough slice before eating.

"You're doing a good job with that toast."

It gives me something to do. What happened after I left?"

"When you radioed at ten o'clock that you had them, we got supercharged. Darna, Rafael, and Glenn kept looking for *Too Cool for School* until they collapsed at midnight."

"Any luck?"

She shrugs. "I don't know. I was too busy dodging McCusker and Gum. They even came by the house, but I wouldn't buzz them in. And then I got your text at three in the morning and drove down here."

"They'll find us. They didn't return my calls for almost a week. At least now we can help Mendoza and Marsh's families."

Trishelle's phone rings. She shows me: *Niall McCusker, LAPD.* We're the only ones in the restaurant this early on Sunday. Trishelle sets the phone down on the table, puts it on speaker, and answers. "This is Trishelle."

"This is McCusker. Is Webb with you?"

"Yes, he is. We're both in San Diego."

Carl leans in. "And I could have used your help last night."

"That's not funny."

"I'm not trying to be funny. I'm pissed. My friends are in surgery. Steven may not make it."

"I already know everything. Both of you go to the FBI Field Office in San Diego and turn yourselves in."

"Turn ourselves in?" Trishelle asks.

My hands wave at her to stay calm. "Do you have information on Swig and Bushnell? "They're the ones behind this."

"We'll discuss this in the Field Office. I'll be there soon. They're expecting both of you. If you don't show up, there will be warrants for your arrest." He hangs up, and Trishelle gives her phone the middle finger.

Wisconsin comes flooding back. My toast tastes sour as a cloud of sadness darkens the room. Julia and Steven are alive, but Mendoza and Marsh are dead, and will always be dead. My job was to protect them, and now I will wake up thinking about them for years to come.

My phone rings next: *Major Glenn Ward.* I put it on speakerphone. "Whaddya got, Major?"

"I found Bushnell and Swig."

Trishelle and I lean in so fast we bump heads. "We're both here. Talk to us."

"We traced the last submission from *Too Cool for School,* when he solved their latitude. It came from an unsecure cell phone, which we traced to a town on the southern coast of Sicily."

Adrenalin recharges my muscles in a second. "Are you tracking that cell phone?"

"Yes. It moved along the south of the coast, as smooth as a yacht on the high seas, then rounded the southeastern tip of Sicily and headed up through the Strait of Messina. Then we lost it."

"*Too Cool for School* is on a yacht?" Trishelle asks.

"Hey, I'm just tracking him," Glenn says. "We called your guys at the National Reconnaissance Office, and they agreed to look at photos of Agrigento from yesterday. Guess what? There was only one mega yacht outside the harbor. I called the harbormaster—"

Trishelle bangs on the table. "The name, Glenn."

"*Reckoning.* She's cigarette-shaped, black and white, totally Bushnell's style. We're trying to locate her with current satellite photos now."

"Glenn, you are the best."

"Thank you, Sergeant Webb."

"Don't let anyone through the gate until someone shows up with a warrant. By then, I'll be on my way to Europe."

"Hurry. Knowing Bushnell, he'll sink the yacht soon." Glenn hangs up.

We toss a twenty-dollar bill on the table and head for the exit. Trishelle opens the door for me. "I guess we're not going to the FBI Field Office in an hour."

"Nope. Glenn is right about Bushnell, and we don't have time to explain it to them."

"Wait. *Too Cool for School* is with Bushnell? That doesn't make sense," Trishelle says.

"It will once I get there," I say.

She chirps open her Audi and slides behind the wheel. "So, handsome, know any Brazilians with a helicopter near the coast of Italy?"

I slide in the passenger seat. "I have some ideas, but we need a private jet to get us there. Got any pull with studio heads, Ms. Producer?"

Trishelle zooms out of the parking lot and turns east back toward Balboa Park and the Navy Hospital. "Not anymore. This experience has been career suicide for Julia. But, I have an idea."

"What?"

She accelerates. "Larry Naythons and *Celebrity Exposed.*"

CHAPTER 58

JULIA TRAVERS

Sunday, March 17, 9:00 a.m. (PST)
California

I wake up in a hospital. My body can't sit up. My head feels
heavy. A nurse, an African-American woman with big curves
in tight blue scrubs, leans over me. She smells like orange
blossom soap. She touches my shoulder and shushes me to lie back
down.

"You'll be fine. Just rest."

That voice. A whisper that I heard in my sleep. My dreams.
Good dreams. She even sang to me. She'll know. "How's Steven? Is
he okay?"

"He's coming out of surgery. I know your boyfriend. He's a sexy
man."

"You know Steven?"

"At the VA Hospital in Los Angeles, after he got shot almost two
years ago. He liked my sponge baths."

"I should treat him to that. He might listen to me more often."

"That's right, sister. He'll stay closer to home. I met you once,
too, when you picked him up after he was released. My name's
Crystal."

I touch my head, just to make sure it's there. My fingers find a helmet of gauze padding on the right side, covering my right eye. "I don't feel anything."

Crystal pulls my hand down. "Don't touch. You're on pain killers. You'll feel everything soon enough. You have visitors."

She dodged the question. A man and a woman float in, backlit against the sunny window. The woman smiles. It's Trishelle, which makes me happy. And Carl. He was on the helicopter. My heart beats fast.

I try to sit up again, but Trishelle's cool fingers touch my shoulder. "Stay down. Listen. We need your permission for something."

Carl moves close. "We found Bushnell's yacht off Italy. Larry Naython's corporate jet will land at the San Diego airport in one hour to fly me there. But he wants something."

"Let me guess. He wants an exclusive interview with me."

Trishelle nods. "And video. And photos. Today."

We have to get Carl on that plane but talking to Larry Naythons would crush me right now. "I need to see Steven."

Crystal shakes her head. "That's not possible."

"You just said he's out of surgery. All I want to do is squeeze his hand."

"You're on an IV."

"Give me a wheelie one. This will happen, Crystal."

Crystal opens her mouth to argue, then sighs. "Let me check."

Minutes later, I'm in a wheelchair with an IV suspended overhead. Crystal pushes me to post-op with Carl and Trishelle close behind.

"You're tough, Julia Travers."

"So are you, Crystal." My teeth are clenched. It's the best way to not scream out in pain from my burned arms and face, my bruised belly, and the bullet hole in my hip.

A nurse pushes away a curtain, and Crystal wheels me up to Steven's post-op gurney. His face is pink, but he's wearing an oxygen mask. His eyes are closed. I find his right hand and squeeze: *1, 2, 3.*

Nothing.

I love you.

Still nothing.

Crystal frowns, feeling my frustration. "He's out, dearie."

"He's in there somewhere." I keep squeezing.

You got us out, like you promised. I am injured, but OK. The doctor said you must fight.

Still nothing. Screw it. I'm going to keep talking.

Carl found Swig on a yacht near Italy. He's flying on Larry Naython's plane.

Steven's eye's flutter. His hand squeezes mine: *Go.*

He squeezed my hand! Crystal and I exchange looks; she saw it, too.

Carl is going, he'll catch her.

Steven squeezes, but the pressure is weak: *You ... go ... too.*

Steven's hand drops away from mine just as Carl appears at my shoulder.

"I'm going with you."

"You've been shot. Your hands and feet have stitches. You have burns."

"It's a private jet. Put a bed and a doctor on too. Larry can interview me there. It'll be a better story. He'll agree. I want to see Tina's face when we catch her."

"What about Steven? Don't you want to be here for him?"

"He wants me to go. He just told me."

317

Carl scoffs and rolls his eyes, then paces and waves his arms and swears, just like he always does. But Trishelle grins at me. That's my girl. She'll make it happen.

CHAPTER 59

STEVEN QUINTANA

Sunday, March 17, 9:00 a.m. (PST)
California

It's lighter. The singing voice is back. It smells like oranges and flowers. The voice holds my hand and squeezes.

"Julia said you squeezed back. So, I know you're in there."

My hand has no strength to squeeze back.

It's up to you now. You have to fight."

The Ferrari explodes. Heyman traps us on the subway. He shoots me with a dart. It's cold and dark. They're beating me. They make me punch Julia. I hate myself. I have to fight them—

A hand touches me. The voice is back. "I was wrong. Don't fight. Rest. Be patient."

Sleep.

CHAPTER 60

TINA SWIG

Sunday, March 17, 7:00 p.m. (CET)
Italy

H e slams into me. "You're hurting me."

He lifts one hand off the mattress and chokes me. If I fight back, he'll know. If I do nothing, he may increase the pain, trying to break me.

So, I fake it. My hips match his thrusts, pretending that the pain he's inflicting is pleasure. My fingers caress his hand around my neck, as if his choking hold is launching me into bliss.

I pretend to orgasm—and it drives him over the edge. He climaxes.

"Slap me." He lets go of my neck and punches the left side of my face again and again. Every punch makes me think of Devon. *Let your anger out on me not him.*

He collapses, and rolls off me. We stare at the ceiling, catching our breath. I can't look at him. "How much do you know?"

My face throbs. "I know how much I love you."

He stays quiet. The ship's intercom whistles. I want to look out the window, but don't dare. We're off the Amalfi Coast. Carlos will be taking Min ashore soon.

"Don't move." Douglas pops off the bed, puts on his underwear, pulls on his silk drawstring pants, and yanks a pullover over his head.

He leaves the master suite and locks the door from the outside. I'm his prisoner, just like Quintana and Travers. Are they dead? Alive?

My body is frozen. My eyes stay on the ceiling. Does he have cameras looking at me? Five minutes pass. The tender motor starts up. I have to see.

My body rolls off the bed and limps to the port window. The houses of Amalfi climb the steep cliff like a set of tiny dollhouses. Devon and I need to get off this yacht and disappear into those tiny streets.

By leaning close to the curved glass, I can see the ship's stern. Min and Elliot are getting into the tender. Both of them are getting off? Then, the captain and first mate get in as well. Then the chef and the housekeeper hop in, whom I've only seen a few times. Douglas stands on the back deck, his hands on his hips, watching Carlos drive the small boat away with six people. Douglas changed the plan. Shit.

He glances back at this window. I step back, even though the glass is tinted black, so he can't see me anyway. Still, he may sense that he's being watched.

He wants answers, and he plans to get them out of me.

I see my reflection in the tinted window. My cheeks are swollen and blue. My eye is swelling up. He beat me, and he's going to beat me again.

The ship's engines start up. The tender couldn't be back already. He's leaving Carlos ashore as well. Douglas, Devon, and I are the only people on board. Douglas will run the ship from his computer tablet. It'll be easy. It's a straight shot to the middle of the Tyrrhenian Sea, where he'll board another yacht and sink *Reckoning*. The only question is whether Devon and I will be on that new yacht with him or sinking with this one.

He'll be back in two minutes. Goosebumps make me realize that I'm still naked. I pull on a terrycloth robe and yank it tight.

Always have a plan.

Maybe there's something in the wet bar. A tool. A knife. The fridge holds only vegetables for juicing, vitamins, and fish oil supplements. My face swells from all the blood rushing to my injuries. It's tingling, but there's too much adrenaline in my body to feel pain.

His bullet blender is on the counter, the one he uses to make his green smoothies, and his coffee with yak butter and MCT oil. I yank it apart and pull out the circular chopping blade.

Next stop is the bathroom. Anything here? There's a mop in the cleaning closet. My mind flashes back to my days mopping up in the Italian restaurant in my late teens. I won't go back to that.

Next to the closet is his hexagon-shaped cryochamber. I open its door a touch. I then face the mirror, place the blade on the counter, then put toothpaste on a toothbrush.

The door unlocks. I wrap a hand towel tight around my hand, and hide the blade under it, then pick up the toothbrush and start brushing. My reflection shocks me. The entire left side of my face is black and purple, and my left eye is swollen shut. He walks into the bathroom and stands behind me, catching my eyes in the mirror.

"Hello, beautiful."

I spit out toothpaste. "Hello, my love."

"You moved. I told you to stay on the bed."

"I was worried about my breath. And I wanted to—"

"What?"

I start to cry. "Put on makeup. To cover my ..."

He makes a shushing sound and moves close behind me. He slides his smartphone out of his pocket and shows me the screen. There's a black and white QR code on it.

"That's the code for our bitcoin account. Pretty, isn't it?"

"Very."

"That's what a billion dollars looks like, turned it into a black and white digital painting. See?" He shows me with his thumb, as if teaching me how to use an app. "Just touch the app on the screen and this pops up, along with our 27-digit code. And, now, we can go anywhere in the world. Be anything. Be anyone."

"Total freedom. We can reinvent ourselves."

"And I can find my Einsteins. And all the money is yours."

"Mine?"

"All of it. I already have money, remember? You earned this. And we won the game. And you remember what I chose for the passcode to my phone?"

"My birthday."

"That's right. Because we love each other." He slides his phone inside his pocket and puts both hands on the counter, trapping me between them. My eyes catch his and he leans close. "The only question is whether it's the three of us, or the two of us. Just tell me what Devon did. You don't want to see him—"

Devon's name is the trigger. My clenched left fist flies back with the blender blade, driving it straight into his left eye. He screams and staggers back. I spin and punch the base of my palm into the same spot, slamming the round plastic base flush with his eye socket.

He staggers back against the cryochamber. The door falls all the way open and I push him inside, close it, then jam the long mop between the door handles. He kicks against the door, almost breaking the metal and wood. I press my back against it, then search with my hand along the outside, find the control panel, and turn it on high. It hums to life, blasting cold air. He kicks again and almost breaks through.

I prop my legs against the marble bathroom counter, bracing my back flat against the cryochamber doors. My thighs are strong from years of running, which I intend to do for years more, once I get off this yacht.

"I loved you, Douglas. Right up until you hurt me."

The chamber is louder now. Frozen nitrogen gas seeps through the crack against my back. It's so cold it burns me, but it's Devon and me against the world again.

He screams and kicks against the doors with new strength. He knows it's life or death for him now. The doors flex and almost open against my back. I lock my knees and push my feet against the marble edge. I can stay this way for hours.

CHAPTER 61

CARL WEBB

I pace the narrow aisle of the Lear Jet, staring at my phone, willing it to ring. This plane lands at the Rome airport in thirty minutes and Interpol is supposed to send a message that an Italian Special Forces team and helicopter is waiting for me. Glenn and my Miami office arranged it, but there's no confirmation. Nothing. Nada.

"Sit down." Trishelle pats the plush leather seat next to her.

"I've called in every favor I have stashed in every country around the world, and, after this, I'll have nothing left. And I'm hundreds of thousands in debt."

"Do you mind?" Larry Naythons asks. "I'm trying to conduct an interview." He swivels in his thick leather chair next to Julia, who's propped up on a medical gurney and wearing a gauze bandage on her head as big as a turban, which then wraps down the right side of her face, covering her right eye.

I hold up my phone. "I'm trying to arrange an international arrest."

"And you're still on *my* jet, Mr. Webb."

I plop down next to Trishelle. She squeezes my arm and smiles. At least she knows what's at stake.

My ear hurts from being on the phone all the way from San Diego to the East Coast. After we refueled in NYC, I couldn't reach anybody, so I slept for four hours—my first solid sleep in three days.

When we got close to Spain, the Italian Army finally called. My company provided expertise when they rescued Italian oil refinery workers kidnapped in Mozambique a few years back. Because of that they have agreed to help me now, but only if Interpol confirms the evidence Glenn submitted about Bushnell and his yacht. It turns out that they've been seeking a positive ID on him and want Bushnell for their own reasons. But for the past two hours it's been silent.

My survival pack is ready, just in case we end up floating on a life raft in the Mediterranean. My Taurus is on my hip, fully loaded with spare ammo on my belt. It's a little gift from the Brazilians as they submitted their invoice for two hundred thousand dollars, plus fifty thousand dollars to the Mexican Coast Guard for looking the other way. They require payment by Friday.

I am so fucking broke.

My headset is around my neck, ready to plug into any walkie the Italians give me. But, no matter how hard I stare at it, I can't make my phone ring.

I look at Trishelle. "If this doesn't ring soon, we're screwed."

"Staring at it won't help."

If McCusker and Gum got their warrant and are inside the Malibu house, it may all be over anyway. They and the FBI could nix our plan with Interpol before we even get to Rome.

Julia laughs, still radiating star appeal.

"How does she do it? She was trapped in a cement bunker a few days ago."

Trishelle nods. "Because she's a pro."

"She must be in pain."

"From the burns? Or from talking to Naythons?"

Naythons glares at us. He heard that. He had a row of seats taken out, so they could fit in the gurney and the beeping machines. The reporter he dragged along is in the closest seat, aiming a smart phone at them. That's all you need to do interviews now.

"I must check her," Doctor Isaac says from the aisle behind me. Naythons forced Doctor Isaac and the nurse, a Navy Ensign named Sarah, into seats in the back, to keep them out of the shot.

Naythons waves him away. "I need ten more minutes."

"Let him do his job," Julia says, and waves him over. The celebrity always wins.

Dr. Isaac darts to her side. He checks her pulse, then slides a blood pressure cuff up her arm. "Your bandages are getting wet again. We'll have to change them."

Larry holds up his hand. "Can't it wait until we land? We're almost there."

My phone finally rings. I answer fast. "This is Webb."

"Carl, it's Bruno." Hearing his voice makes me smile. Colonel Bruno Cappello and I have helped each other several times over the past decade.

"I'm glad it's you, Colonel. What's the news?"

"We're in contact with Major Glenn Ward. *Reckoning* is headed toward Sardinia, two hundred miles west of Rome, and they're moving fast."

"What are you flying?"

"An A129 Mangusta. We can cross the Tyrrhenian with it, but we cannot crisscross the sea looking for them. And we're going to burn fuel going full speed."

"Understood. Glenn says the yacht has a helipad. We can touch down, get them, then go on to Sardinia."

"Interpol says that the FBI wants to arrest you when you land in Rome."

Naythons waves at me. "Mr. Webb? Can you sit down and be quiet please?"

I keep talking. "Can they wait and arrest me in Sardinia? After we catch Bushnell?"

"I'll see you on the tarmac," he says, and hangs up. Bruno didn't say "yes," but he didn't say "no," either.

The landing gear clunks into place. The steward touches my arm. "Please sit down, sir, we're landing."

I buckle in, then watch Naythons pepper Julia with more questions. He never lets up, and she doesn't fade. I don't understand the celebrity game, but I have to admit they're both pros.

"Be honest, is all this real?"

"What do you mean?"

"You're an amazing actor and a successful producer. The explosion at your Malibu press conference was only nine days ago. Some people doubt it even happened."

"You saw the episodes. Of course, it happened."

"People are saying you produced it all. The explosion, the kidnapping, *The Danger Game, The Rescue Game*—even the bandages and this plane ride. It could all be an elaborate hoax designed to make money, or a brilliant new kind of entertainment. What do you say to your critics?"

Julia stares at him with a frozen blank face. But knowing Julia, she can't be stunned. She finally laughs.

"The same haters said I was a dumb blonde who just got lucky. Now, they say I'm an evil genius capable of constructing a gigantic secret conspiracy. That would make me a brilliant dumb blonde, wouldn't it?"

Naythons didn't get the answer he wanted…until he laughs too. The wheels touch down. When the cameraman lowers his smart phone, Julia makes a cutting motion. "Interview over. Done."

"No, it's not." Larry wags his finger at her.

"Yes, it is, love. We've arrived. That was the deal."

"And you're here because of me. Quid pro quo, Julia Travers."

"True. We need each other. So, thank you."

He puts his hands in prayer position. "You're welcome."

Julia smiles, then stares out the opposite window to avoid looking at him.

We taxi to an isolated section of the airport, where a Blackhawk helicopter is waiting. Colonel Bruno Cappello stands by the open door of the sleek, green, Italian Army chopper, already in his flight suit with his helmet under his arm.

I slide on my survival pack and tighten my vest. The moment the steward lowers the staircase, I'm down the steps with my headset on. Cappello tosses me my walkie talkie, and I plug in.

His voice crackles. "We leave in sixty seconds."

"Copy." I flash him the thumbs up as he boards the chopper through the copilot door. With Bruno, the pilot, copilot, and me, it's a four-man operation. He probably didn't even file a proper flight plan.

"Carl!"

Trishelle runs toward me. Behind her, Dr. Isaac, Ensign Sarah, the two stewards, and even Naythons are lifting Julia on her gurney out of the plane and onto the tarmac. The reporter is still shooting it all.

Trishelle gets close. "Julia insists she gets to go. She wants to stare at Tina Swig in handcuffs as you fly them to jail."

Shit. I forgot that was the deal. The helicopter starts, and the blades whip up wind around us. Julia stares at me with one blue eye, her hair on the left side of her head flapping alongside the bandages. Even with one eye, her thousand-yard-stare could drop a gazelle on the Serengeti.

I have to admit, I'd like to see that too. I click my walkie. "Requesting permission to bring a doctor, nurse, and patient on a gurney."

Inside the chopper, Bruno leans between the pilot and copilot as they gesticulate like frustrated Italians. Bruno crackles back on. "Six max. Only the patient and the doctor."

"Thank you, Colonel."

"Carl, *dopodiché, siamo pari.* After this, we are even. *Capiche?*"

It helps that I rescued his men before. "*Capiche. Grazie.*"

I walk back to the group. The reporter lifts his smartphone to record me, but I shoot him one glare and he lowers it. "Julia and Dr. Isaac only."

Dr. Isaac and Ensign Sarah get Julia, her gurney, and the first aid kit onto the helicopter in record time. Navy medics know their shit. Ensign Sarah backs away. I climb on after the doc. Of course, the reporter is recording video as the chopper revs up. Trishelle, my guitar-playing muse, blows me a kiss as I close the door.

CHAPTER 62

JULIA TRAVERS

Monday, March 18, 11:00 a.m. (CET)

My face and scalp feel like burnt meat. My body screams for pain killers.

Why did I look when I slammed down that rock? Steven told me not to look.

Steven, where are you right now? Are you awake? Alive?

The wind screams through the open side window of the helicopter. Water is far below. The bandages are too tight to turn my head, but Carl and Dr. Isaac are just a foot away. The wind shakes us like a toy.

Dr. Isaac yells in my ear. "I'm changing the bandages!" He peels off the layers of gauze surrounding my skull. When he reaches bare skin, the shock of the wind hurts at first, and then numbs me.

"How do I look?"

"I've seen worse." He applies fresh gauze and wraps me up with new bandages. He does it perfectly, even with the wind blowing in the helicopter. He has bandaged wounded people on windy helicopters before, probably with people shooting at him.

No more self-pity. Steven looked worse after our last adventure, when Heyman made him look like a turtle. I shot him as we were lifting off, and I'm glad. I hope he's bleeding to death under a cactus. I wish I had that rifle again, so I could shoot both Tina and Bushnell and watch them die.

No. That would make me worse than them. Just watching her get handcuffed will be enough. Then, I'll stare at her the entire way back to shore.

Minutes pass. The pain increases. Dr. Isaac stares at me. "I'm going to give you a painkiller. To rest."

"No! Give me something to keep me awake."

He glances to the side and confers with someone on my blind side. It must be Carl. Isaac nods and turns back to me. "Okay. You will feel invincible, but you're not. You're wounded. Understand?"

I nod. He preps the needle, and it goes into my arm.

Walkie talkies crackle, then Carl's face leans in front of mine.

"We spotted the yacht. We're landing in five minutes."

Steven, if you can hear me, it's happening. It's ending now.

CHAPTER 63

STEVEN QUINTANA

Monday, March 18, 2:00 a.m. (CET)

The ocean is warm. The water rises and falls under me, just far enough off the beach that the swells haven't turned into waves yet. A turtle pops his head up next to me, then another. It breathes through its black beaked nose and blinks…then goes back under.

Honu. Hawaiian for turtle. My leg is bleeding. The water around me turns dark as wine. A huge fin passes by. A shark. They always show up whenever I'm hurt and in the water.

Someone squeezes my hand. It's the turtle again, except turtles don't have hands.

"Steven, you're in a coma. But I know you can hear me."

The turtle sounds just like my brother Anthony. In fact, he transforms into Anthony right before my eyes. Except he's a thirteen-year-old version of Anthony, and our family's camper van is on the beach, and my parents are waving next to the campfire because dinner is ready. We're on the beach in Baja, one of the best trips of my life, when I learned how to surf, speak Mexican slang as good as my father, and we saw turtles.

"If you can hear me, squeeze my hand."

What's the big deal, Tony? I squeeze his turtle hand as we float there in the water.

The sky pulses. A vibration moves through me.

Steven, if you can hear me, it's happening. It's ending now.

That's Julia's voice, barely there, but it vibrates through the water. No. It's part of the breeze. The sky moves like a sheet that someone's shaking.

"You're going back into surgery," Anthony says, and he lets go of my hand.

My body sinks under the water and falls back asleep.

CHAPTER 64

Monday, March 18, Noon (CET)

Devon and I are not starting over. That money is ours.

I left the cryochamber running while I spent the night with Devon. When he saw my battered face and no Douglas, he knew what I'd done without having to ask. He's a smart boy and trusts his mother.

The machine's been off long enough. Time to do this. Fast.

I yank open the door. Douglas is crouched at the bottom, hugging his knees, his eyes closed, like he's relaxing at the end of one of his yoga sessions. He's like a peaceful white marble carving, except for the blender blade still embedded deep inside his left eye.

His frozen phone is still in his pocket. If there's justice in the world, it'll work again.

I whisper to Douglas. "I will always love you. There will be no other. And I promise to put this to good use."

I race up the stairs to the bridge. Douglas took me up here only a few times, and always with the captain. The wide windows give a perfect view of the whole front end of the ship, rising and falling against the waves. It's either on automatic pilot or someone is driving this thing remotely. We're moving fast with no land in sight.

Devon and I need to get off this ship, and I don't have a plan.

A dozen screens are embedded into a long panel under the windows. Each is a console that communicates something—location, wind speed, wave size, fuel levels. *Reckoning* is tiny on one of them, a dot in the vast Mediterranean Sea. *Reckoning* is huge on another, with the engines lit up orange, the cooling system lit up blue, the electrical system red. What do I push? I'm on a goddamned spaceship.

Typing appears across a screen. The engine noise changes as the ship slows. The remote captain and first mate are probably looking at the same images on their screens, somewhere else in the fucking world, steering this yacht like it's a drone.

I don't have a plan.

Douglas would know what to do. Except he's dead and frozen in his cryochamber, killed by the machine that was supposed to help him live forever.

No, I killed him.

He knew better. He made me react. I wish he were here now, so I could tell him—

Get a grip, Tina. Think.

The screens hold the answer. The one in the middle shows our heading. We're not heading to Malta, like Douglas promised. We'd be going south now, but the yacht is pointed straight at Sardinia.

Douglas was always planning on sinking this ship once we were done.

How would he do it? Think.

He'd do it elegantly. He wouldn't lift a finger. It would just seem to happen. Another yacht would appear on the horizon. *Reckoning* would stop. The new yacht would send over their tender. We'd board the tender with just a laptop and an overnight bag, with enough extra space for Devon and his wheelchair. The new yacht would already have everything we'd ever need, including new clothes. Our new suites would look exactly like the ones on *Reckoning*, right down to the posters on Devon's wall. We'd sail away on the new yacht and watch *Reckoning* blow a hole in its hull, nothing dramatic, and it would sink beneath the waves.

He already did all the work. All he would have to do now is send a signal, probably with his smartphone or tablet. Maybe he already has. Or maybe they're waiting for the final signal. Maybe they don't need a signal, maybe they're tracking *Reckoning* via radar, and know to meet us when we get to a certain longitude and latitude.

I need a plan.

The walkie talkie crackles, making me jump. Who's on board?

"Mom, I'm scared," Devon says through the walkie. He uses a typical boy's voice, one I haven't heard before.

I grab the walkie and hit the button. "I'm here, my love. We're fine. We're safe. I'm just trying to figure something out. We're leaving the ship soon."

There's a pause, then I hear one click for yes.

I click again. "I love you," I say, and he clicks back once. He loves me, too.

My heart aches. He's been alone for hours. He went searching for me, got on the elevator, found a way to push the button with his one good hand, found a walkie in the galley, got it onto his laptop table somehow, and found a way to push the button while still using his mouthpiece. It must have taken every ounce of energy and effort his twisted body could manage.

I must hail that new ship. The ship's computer and keyboard are right in front of me. The Wi-Fi and router are turned off just as Douglas demanded. Could it be this easy? I turn them both on and see the reception jump from zero to four bars.

The computer screen dings with six instant messages from Navionics, from Boat Beacon, from Seapilot…what are those? They all say the same thing.

We will be waiting at the transfer point. Copy?

My heart jumps. We're going to make it. My fingers fly across the keys.

Sorry for the delay. We're programmed to slow when we reach you, correct?

My heart skips a beat when the answer comes.

Yes. Our tender will come to you. Please be waiting on the lower aft deck. Our bosun will invite you down onto the swim platform and onto our tender once we tie alongside. There will be a swell. Help from your bosun will be appreciated.

I have no bosun. He got off at Amalfi. Douglas is dead. Time to lie.

Our bosun fell ill and left the ship in Amalfi.

There is a long pause, then their answer. *Understood. Please give us your confirmation code per your instructions.*

Douglas thought of everything. My brain searches for an answer.

Understood. I will send the code prior to the transfer point. Look for us on the aft deck.

There is another long pause. *Understood.*

How much time did that buy me? And what the fuck is the code?

A low whipping noise starts. Helicopter blades? A side console shows all the ship's cameras. An Army helicopter is approaching. It's about a quarter mile away.

A belt tightens around my chest, squeezing my ribs with every beat of my heart.

"Fuck, fuck, fuck, fuck, fuck!"

The walkie crackles. "Mom, did you hear that?"

My thumb presses the call button. "Devon, meet me on the aft deck."

He clicks once for yes.

I need a gun. I rip through the wood cabinets against the back wall. No gun. I open more cabinets. No gun. Fuck.

The cameras show that the helicopter is right overhead. The ceiling whines and then clunks like it's about to collapse. I scream and cover my head—but it's the runners of the helicopter landing on the helipad roof above me.

Think.

There's one last cabinet by the captain's chair. I flip it open. My left eye is too swollen to see. My right eye spots a flare kit. Inside is a flare gun with two flares. I load one, keep the other in my hand, and head down the bridge stairs to the middeck.

I pause under the lip of the sunroof. Prepare. Inhale. Remember hunting for deer in Wisconsin. Step out, spin, aim, hold your breath and squeeze the trigger on the exhale.

I step out and turn—and a force rips into my left shoulder, flinging the flare gun out of my hand and down the stairwell to the aft deck. I'm bleeding.

Webb is on the sunroof. He aims his gun at me while the helicopter blades slow to a stop on the helipad above him.

Webb flips over and lands on the deck in front of me like a circus acrobat. "Lie down, Tina. Now."

No way.

In two seconds, I'm down the stairs and on the bottom aft deck. Where's that flare gun? The yacht lurches. Shit, that's right. It's programmed to slow at the transfer point.

I run to the railing. Another yacht is a quarter mile away, a beautiful blue and gold behemoth twice the size of *Reckoning*. It's sleek and gorgeous and fast, and it's coming to rescue us! I wave with my good hand, jumping so they can see me.

The ship turns.

"Come back!"

"Mom."

Devon is on the aft deck, waiting for me just like I told him. He seems calm. Not playful, not resentful, not pouty, none of the faces that make my heart fill with love.

He looks disappointed. In me.

"Lie down, Tina." Webb comes down the staircase, his pistol aimed at my head. Behind him, six steps up, is a woman in a hospital robe with gashes on her hands and feet and a bandaged face and head. She looks like a zombie, but with one piercing, blue eye.

"Julia."

She smiles when she hears me say her name, then limps down the staircase. Webb doesn't turn; he's too good to be distracted by anything.

She stops on the last step behind him. "I beat you, Tina. Twice."

"Lie down! Now!"

Devon opens his eyes wide and gestures for me to stop.

"I can't lose you."

His eyes tell me that I already have.

My head bows. The flare gun is two feet away. "Devon, look the other way."

I turn back to Julia and stand tall. I'm not lying down for anybody. Our eyes lock. She did beat me. Twice. Better than any man could do. "Devon is my only child."

Carl moves closer. His gun is four feet away from my face. There must be another way. Devon can't see his mother making a mess.

"Lie down now."

My fingers move toward my jeans. "I'm taking a phone out of my pocket." I lift it out with two fingers. "It was frozen. The passcode is my birthday."

"Drop it."

My eyes lock on Julia's. "Take good care of him."

I pick up the flare gun and run at Carl Webb. His gun explodes as the force sends me flying backward. My spine hits the railing and flips me over the side. My eyes glimpse Devon in his chair for a microsecond before I fall. He's facing away. Good boy.

A sea swell flies up to grab me. It's cold. My lungs gasp for air but water floods in. The moving yacht sucks me under. A propeller blade slices into my head.

That does the trick.

EPILOGUE

STEVEN QUINTANA

September 18, 4:00 p.m. (EST)
Lake Shebandowan, Ontario
Six months later

Devon adjusts his mask and looks at me through the brackish water. We exhale our bubbles through our regulators and trade the "OK" sign. After checking our gauges, I shoot him a questioning look and a "thumbs-up," asking him if he wants to ascend. He signs a reluctant "thumbs-up" back.

This kid would live underwater if he could, but it's cold and I've seen enough pike drifting past us in this dark, Canadian lake.

He smiles with his eyes through his mask. I have to give the kid a break. He's done damn well this summer, considering his life got blown apart.

We ascend slowly, letting the bubbles float ahead of us. Only rise as fast as your slowest bubble. We're only twenty-five feet deep. Any deeper and we'd lose too much light.

When we break the surface, I tug our masks down around our necks and inflate our buoyancy vests. "That was fun."

He moans back with enough of a "y" sound that I know he means "yes."

"It's like flying. You'll get that in outer space when we get you there."

He starts chattering, expecting me to keep up. We catch most of what he's saying. Half the trick is just concentrating as we listen, which we do a lot since he refuses to use any digital voices unless it's absolutely necessary. The other half is just knowing how he thinks.

He already knows how I think. He was the one who saw my clues in Baja and interpreted them. It was like I was sending them directly to him.

He talks some more.

"Yes, I'll look at the Hodge conjecture paper one more time. It's not like I can add much more, aside from spotting typos." I grab his vest by the collar and tow him towards the shore. He stares up at the sun and laughs.

"Kick, dude. Your legs work a little. I'm not your servant."

He laughs some more and kicks his legs closer to the surface. All this exercise is helping him get stronger, and he seems to be enjoying life for the first time since we met.

"We'll do it in the ocean next. Finish your certification."

He grunts in agreement. He then stops kicking. He's stares at the white clouds, drifting across the blue sky.

"What about a paper on chaos theory next? Predicting patterns for cloud formations could help with weather prediction."

He doesn't answer. He does this a lot. He freezes in the middle of a conversation and locks his gaze on something. Julia and I don't know what's going on. He could be having a seizure, be lost in thought, be sad, or remembering his pain. It's hard to break through to him.

Julia is convinced she can do it. This is her new quest. After I survived *Six Passengers, Five Parachutes,* she insisted on making a movie, getting married, and having a family—1-2-3, as if she could transform tragedy into a successful life through sheer will power.

Since *The Danger Game,* she's changed her vision. Now, she wants Devon and me to be that family. Is Devon all for it? He says he is, but I can't tell.

He breaks his gaze and mutters something too low to understand.

"I'll drag us in."

Julia waits for us on shore. We're at her family's summer cottage on Lake Shebandowan in Northern Ontario. It's been a long six months, but life feels good.

"How are my powerful magicians? Did you have fun?"

"We did! And we hail the queen upon our return!"

When the water is six inches deep, I plop us down on our butts and get our tanks off. Then, we roll onto our bellies and crawl out of the water onto a strip of sandy beach.

My challenges return. Gravity is my enemy. My right leg hurts like hell when I put pressure on it. My left hand still burns with phantom pain from where my pinky finger once was. It will take months of rehab to get through both challenges. But I don't dare complain. Devon doesn't, and his entire body betrays him, every day.

Julia and I pull him onto the white sand and help him get his fins off. He sighs. He hates gravity too.

"I want you to spend thirty minutes in your hyperbaric chamber," Julia says.

"Are you talking to Devon? I already did mine this morning."

"Devon. And it's working. He's breathing completely on his own now, and his muscles are gaining strength."

Devon purses his lips and does something he couldn't do four months ago. He whistles. His robot wheelchair bumps down the rocky grade, each wheel adjusting for the terrain. It stops in front of us and Julia and I lift him into his seat.

He gets his lips over the mouthpiece and uses the new voice he designed, a mix of six people talking at once, representing the six sides of his personality. "Steven. Let's do that again tomorrow."

"Sure. The water will stay warm enough for another few days."

He turns his chair and heads back up the slope to the cottage.

"Does he need any help?" I ask.

"He's fine. He's eighteen now. An adult. You know that he worked with JPL to write the software for his AI wheelchair."

"He told me. And Professor Carlton arrives tomorrow to go over their joint paper on the Hodge conjecture."

"Who knows? He may still win the Millennium Prize."

Her face, scalp, and hands are healed. Her hair is taking a while to grow back, so she keeps it in a buzz cut for now. If need be, she'll get hair transplants. Everything else is fine. She's lucky, but I miss her hair.

My bad thoughts return. She was burned because of me. I made a mistake on the numbers. My hand was infected, which made my brain cloudy. I also made her shoot that gun, and she may have killed three men. If she resents me for it, she doesn't say.

"Yo!" Carl yells, waving from the lawn with Trishelle next to him. "Glenn is here too! Are you ready to start this party?"

"After I shower! Ten minutes!"

My skin got "duck itch" at the start of the summer because I didn't shower enough after swimming in the lake. I learned my lesson, so I scrub my skin hard.

My left hand sends a fiery thunderbolt zooming up my arm.

Shake it off. Always move forward. Julia is right. We create our own futures.

We all meet on the screened-in porch. The afternoon sun shines through the tall trees, sending dappled light across the walnut dining

348

table. Julia, Carl, Trishelle, Glenn, and my brother, Anthony, are there already, along with a cold Molson waiting in front of my chair. We clink bottles and sip.

I look around. "Where's Devon?"

Julia sighs. "He says we're boring. He wants to watch tonight's JPL launch online from Vandenburg."

Julia serves us a delicious meal of lemon chicken and rice, which Anthony declares is as good as our mother's.

"That's sacrilege, bro. Don't ever tell Mom you said that."

"Are you kidding? I don't want to die."

It ends with black coffee and rhubarb pie. A sour vegetable stalk turned sweet with tons of sugar, a family recipe of Julia's. An acquired taste, but one that I now enjoy.

After dinner, I help Julia clear the table. We set our dishes down by the sink in the kitchen. I hold her close. "Six months ago, on that rock in Baja in the middle of the night, you dared me to dream of this dinner. That gave me hope and got us home. Thank you."

"You're welcome. And now I have a new dare."

"Say it."

"A quiet life with love, marriage, a home, and a family."

I kiss her long and hard. "So do I. More than anything."

We stare at each other. Is a quiet life even possible for us? Or, are we addicted to our respective high-wire acts too much? She thrives on the chaos of Hollywood, while I'm at my best, when people around me are in danger.

She touches my face. "We'll find a way."

"I'll start by taking photos again. I miss it."

We head to the screened-in porch to join the others, who are sipping the last of their coffee and wine. The lake is dark on the other side of the screen. Crickets hum, it seems, in rhythm with the squadron of fireflies hovering over the water.

Julia breaks the serenity. "So, should we get down to business? Carl? Any news?"

"I spoke to McCusker. Swig is the only suspect for the murders of Marsh and Mendoza. A revenge killing after *Six Passengers, Five Parachutes*. They're still not linking her to Baja."

Devon comes down the ramp from the house. "What are you all talking about?" he asks clearly, with his real voice.

None of us answer. Devon and Julia have just started to talk about Tina, which is a conversation that doesn't include me. Devon and I talk about clouds and the next JPL launch, not our feelings.

He raises his eyebrows. "I'll ask again. What are we talking about?"

"We're talking about what we should do with over a billion dollars in bitcoin. Any thoughts?" Julia didn't say it was her billion dollars, even though she could. She didn't say it was his billion dollars either.

No one is trying to take it, so it seems safe to keep it. And ever since Larry Naythons published a piece in *Celebrity Exposed* saying that Julia and Trishelle are producers of the year for creating *The Danger Game*, law enforcement doesn't seem to care at all.

Anthony leans forward. "Steven, all of this happened because you snapped a photo of the glamorous Julia Travers five years back. What do think we should do with a billion dollars?"

"Take care of Mendoza and Marsh's families."

Julia nods. "We will. And you, too, Carl. We'll pay you back, and then some."

"Let's use it to make a difference," I say, and for the first time in years, I feel like I have a place in the world.

—THE END OF BOOK THREE—

Acknowledgments

I wish to thank Robin Berlin, Joe Weiss, Toni Gallagher, Deni Siedschlag, Douglas Gorney, Alitha Rodgers, Lisa Cerasoli, Dr. Ken Atchity, and Alexios Saskalidis.

The Danger Game is the third installment in The Quintana Adventures. *The Picture Kills* and *Six Passengers, Five Parachutes* are the first two books in the trilogy.

Ian Bull is also the author of the romantic thrillers *Liars in Love* and *Facing Reality*. He also writes nonfiction under his full name, Donald Ian Bull.

If you're interested in reading more of his work, email him at:

IanBullAuthor@gmail.com

Or visit:

www.IanBullAuthor.com

And, please, write a review of this book!

THE DANGER
GAME

Made in the USA
Monee, IL
06 August 2020